The Conglomerate:

A Luxurious Tale

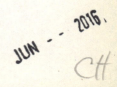

The Conglomerate:

A Luxurious Tale

Danielle Santiago

URBAN
BOOKS

www.urbanbooks.net

Urban Books, LLC
97 N18th Street
Wyandanch, NY 11798

The Conglomerate: A Luxurious Tale
Copyright © 2016 Danielle Santiago

ISBN 13: 978-1-62286-778-3
ISBN 10: 1-62286-778-5

First Trade Paperback Printing July 2016
Printed in the United States of America

10 9 8 7 6 5 4 3 2 1

This is a work of fiction. Any references or similarities to actual events, real people, living or dead, or to real locales are intended to give the novel a sense of reality. Any similarity in other names, characters, places, and incidents is entirely coincidental.

Distributed by Kensington Publishing Corp.
Submit Orders to:
Customer Service
400 Hahn Road
Westminster, MD 21157-4627
Phone: 1-800-733-3000
Fax: 1-800-659-2436

Chapter One

"Oh my God! Joey, how much longer are you going to be?" Cee questioned angrily. "I don't know why you had to change anyway. There was nothing wrong with the first dress you had on." Cee looked over at Evan. "Right?" she asked, hoping to get support from their best friend.

Evan refused to side with Cee, even if she was right. All of Cee's complaining and rushing was irking her. "Just chill, Cee." Evan sighed. "We're still on schedule." She went over to the small bar in the corner of the dressing suite. Dressed in a gold one-shoulder Grecian-style Oscar de la Renta dress, with her long blond hair twisted in a neat chignon on the side of her head, Evan looked like beauty in motion. Large gold chandelier earrings adorned her ears, radiating Evan's toasted-almond skin. After making a dry martini, she sat down in a wingback chair on the other side of room, crossed her legs, and sipped her drink.

Cee cut her eyes in disgust at both of her best friends. Unfazed by Cee's glares and comments, Joey stared at her reflection while adjusting a gorgeous eighteen-karat yellow gold Marco Bicego necklace. Once it was rested perfectly on her well-defined collarbone she admired the $18,000 gift that she'd purchased for herself.

Joey stepped back and gave herself a once-over. She was stunning in a deep burgundy floor-length St. John's two-piece gown. Her silky top hung seductively off her shoulder, revealing just the right amount of cleavage.

Gold specs accented the long sequined skirt. It hugged her tightly from the hip to the knee then let out elegantly. Joey moved in closer to the mirror, tousling her large red curls with her fingers and checking her makeup. She motioned for her makeup artist to come over. "I need little more blush please."

"Are you fucking serious?" Cee snapped loudly, jumping up from her seat. Clutching the side of her long cream strapless gown, she stormed toward the door with her gold Casadei heels clicking loudly against the polished floor.

Cee's exit was blocked by Evan, who stepped in front of the door just as she reached for the knob. "What is your damn problem, Cee? You've been acting like an impatient, spoiled child for the last hour with your whining and complaining."

"Look, I'm tired as hell and—"

"Whoa!" Evan held up her hand, cutting Cee off. "You think me and Joey are not tired? We've been working just as hard as you if not harder."

"Well, before you so rudely interrupted me," Cee said, and rolled her neck, "I'm ready to go home with my husband and see my kids. You might know something about that if you had more than your white furniture and glass tables waiting on you at home."

"Fuck you! You selfish bitch! Joey has kids too who she hasn't seen in days, yet we both stayed after the ribbon cutting to personally work your grand opening, when it was over." Evan pointed her finger directly in Cee's face, nearly grazing her nose.

"Watch your finger," Cee said, knocking it away with the back of her hand.

Evan placed it right back in her face. "You ran your wide ass up out of here like it was on fire. We had to finish working, then take a quick shower here while you

got to go to the comfort of
and dress. So you can go su(
rushing shit."

The hairstylist and make
glances as they packed thei
nessed arguments between
with low blows slung back a

"You can miss me with
showered in a brand new tw
bathroom and not at the M(
tell me to go suck a dick," C.......... ....,
"be prepared to throw hands."

"That's enough already!" Joey said, easing between
the two. "This is the exact reason I didn't say anything
back to Cee. This is our night and there should be zero
arguing, especially over petty shit." She looked at Cee
then at Evan; both of them were frowning hard. "Now fix
your faces and let's go."

Once outside the room any evidence of internal strife
among the friends was undetectable. The ladies were all
smiles as they entered a ballroom to a waiting crowd of
close to 1,000 people who had come to celebrate their
current success at a $250-a-plate charity dinner.

2010 had been an extraordinary year for the three
best friends from the west side of Charlotte; apart
they each had thriving profitable careers. Joey was
one of the top club and concert promoters on the East
Coast. Evan was highly sought-after wedding planner
and the owner of a PR firm that specialized in event
planning. Cee, a master hairstylist to more than a few
celebrities, also had a stable clientele list of 500-plus
clients. The trio constantly worked together in some
capacity, whether it was Evan doing PR for Cee's and
Joey's projects, or Cee's glam squad providing hair
and makeup for Evan's events. Since their businesses

...ng they decided to form a conglomerate ...Luxe Group. A year earlier they broke ...d began building their company's home on a ... land that Evan inherited from her father.

...day they were celebrating the grand opening of ...e Luxe Enclave, a semicircle of three buildings. At the entrance was Evan's brainchild, the L Room: an event hall that consisted of five ballrooms, five dressing suites, a kitchen, and Evan's PR firm's offices. Next door to the L Room sat Cee's creation, Luxurious: a two-story salon and full-service spa. The Luxe Group's headquarters would be run from the fourth floor of the third building. It was five stories and it housed Club Luxe, a posh three-level nightclub only comparable to the nicest spots in Miami or Vegas. The Luxe Penthouse was a private membership club located on the fifth floor. Its grand opening would be later this week. Both clubs were created and executively managed by Joey.

Joey, Cee, and Evan held hands as they took the stage at the front of the room. The crowd was filled with family, friends, politicians, supporters, and celebrities. Evan took the microphone from the stand.

"I would just like to welcome everyone to the L Room and thank you for coming out to celebrate this special day with us. A special thank you to those of you here who also joined us for the ribbon cutting this morning. This night is . . . um," she stuttered nervously as her eyes focused in on a man at the rear of the room who was giving her an icy stare. All of the color flushed from Evan's face and it became covered with perspiration. "This night . . ." She tried to continue, but paused again as she fought the urge to panic. "I'm sorry but the staff is calling for me," Evan lied. "I believe it's important. Thank you and please enjoy the dinner."

She handed Joey the mic and rushed off the stage. Cee and Joey exchanged curious glances. "That's how it is when you're the boss," Joey joked while trying to figure out the cause of Evan's sudden departure. "I would like to thank you for not only celebrating the opening of our Luxe Enclave, but also purchasing a two hundred and fifty dollar plate. As you know one hundred and seventy five dollars from each plate was set aside for the charity of our choice. We chose the Westside Boys and Girls Association, a place that Cee, Evan, and I credit for keeping us out of trouble with year-round sports programs." Evan passed the microphone to Cee.

"Due to your generosity," Cee said, and pointed at the crowd, "we raised $157,000." The crowd roared with applause and two formally dressed models came out with a poster-sized check. "With pleasure we present this check to Westside Boys and Girls Association."

An older lady and gentleman, representatives of the Westside Boys and Girls Association, came up to receive the check. After taking a few photos with the representatives Joey returned to the microphone. "Once again thank you, please enjoy your meal, and when you are done please come over to Club Luxe for the grand opening. The first two drinks are on me and we have free champagne all night."

"What the hell is wrong with Evan?" Cee asked Joey as they stepped off the stage. "She looked like she saw a ghost."

"I don't know what's going on with Evan. We rode to the gym together the other morning. I swear to God we weren't there twenty minutes when she gets a call and just like that"—Joey snapped her fingers—"she got all jumpy and was ready to leave, but she absolutely refused to tell me what was wrong."

"Well, she needs to tell us something right now, because that little episode just now was crazy." Cee scanned the room. "Look, there's Evan coming back in now. Come on. Let's find out what's up."

"No," Joey said. "You go start making the rounds and I'll talk to Evan, because I don't want the two of you to start going at it out here." Joey went over to Evan. "Is everything okay?"

"Yeah, everything is fine." Evan smiled weakly.

"Oh, really? Well, why did you almost fall to pieces on the stage?"

"I thought I saw someone I knew from a long time ago and it shook me up a little, but I'm okay now."

"All right. I'm going to let it ride for now," Joey said, deciding not to push for the moment, "but I know you like I know myself and something isn't right."

"I'm good," Evan assured her, walking away.

Yeah, right, Joey thought, and walked in the other direction.

After going around the room to personally greet guests at each table, Cee and Joey sat down briefly with their families. Instead of eating, Cee doted on her husband, Petey. Between their careers, and five children, the high school sweethearts didn't get to spend much time together. Therefore, any time they got a moment to just sit together Cee would give him all of her attention. Petey was a great husband and a wonderful dad, and Cee never failed to show him how much she appreciated him.

Cee's marriage was the envy of many women, but most didn't know of the couple's turbulent beginnings. At the age of thirteen, Cee had the great misfortune of becoming pregnant by a fourteen-year-old Petey. The fact that she was pregnant with triplets complicated matters exponentially. Both Cee and Pete were blessed to have big, supportive families. Although their mothers were furious at them, they banded together and helped out with the triplets so that the two young parents would be able to continue their education. Of course, Cee faced ridicule and gossip from the people in the community, especially her peers. She paid them no mind. Cee had been cornrowing and curling the neighborhood girls' hair for free or candy since she was ten. Once she gave birth to a set of triplet girls, Taleah, Talia, and Tanine, the freebies went out the window. From then on out she charged every time she picked up her comb.

Pete went to work doing odd jobs for his grandfather's towing and trucking company. At age sixteen Petey got his work permit and went to work full time at the trucking company. At this point Cee was enrolled in the cosmetology program at West Charlotte Senior High and worked as a stylist assistant. Upon graduating Cee became a licensed cosmetologist and Petey took on more responsibilities at the trucking company while attending UNC Charlotte as a business major.

At twenty the couple married and moved into one of Petey's father's rental properties. The early years of their marriage was no fairytale. Cee struggled with balancing her successful career and her young family. There was also infidelity on both their parts, in some aspect to be expected in their situation. Neither had experienced anyone else before taking their vows. In the long run both learned from their cheating that they only wanted one another.

Though it had been a rocky road, life had come full circle. Cee had become an übersuccessful stylist and salon owner. Petey was now the owner and operator of his family's truck business. He'd expanded and taken the trucking company to heights his grandfather never even dreamed of. The triplets, or trips, as they were affectionately called, were in their freshmen year of college. In addition to the trips, Cee and Petey were the proud parents of a seven-year-old boy, Petey Jr., and a four-year-old daughter, Shelby.

Joey didn't have much conversation for Zay, her husband of ten years. Yes, she'd been away from him more than usual lately, but this was the first meal that she'd had in two days and she was beyond starving so there wasn't much time for talking. In a matter of minutes it would be time for her to head to over to the club to complete last-minute preparations before the grand opening that was only an hour away. While eating Joey did manage to keep a close watch on Evan, who had yet to sit down.

Although Evan was single and both of her parents were deceased, she did have aunts, uncles, and cousins in attendance. She zoomed around the room like a Tasmanian devil busying herself with the smallest things: things that Evan's highly skilled staff was more than capable of handling. The dinner was flowing smoothly without a hitch just like all the events that Evan planned. Evan's movements only confirmed Joey's suspicions that Evan was hiding something serious.

"Slow down, baby," Zay whispered to Joey. "Can you even taste the food?"

"I don't need to." Joey blushed. "Besides, I have to get over to Luxe to make sure everything is straight before the doors open."

"There is nothing more for you to do. I stopped by there before I came in here. Everything is good, so slow down and enjoy your food." He kissed her cheek. "When you're finished, don't take off like your girl ran off the stage for no apparent reason." Zay chuckled.

"You caught that too?"

"Hell, yeah. I was standing at the back of the room and not one person motioned for her. I've been telling you for years something not right with ya girl."

"Oh, Zay, please. There is nothing wrong with Evan. Just admit you don't like her and you haven't from day one."

"Not true at all. I don't dislike Evan. My instincts have just always told me that she got some extra shit with her."

"The street nigga in you tells you she got extra shit with her." Joey shook her head. "That has been my bestie for over twenty years. She has never done anything for me not to trust her and for the ten years that you've known her you've been trying to find something wrong with her."

"I've been telling you for a long time you can be down with someone for thirty years and they will betray you like they never knew you. Anyways," he said, changing the subject. He wasn't going to waste his time arguing over something petty. "You are beautiful in that color."

"Thank you, honey."

"I meant to tell you that when you first sat down, but you went in on that plate like a beast."

Laughing, Joey nudged him with her elbow. "Shut up, boy." Biting her bottom lip sexily she eyed him up and down. "You are looking real presidential in that tux. If I had fifteen minutes I would take you in my office and do you real good."

"Ain't no 'if' about it. You got time."

"Nah, I don't have time. As a matter of fact," Joey said, and looked down at her gold Rolex, "I have to go change my clothes right now. I'll peel you out of that tux tonight and give it to you until the sun comes up."

"That ain't happening," Zay spat.

Joey frowned. "Why not?"

"First of all, I'm coming up out this monkey suit before I go in Luxe. And you know the sun will be up by time you get home. But, hey, we haven't fucked in two weeks so what's another day?" He winked, taking a sip of Hennessy.

"Really, Zay? You wanna do this right now?"

"Not at all. I'm only messing with you, baby. I know how hard you've been working and it has definitely paid off. I'm proud of you."

Joey cupped his face in her hands. "I'm going to make it up to you. We're going to leave together early." She kissed him adoringly, and then said, "I gotta go. I love you."

"Love you too."

With fifteen years of club management experience in Miami and Manhattan, Bev Garcia, the operations manager of Club Luxe, ran a tight and efficient operation. Bev's expertise came with an expensive price tag but it was well worth it. She had the club's staff well prepared for the huge grand opening, which included: performances by three of the biggest stars in hip-hop and R&B; a two-hour open bar; and free flutes of champagne all night for VIP guests.

Two hours after the doors opened, the club was filled to the maximum capacity of 3,000. This forced the bouncers to turn away a line of hundreds. Clad in a short silk white romper and fuchsia platform pumps, Joey moved through her club, greeting guests, checking the five bars, and constantly making sure that celebrity guests and performers were okay.

When Bev went into the stock room, she found Joey loading bottles into a box she had tucked beneath her arm. "What are you doing?" Bev asked.

"I am getting some vodka and Patrón for the first-floor bars. They're both almost out."

"I know," Bev said, then took the box from Joey. "That's why I came to pull bottles. The bar hands are on their way to pick up the orders."

"Well, I can at least help you pull bottles so the boxes will be ready when they get here," Joey replied, reaching for the box.

"Joey, I have everything, and I mean everything, under control. I just sent three bottles of Ace up to your VIP section. Go celebrate your night to enjoy all of the hard work you've put in."

Joey checked her watch. It was a little after midnight. "Okay," she said reluctantly. "Thank you, Bev. You are doing a wonderful job. This night turned out much better than I ever imagined."

"That's what you hired me for," Bev replied, smiling brightly.

"What kind of Ace did you send?"

"Two gold bottles and one rosé."

"I'm going to get another bottle of rosé from the bar. That's Cee's favorite so I know it's probably gone already."

"All the bars are out of rosé. My next stop is the cooler to pull some more of that, too. When I get them I'll send you some over by the waitress. Now go have fun."

Joey slipped, unnoticed, into the largest VIP section on the second level. She snuck up behind Zay, who was standing next to Petey, watching the performances. Joey wrapped her arms around his waist and hugged him.

"Hey, baby, I'm done working already and the night's not over yet."

"That's what's up," he said, turning to face her. "I hope you still planning to give it to me until the sun come up."

"I sure am. What's up with Cee?" Joey asked, pointing at her best friend. Donning a slinky white off-the-shoulder minidress, Cee was standing on top of an oversized ottoman with a bottle of champagne in her hand, dancing and singing.

"You know what's up with her." Zay laughed, shaking his head. "She's wasted."

"I'm about to get just like her," she said, dancing side to side. Joey looked around. "Where is Evan?"

"Hell if I know. I thought she was with you."

"No." Joey frowned. "I've only seen her twice since we've been in here. Whatever." She shrugged. "She'll surface eventually." Notorious for hard partying, Joey had the bottle server pour her three shots of Cîroc, which she quickly downed and chased with a big swig of champagne. Minutes later she was up dancing on the ottoman next to Cee with her own bottle.

Evan smiled as she peered down at her two best friends from a restricted area on the third level of the club. She could tell that they were having a really good time. Normally she would be right there in the middle getting twisted with them. Due to recent, strange events she needed to be focused while in public.

Evan felt a tap on the shoulder and nearly jumped out of her skin. She spun around. "Oh, God, Bev," she exclaimed, holding her chest. "You scared the shit out of me."

"Sorry, but why are you not down there celebrating?" Bev questioned, wondering why Evan was in a secluded area of the club by herself. "Do you need a bottle of champagne or something? I'm about to go in the cooler room now."

"No, I'm fine. I just needed a moment to myself. I'm not really in the partying mood right now." Evan paused. "You know, Bev, I'm gonna break out. Can you tell Joey and Cee that I left?"

"Sure."

Evan walked briskly through the Enclave parking lot to her reserved spot in front of the L Room. Once she was in eyeshot of her white Maserati, she spotted a blue Tiffany's box atop the roof. "What the hell is this?" she muttered.

Evan snatched the box down and looked around the parking lot. A few drunken partiers were straggling to their vehicles and the security guards were patrolling the lot on golf carts. Evan hurried into her car, locked the doors, and cranked the engine. She reached beneath the passenger's seat, retrieved a Glock .380, and placed it on her lap.

Before pulling out of her space she opened the box. Evan gasped at the sight of the contents: a silver bullet with her name engraved in it. A small note beneath it read: ESPECIALLY FOR YOU. Over the last month she'd been receiving subtle to not-so-subtle notes, texts, gifts, and e-mails that could easily be perceived as threats. In the beginning she thought it was some scorned female mad at her for messing with her boyfriend or husband. Not long after the threats started she realized that it wasn't some vengeful woman. Evan received a text that stated: I'm coming for my money, on my terms, when you least expect it.

After receiving that text she started to think the anonymous threats were most likely from one of the many men she'd played while leading a different life a decade earlier. She always thought that one of them would come after her, but she thought it would be within the first two or three years, not ten years down the road. Someone coming after her didn't bother her as much as not knowing who it was. The situation was torturous, which she figured was the person's intent.

A light tapping on the driver's side window startled Evan. She looked up and a saw Rhamel, the security guard. He was forty-something, with brown skin, and stocky. His claim to fame was that one year he played for the Cleveland Browns. It was no secret that he had a huge crush on Evan because he was always flirting with her. Evan rolled the window down halfway.

Rhamel flashed a wide gold-toothed smile. "You need something, Ms. E?"

"No, Rhamel. I was just leaving."

"So soon? I thought . . ." He spotted the gun on her lap. "Is everything all right, Ms. E?"

Evan glanced down at her lap then back at him. "Oh, this is nothing. I always take it out when I'm driving home late at night," she lied. "You know this city can get dangerous for a lady late at night."

"Well," he said, rubbing his chin between his forefinger and thumb, "if you ever need me to accompany—"

"No, thanks," she spat, cutting him off. "I'm good with my boyfriend." She held up the Glock. "So, good night." She pressed the window button up and drove away.

Driving in silence, Evan tried desperately to figure out who was the culprit behind the threats. Faces and towns raced around her mind until her head began to throb. *That's enough,* she told herself as she pulled up to the entrance of her gated neighborhood. Familiar with her car, the guard waved her through without looking at her face.

Chapter Two

"Damn it," Evan screamed, struggling to disable the newly high-tech alarm system complete with cameras, yard sensors, and a fingerprint scanner. She was ready to rip the keypad from the wall when she realized that she was putting in the code to her old system. Evan punched in the correct code and scanned her right thumb. "Thank you, Lord." She sighed when the green light appeared.

Evan reset the alarm and removed her heels. Her 8,500-square-foot home was a palatial palace. It had seven bedrooms, five and a half bathrooms, several living and dining areas, a pool, and a pool house. Handcrafted crown molding lined the ceilings while Swarovski crystal chandeliers hung from it. Marble flooring adorned the halls, kitchen, bath, and dining rooms. Gleaming snow white carpet lay in the rest of the house. All of the couches and chairs were white, light beige, or a mixture of both. Expensive glass pieces, paintings, and sculptures perfectly decorated the home. Evan's place was undeniably stunning, yet it was cold and uninviting.

Exhausted from the long day, Evan knew the only thing that would ease her mind enough to sleep was a good, strong drink. She scanned the shelf of her entertainment room's fully stocked bar. Wanting something with a quick one-two punch, Evan decided to make Texas Tea. She grabbed a small glass pitcher and poured in a mix of tequila, rum, vodka, gin, and bourbon. Trying to remember the final ingredients she studied the bar. It had been a long time since she made it. Champagne and vodka martinis were her usual drinks of choice.

"That's it." Evan snapped her fingers then grabbed the triple sec, sour mix, and a can of Coke. Stirring the pitcher of liquid Evan suddenly thought of Reza, the man who taught her how to make Texas Tea. *Could he be the one behind all this nonsense?* He could easily be number one on the list of suspects, considering that when they parted ways it was not pretty at all. Standing behind the bar, Evan took a few sips of her drink as her thoughts took a trip down memory lane, back to her time with Reza.

Hampton Roads, Virginia
2000

Evan attracted the attention of males and females as she roamed around Club Shadows in a brown, cream, orange, and gold Coogi sweater dress. Not the awful cheap ones that were sold; she was donning a $700 dress paired with a pair of brown knee-high boots and a large Fendi bag. It was a Wednesday night, the club's most crowded and busiest night. All of the area's elite were in the building. When Evan walked past the VIP area, someone grabbed her wrist. She turned around and frowned at the short, light-skinned guy who was holding on to her. He leaned over the red rope and said to her, "My man wants to holla at you." He pointed over his shoulder.

She looked past him and saw a gorgeous brown-skinned man, with shoulder-length cornrows, dressed in all black Iceberg. He raised his glass to her. Evan smiled at him then said to guy who'd stopped her, "Tell your man he should've hollered at me himself." She yanked her wrist from his grasp and walked away.

Evan squeezed through the tight crowd and found a spot at the bar. The six bartenders were getting slammed from every angle, making it hard to get their attention.

Evan took out a twenty dollar bill and flashed it at the bartenders. It was a trick that usually worked in this type of situation, but fifteen minutes later she still had not been served. Mr. Gorgeous from the VIP came and stood next to Evan at the bar. Immediately two bartenders nearly knocked each other down running over to take his order.

"You've got to be fucking kidding me!" Evan scoffed.

Mr. Gorgeous leaned over and said to her, "Tell 'em what you drinking."

"A Cosmo with Grey Goose," she said to the bartender with her mouth twisted.

"And," Mr. Gorgeous interjected, "let me get a double shot of Rémy."

"You must own the place," Evan said to him.

"Nah. Why you say that?"

"'Cause I've been here for close to twenty minutes and not one of them ass wipes has even looked at me. You walked up and they ran over like the king arrived."

"They like me in here. I'm such a friendly guy." He extended his hand. "My name is Reza."

Evan shook his hand and took a quick glance at his iced diamond watch. "I'm Mika," she replied, using her favorite alias.

The bartender returned with their drinks. "That will be twenty-five dollars."

Reza pulled a large wad of money out of his pocket. Evan checked it from the corner of her eye as he rifled through it. The roll of money consisted mostly of fifties and hundreds. He found three twenties and tossed them on the bar.

"Hmm, thirty-five dollar tips," Evan remarked. "No wonder they think you're such a nice guy."

"That's light money," he said, tooting his own horn. "My bad if I offended you by having my homeboy stop you. I didn't want to let you get away."

"All is forgiven."

"Are you here with your friends or your man?" Reza asked.

"Neither," she replied.

"You're alone?" he questioned with a raised eyebrow.

"Yes."

"You wanna come chill in the VIP? It's a little more comfortable in there."

"Sure."

All eyes were definitely on Evan now as she sat down next to Reza, the man almost every female in the club wanted to get with. Some of the girls already in the VIP were pissed that Evan was receiving all of Reza's attention. They were sure to let her know with mean glares, eye rolls, and twisted lips. There was a tall, slim, expensively dressed female who looked like she was about to burst in tears. She was the one throwing the most shade at Evan.

"I don't think your little girlfriends appreciate me being here," Evan told Reza.

"Pay those thirsty hoes no mind," he said with a dismissive wave in their direction. "You want me to put them out, Mika? 'Cause I will."

"No, you don't have to do that. I like making people jealous," she said, then smiled at the slim girl.

Just then the DJ dropped Jay-Z's "I Just Wanna Love U." The club went crazy. Evan stood up and began dancing as if she were having the time of her life. And just to make the girls even madder she went over and did a seductive dance in front of Reza.

When she sat down Reza said, "You do enjoy making people jealous with your fine ass. Ay, how come I've never seen you around here before? You go to Norfolk State or Hampton?"

"No. I came up from Florida with my mom to visit my auntie in the hospital."

"How long will you be here?"

"A week. My mom had to go home to take care of some things. I will be here until she gets back."

"A week." He downed his shot of Rémy. "That gives us plenty of time."

"Plenty of time for what?"

"To get to know one another."

"You're pretty confident that I want to get to know you," Evan remarked.

"Everybody wants to get to know me."

After having a few more Cosmos, Evan decided it was time for her leave. "I'm out," she notified Reza as she stood to leave.

"But I don't want you to leave yet."

"I have to leave now. Those Cosmos are starting to come down on me hard and the highways here are really confusing."

"Where are you staying?"

"The Marriott, in downtown Norfolk."

"I can drop you off after we have breakfast."

"Breakfast," she exclaimed with a screw face. "What are we are supposed to do until breakfast? I don't know you."

Reza chuckled, shaking his head. "I'm talking about going to breakfast now. It is one o'clock in the morning."

"Oh, my bad." She smiled, feeling a bit silly. "I'll go to breakfast with you."

Reza took a hold of her hand and led the way out. As they passed the two guys who had come with him, he pointed toward the exit. The pair promptly walked away from the women they were conversing with and followed Reza.

Outside, Reza made a very informal introduction: "These two lame-ass niggas are Reggie and Stef." He pulled Evan close to him by the waist. "This is Mika."

She greeted them with a quick, tight-lipped smile. Evan recognized Stef as the guy who grabbed her earlier for Reza. Stef stared at her with a wide grin, displaying a mouthful of yellow gold.

"Damn, nigga," Reza said to Stef. "Stop staring at her like that before you scare her."

"My bad, A." Stef guffawed. "I was just admiring her beauty."

"I don't give a fuck why you were doing it! I told you stop eyeballing her."

Stef lowered his eyes and looked to the ground. Reza looked at Evan. "What you driving, Mika?"

"The silver Diamante over there." She pointed.

"Let me get the keys."

Evan retrieved the keys from her purse, and then placed them in Reza's hand. He tossed them over to Reggie. "Y'all go by the spot. Get the Explorer, and then drop her whip off at that Marriott in downtown Norfolk."

Straight do boys, Evan thought, watching them as they marched away with their orders.

Reza guided her to his burgundy Range Rover 4.6. Sitting on custom chrome twenty-two-inch rims, it was the prettiest car in the lot. Smiling inwardly, Evan thought, *Yes! I got the right one.*

Out of nowhere, Evan heard a loud commotion. She turned around and saw the slim girl from inside the club charging toward her, yelling, "Reza, who is this bitch?"

Evan dropped her purse and rapidly got into a fighter's stance. Reza stepped in front of Evan, blocking the girl's access.

"What the fuck is up, Reza?" the girl screamed. Her face was drenched with tears.

Calmly Reza told her, "Tam, you're drunk. You need to go home before you play yourself out here."

"I've already played myself by allowing you to play me in front of my friends with this bitch!" She swung her fist at him.

Reza caught her by the arm while it was in the air. Squeezing it tightly, he told her, "Ho, don't you ever raise your hand to me. I didn't play you! You played yourself, out frontin' like you my girl when you not even my number two bitch." He flung her violently to the ground. Reza picked up Evan's purse and handed it to her. "Let's go."

"Are all your nights always this eventful?" Evan asked Reza, sitting across from him at IHOP.

"That was nothing."

"Oh, really? I've never had to fight over a nigga I just met." She laughed. "So where are you from?"

"Hartford, Connecticut," he replied.

"What brought you to Virginia?"

"A better life for my kids."

"So what do you do?"

"I'm an independent entrepreneur." He smiled coyly. Evan burst out laughing. "What's so funny?"

"Your answer, but I'm going to leave it alone."

"So what's your story, Mika?"

"I'm from Miami. I go to FAMU, but I sat out this semester to help my mom with our family's manufacturing business. Since my auntie got diagnosed with cancer my mom has been running it by herself."

"Your aunt is not from Virginia?"

"No."

"How did she end up in the hospital here?"

"Sentara is the only hospital on the East Coast with a special program for the type of cancer that she has."

They continued to talk during and long after their meal. The more Reza learned about the girl he knew as Mika, the more he liked her.

"What time will you be back from seeing your aunt?" Reza asked Evan when he pulled in front of the Marriott.

"I usually drop in on her about twelve thirty and stay about an hour. So I guess like one thirty."

"How about doing some shopping with me when you're done? I wanna check out that new McArthur Mall then swing up to the outlets in Williamsburg."

"Sure, I'll be ready at two."

Reza bought whatever Evan wanted. At the end of their shopping date, the back of his Range was filled with bags from the floor to the ceiling. The majority of the bags belonged to Evan.

Over the next few days, they were inseparable. Reza even convinced her to check out of the hotel and spend the remainder of her trip at his townhouse in the historic Ghent section of Norfolk. His home was beautifully furnished and decorated. However, it paled in comparison to his minimansion in Chesapeake. Evan caught a quick glimpse of the house by accident. Reza's mother had locked her keys in the house while she took his kids to the park. He didn't have time to drop Evan off before going to let them in. It would've taken too long.

"Nice digs," she told Reza when they pulled away from the house. "That must be where wifey lives."

"No, that's where my mother and my kids live."

"If you say so," she replied with full knowledge that his mother was there watching the kids because his children's mother was out of town. That bit of information came from ear hustling while she pretended to be asleep.

Evan also knew that the townhouse was actually Reza's stash house for his drugs and money. One of the bedrooms had a steel door and three deadbolt locks. Reza kept it locked, but one day he slipped up. While rushing out to meet someone who owed him a large sum of money, Reza left the door wide open. During the time he was out, Evan went in and looked around. There were two wide black chest-height safes against the back of the wall. A large trunk sat in the middle of the room. When Evan looked inside the trunk, she was speechless at the sight of at least thirty kilograms of cocaine. She closed the trunk and ran out of the room. Evan never said a word about what she saw to Reza.

In the meantime, Reza was falling hard for Evan. He hadn't even had sex with her and he found himself contemplating leaving his baby mother and giving up his side chicks for Evan. To him she was worldly, classy, book smart, and street smart. Evan could fit in anywhere, unlike his children's mother, Ladon. She was loud and ghetto.

Reza kept Ladon laced in the best designer labels. He moved her from the projects of Hartford into a $600,000 home, and put her behind the wheel of a Benz 600. None of those things mattered to Ladon. She frequently made trips to Hartford to hang with friends from her old neighborhood against Reza's approval. He was growing tired of Ladon long before he met Evan, but Evan was just the right motivation Reza needed to throw the towel in on their relationship.

On the night before Evan was set to leave, Reza took her out to a five-star restaurant on Norfolk's Waterside Drive. "Mika, I don't want you to leave me," he told her over a candlelit dinner.

"I don't want to leave you either. I'll be back next week, before you even have a chance to miss me."

"You'll be back to visit your aunt. That doesn't mean you'll come back to me." He set a little red velvet box on the table. "Hopefully these will be a little incentive for you to come back to me."

Evan picked up the box. "What are these?"

"A gift for you. Go ahead and open it."

Evan popped the box open and her eyes lit up. Inside
was a beautiful pair of two-karat brilliant solitaries set
in platinum. *Lord, I swear this nigga gon' make me
fall in love with him.* She quickly reminded herself, *Ain't
no money in love, though.*

"They are so pretty." She got up and hugged him.
"Thank you, but you didn't have to give me these."

"I wanted to. Consider them a token of my appreciation for keeping me company. What time does your plane
leave tomorrow?"

"At four forty-five in the afternoon."

"I didn't know you were leaving that late. That means
we can hang out and hit a few spots tonight."

"I want to stay in tonight," she purred, rubbing his leg
with her foot beneath the table.

"And do what?"

"I was thinking you could make some of that Texas
Tea you turned me on to and I could model some of the
lingerie you bought me from Vickie's."

"I'm with that! Ay," he called out to their waiter. "Let
me get that check right now."

Carl Thomas's *Emotional* pumped out of the surround
speakers spread throughout Reza's townhouse. Wearing
only a pair of basketball shorts, Reza held Evan firmly
in his arm as they slow dragged in living room. She was
scantily clad in a purple sheer one-piece thong bodysuit.
They both were feeling good and tipsy from the glasses
of Texas Tea they'd consumed. Reza was all over Evan,
kissing and licking her mouth, ears, neck, and chest while
rubbing her body.

Reza spoke softly in her ear: "Enough of this dancing.
Let's go upstairs and lie down."

"Okay," she replied.

Holding Evan's hand, Reza led her up to the bedroom.

"Damn it," Evan hissed, "I left my glass downstairs."

"I'll go get it," Reza said.

"No, baby." Evan placed her hands on his chest. "I can get it. You lie down and relax."

Evan returned moments later and lay down next to Reza. He didn't waste any time getting back to business. Reza massaged her breasts while glazing her lips with his tongue. He slipped his hand between her legs, feeling her wet, warm middle through the thin, sheer material.

All of a sudden, Reza felt a painful whack on the back of his head, then the cold muzzle of a gun against his temple.

"Do not move. If you move one inch," a gruff voice said, "I will put a bullet in your head."

Gripping the back of his head in pain, Reza followed the gunman's directions. Evan leapt out of the bed. She yanked open the nightstand drawer and grabbed Reza's nine millimeter pistol. *Whew,* thought Reza, *Baby girl is on point.* Then he realized that Evan had the gun aimed at him.

"Put the gun on him," Reza barked.

Evan stared at him blankly with a stoic face. Between the Texas Tea and the blow to the head it took a few extra seconds for him to process the situation. "What's up with you, Mika?"

"You know what it is," she said coldly.

"Damn, bitch, you sure had me falling for your grimy ass."

The gunman struck Reza in the head once more. "Shut the fuck up!" He tossed a pair of flex-cuffs to Evan. "Restrain your pretty-ass boyfriend then put some fucking clothes on."

"He is not my boyfriend," Evan snapped at the gunman, who was actually her boyfriend, Gage. Lately he was becoming difficult to deal with.

"Shit, you act like you feeling him. If I would've waited another minute his dick would have been inside of you."

"Whatever." She got the cuffs on to Reza and pulled them tight. Reza was scared, nervous, mad, and humiliated at the same time.

Evan threw on a black Juicy velour suit. She picked up a set of keys from Reza's dresser, and told Gage, "Bring him down the hall. We're going to need him for the safe combination."

"Okay, pretty boy," Gage said, "get up and don't do nothing to make me blow your head off."

Reza looked on helplessly as Evan unlocked the deadbolts on the door to his stash room. She went straight to the trunk that held the cocaine. By now, there were only ten kilos of cocaine in the trunk. Evan tossed them into a black leather duffle bag then moved over to the first safe.

"What's the combination?" she asked Reza.

"Fuck you, bitch," he spat.

Gage hit Reza in the jaw with the gun. Blood gushed from his mouth as he crumpled to the floor. "Tell her the fucking combination!" Gage ordered.

Reza spit out the thick blood that was filling his mouth. "Y'all better take those bricks and be happy 'cause I'm not telling you shit. I don't care what you do to me."

"A'ight, tough guy." Gage laughed. "Will you care what I do when I drive over to 11457 Prescott Lane? You know, that real nice mansion where your mama and your kids at?"

Reza cut his eyes at Evan. "You conniving bitch. You told him where my kids lived?"

Gage kicked Reza in the side. "Kids or the combination."

Reluctantly, Reza said, "Twelve, nineteen, eighty, nine."

Evan punched the numbers on the electronic keypad. She raked the stacks of money into the duffle bag and moved over to the second safe. She simply looked at Reza with a raised brow. He didn't say a word. Gage kicked him harder than the first time. Reza spit out the combination. Moving fast Evan cleared out safe number two, then dragged the heavy duffle bags out to the hallway. Gage bound Reza's wrists to his ankles with another pair of flex-cuffs.

When Evan walked back into the room, Reza glared at her hatefully. He could not believe that a chick he really liked had played him so badly. "When I catch you," he said to Evan, "I'm going to kill you."

Gage pulled his gun and aimed it at Reza's head. Reza's eyes widened as fear gripped his body. Evan pushed Gage's arm down.

"Why the hell did you do that?" asked Gage. "Because you feeling this nigga just like I said?"

"No, because of the rule: no killing unless it's necessary."

Gage shoved his gun back into the small of his back, snatched up the two duffle bags, and stormed out. "Hurry the fuck up so we can get out of here," he barked over his shoulder. Evan reached for the knob to close the door.

"I will kill you," Reza said.

"You should show some gratitude. I just saved your life."

"Fuck you. On my kids I'm going to kill you."

"You have to catch me first." Evan cut the light off, slammed the door, and locked the three deadbolts.

"Did you kiss your boyfriend good-bye?" Gage questioned Evan from the passenger's seat as she drove down I-85 in North Carolina. He had been silent for the first two hours of the ride. Evan wished that he would stay quiet for the remainder of the ride.

"That's not the first time you've seen a nigga all over me when we're working. Why are you tripping so bad about this one?"

"I saw how you were all into it. Like it felt really good to you."

"I was acting like I always do. If you think I'm starting to like these niggas out here I can stop doing these stick-ups. Quite frankly, I'm getting tired of this shit anyway."

"Maybe I am tripping," Gage said, changing his tune. He couldn't afford to lose Evan's help. She was critical to his operation. "I'm sorry, baby."

Whatever, Evan thought. *As soon as I graduate, I'm done with him and these robberies.*

At twenty-one Evan was living a double life. She was in her senior year at Clark Atlanta University. Evan was set to graduate with honors in the spring of 2001. Never in a million years did she imagine that she would be one half of a stickup team. However, life had thrown her a few curveballs that had rendered her indigent. Growing up, Evan was an only child. She was the classic daddy's girl. Her father, Richard Teague, started out in midlevel management of a Fortune 500 company the year that Evan was born. Seven years later, he worked his way up the ranks to CEO and a $700,000 base salary plus bonuses. When it came to Evan and her mother, Sherlynn, he spared no expense to make them happy.

Sherlynn had every major credit card, charge card, and department store card. Sherlynn loved to shop and she did it without a conscience. When the credit card bills came in from his wife's insane shopping sprees he paid the bill and never once discouraged her reckless spending habits. The good pay wasn't the only thing that came with Richard's CEO job. It also came with an enormous amount of stress. That only worsened with each passing year.

During Evan's sixth grade year, Richard suffered a massive heart attack and died at the young age of thirty-eight. His death devastated his wife and daughter. Sherlynn dealt with her grief by exercising retail therapy. She also splurged even more on Evan, hoping that would take her mind off her father's death.

Sherlynn had not worked since she gave birth to Evan and had no means of income. Therefore, there were large amounts of money going out and nothing coming in. It only took a little under three years for Sherlynn to burn through the insurance money, their life savings, and Evan's trust fund. The only money that Sherlynn was unable to get her hands on was Evan's college fund. Sherlynn hid her money problems from Evan and just as the money ran out, she married a prominent pediatrician. He had three successful practices in the Charlotte area.

Once again, Sherlynn had access to plenty of money. She resumed her wild shopping sprees, but now with Evan by her side. Now that Evan was in high school, she only wanted the freshest and most expensive designer clothes. Her mother was all too happy to oblige her daughter's wants. She even put her daughter behind the wheel of a Lexus GS 300 for her sixteenth birthday.

Sherlynn's new wonderful world came crashing down only a week after Evan graduated from high school. Multiple parents began alleging that her husband had molested their young daughters during physicals. He was arrested after a nurse gave the police videos that corroborated the allegations. The good doctor was shot and killed as he walked out of the courthouse on $1 million bail. The shooter was the father of a five-year-old girl the doctor had molested.

Unlike when Richard died, there was no money at all for Sherlynn. The doctor had willed everything to his children from his first marriage. There was no certainty that his children would receive anything. The court froze his estate, because it was facing multiple lawsuits by the victims.

Sherlynn was embarrassed, hurt, and humiliated by the scandal surrounding her late husband. The thought of being broke sent her into deep depression. Unable to cope with the circumstances, a month after burying her second husband she took sixty Xanax pills and lay down to never wake again.

After Sherlynn's suicide, Evan learned the truth about her financial situation. She was broke, and no job at the mall or waiting tables would provide the lifestyle that she was accustomed to. Before Evan left for college, she sold a few pieces from her mother's fine jewelry collection. She made a nice sum of money, but not enough to carry her through the first year of college.

At the beginning of the second semester of Evan's freshmen year, she met and began dating Gage. He always had money, dressed nice, and drove a new Chevy Tahoe. Gage didn't work, so naturally Evan assumed that he was a dope boy. After only a few dates, she knew that she had him wrapped and he was into her heavy. Evan liked Gage, but she wasn't crazy about him. Gage didn't mind spending money on her so, for at least a little while, he was a temporary solution to her monetary problems.

It would be a few months into the relationship before Evan learned that Gage wasn't a dope boy, but the person who robbed the dope boys. That's how he earned the nickname Gage. It was short for twelve gauge: his weapon of choice. The crime partnership between Gage and Evan happened by chance. The two girls he used to lure drug dealers with had been arrested before they were set to travel with Gage to Jacksonville, Florida. He desperately needed a female for this particular trip. It never crossed Gage's mind to ask Evan to go with him; he would never put his girl in harm's way. Although, when she volunteered to make the trip with him, he did not say no.

All it took was that first trip to turn Evan out. Pretty, classy, and well versed, Evan could lure in the major drug dealers with long money. Adding Evan to his team changed the entire game. Now in her senior year Evan was ready to leave the robbery game. She had amassed enough money to start up her own public relations firm and enough money to live off until the firm turned a profit. Once she crossed the stage in the spring, she would be done with her life of crime. Gage's days were numbered, too. Evan did love him but he had no dreams or aspirations, and if he did he didn't share them with her. She often wondered if he thought that he was going to get away with robbing drug dealers forever.

Evan felt a little relief when she drove into the Charlotte city limits. The ten kilos in the trunk had her on edge during the entire ride. She was ready to unload them and get back to school. Evan pulled out her Startec and dialed up her best friend.

"Hello?" a groggy voice answered.

"Joey, are you up, honey?"

"I can be. What time is it?"

"Five thirty."

"Evan, you pick the most fucked-up hours to come through."

"So, what, you want me to come between nine and five?"

"I sure do. Anyway how far away are you?"

"I'm pulling into your complex."

"Do you remember the code to the gate?" Joey asked.

"I just punched it in. Unlock the front door."

"You look like shit," Evan said to Joey as she entered the apartment carrying the duffle. "I thought you were asleep."

"I was."

"In your clothes?" Evan frowned.

"Yes, I just got home an hour ago," Joey responded, standing by the door. "Is your boyfriend coming in?"

"No, his ignorant ass is asleep." Evan set the duffle on the kitchen counter. "I have to go to the bathroom."

Joey began removing the kilos from the bag.

"So, who were you with all night?" Evan asked as she returned to the kitchen.

"About five hundred people," Joey said, inspecting the packages of cocaine. "I threw a party at Mythos last night."

"How was it?"

"It was straight. I made a nice chunk of change. How much y'all want for these bricks?"

"Fifteen five apiece. Gage said this is some good, quality coke so you can work your magic." Evan winked twice with a slick smile.

"How long y'all gon' be here?"

"All day. We're about to get a room and rest for a little while. Then I'm going to the shop so Cee can do my hair."

Joey walked Evan to the front door. "I'll have the money for this in a little while. I can bring it to the shop if you want me to."

"That'll work."

Joey returned to the kitchen and she retrieved a five-gallon jar from the pantry. Inside was a special blend of lactose, baby formula, baby laxative, and a protein supplement that Joey used to cut cocaine. She wasn't a drug dealer. She just happened to come from a family of drug dealers.

At the early age of twelve, she learned how to cut and package various narcotics from her older cousins. Joey also knew many hustlers. Therefore, whenever Evan came across drugs during a robbery she would bring them to Joey.

Joey was something of an expert at cutting cocaine. She could take four fair-quality kilos of cocaine and turn it into eight. Any time Evan brought good-quality product to Joey she would double it and they would split money for the extra ki's. Gage knew nothing about these side deals between Evan and Joey. At the same time, Joey had no clue that Gage and Evan were out robbing drug dealers.

Joey turned those ten kilos into twenty, repressed them, and repackaged them. She managed to get in a shower before Zay arrived to pick them up.

"What's the ticket on these?" Zay asked, thoroughly examining one of the bricks.

"Fifteen five apiece," Joey replied.

"Fifteen five." He laughed, shaking his head. "Where your homegirl be getting this coke from?"

"Her man. Why?"

"Her man hitting somebody in the head for it."

"What are you talking about, Zay?"

"It's a drought right now. And even if it wasn't fifteen five is a wholesale number. Don't no regular nigga have numbers like that for coke this good," he said, holding one of the bricks up. "Then they come through every now and then with work."

All Joey wanted was for Zay to purchase the work and get out so that she could catch a nap. "So does this mean you're not getting it?"

"Fuck no; it means I want you to be careful. I know that's your homegirl but her man is a robber and I wouldn't doubt that she down with him."

"Negro, please, I been knowing that high sidity chick since preschool. Trust and believe she don't get down like that."

"Just because her daddy got that good job and moved them out the hood don't mean she ain't got that shit in her. I know this," he said, waving his hand over the kilos, "is not really your thing, but even if you only fuck with it from time to time you can't let friendship or family ties blind you to the facts." Zay reached in his pocket for his vibrating phone. "I'm coming out now," he answered.

Joey watched from the window as he tossed the duffle bag of kilos in the rear of a minivan. The driver was beautiful girl who resembled a young Beverly Johnson. She handed Zay a gray Prada knapsack. He kissed her on the cheek then she drove away. He came back in and sat on the couch. Joey sat on the chair in front of him.

"You keep an ol' model-looking bitch around," Joey said.

"You jealous?"

"Never that," Joey replied.

"You need to stop frontin' all the damn time. Just admit you into me heavy. I don't know why you won't give me a chance."

"'Cause you got too many hoes. They be all out in the street fighting over you. I'm not with none of that shit. I'd been killed a bitch."

"I'd give all them up if I had you."

"You already know I'm not falling for that weak game of yours."

"You'll give in eventually." Zay nodded. "This is $310,000." He stood up. "It was good doing business with you, baby girl."

"Likewise," Joey replied, reaching for the doorknob. Zay leaned against the door, preventing her from opening it. Joey eyed him up and down. "What are you doing?"

"I really want to take you out."

"Zay, honestly, I can't have all that drama. I'm trying to grow my promotion company. I can't be seen out with you, and then your little chickenheads will be showing up to my events trying to fight me. That shit is bad for business."

"If being seen in Charlotte is the problem you can go to Miami with me for a few days next week."

"So now you want to slide me out of town like them other chicks, spend some money on me, and smash me. Then when we come back you flip."

"You the one be acting like we've never fucked before," Zay said.

"Man, that was five years ago. I was a little fast-ass seventeen-year-old and you were a shell twenty-three-year-old fucking everything moving. Not much different than what you're trying to do now."

Zay liked a challenge. "Come to Miami. I'll put you in your own suite and you'll see it's not about that with me and you."

"I'll think about it," Joey replied, even though she had already made up her mind to go.

"Do that," Zay said. Suddenly he leaned in and kissed her as if he loved her. Joey was shocked but it felt good as his tongue moved rhythmically around hers. Her nipples stiffened and her vagina jumped. Just as unexpectedly as he began kissing her he stopped and stared at her briefly. Without saying a word, he opened the door and left. Joey stood frozen for like thirty seconds; then she pushed the door closed and leaned against it, thinking, *God, what am I getting myself into?*

Atlanta, Georgia
Spring, 2001

"Where is he?" Evan muttered then rang the doorbell a fourth time. She was standing at the front entrance of a spectacular mansion in the Sugarloaf section of Duluth County. The home belonged to Marshawn Griggs, one of the biggest drug traffickers in Atlanta. Evan had been at the door for more than five minutes. *I could be with Joey and Cee right now.* She should've been at dinner with her two best friends celebrating her graduation that took place earlier in the day. Instead, she was attempting to commence another robbery. This was the last thing that she wanted to be doing on such a special day, but Marshawn was hard to get with because he was rarely in town.

Gage and Evan never robbed drug dealers in or around Atlanta. However, once they made plans to move out of Atlanta the same weekend of graduation, Gage set his sights on robbing Marshawn. Gage had wanted to rob the braggadocios New York transplant for a long time for two reasons: he knew that he was sweet and he just plain didn't like him. So when the opportunity presented itself he jumped on it.

Evan reached to press the bell a fifth time, but decided against it. *Fuck this. I'm going to get with my friends.* Evan was radiant in a navy knee-length halter dress and strappy pale pink five-inch Manolos. Her long golden blond hair crowned her face in Farah Fawcett curls.

"I'm out of here," Evan said aloud. She walked carefully down the large brick steps and down the stone walkway to her white-on-white Mercedes CL 500, a graduation gift that she'd bought for herself. Evan opened the door, tossed her purse inside, and eased down into the car.

The front door of the house flew open and Marshawn ran out yelling, "Tiff," the alias that he knew Evan by.

Evan got out of the car. "I was just about to leave. I've been out here ringing the bell for ten minutes."

"I'm sorry about that," he told her. "My alarm shorted out today and the doorbell is connected to it. The alarm company can't straighten it out until tomorrow."

"Oh. I thought you were playing games."

"Not at all. You wanna get something to eat?"

"I ate with my parents before they flew back to Cali." Just like Evan's other aliases, Tiff came complete with a background. This time she was a student at Georgia Tech who came from a wealthy California family.

"What about a movie and drinks?"

"Sure," Evan replied and followed him into his home theater. The room was like a mini theater equipped with an authentic popcorn maker and a wet bar.

"You wanna watch *Ali, Baby Boy,* or *Exit Wounds?*"

"Bootlegs?" Evan shrieked. "I don't do bootlegs, sweetheart. None of those movies you named are out on DVD."

"I got guap, ma, so I get my shit when Regal and AMC get theirs."

What a cornball. "I want to see Baby Boy."

"Good choice. Fix yourself a drink while I put the movie on."

"I need to run out to my car and get my purse."

"Go ahead. I won't start the movie until you come back."

Evan moved briskly out to her car. She got her bag then placed a quick call to Gage. "The door is open," was all that she said and went back into the house.

Not twenty minutes into the movie, Marshawn was all over Evan. He was smothering her with wet kisses while his hands explored her body. Marshawn knew all the right places to touch. Evan tried hard not to get lost in pleasure but he was making it hard. Especially when he dropped to his knees, pulled her ass to the end of the chair, and spread her legs apart. Using his tongue, he pushed her thong to the side and sucked on her swollen clitoris. He then slid two fingers inside of her. Marshawn moved them in and out while tracing her clitoris with the tip of his tongue.

"Oh, God," Evan screamed out in pleasure, closing her eyes and tossing her head back.

Gage's blood boiled as he stood in the door watching them. Enraged, he ran over and backhanded Marshawn with a closed fist, dazing him. Gage yanked Evan by the hair and flung her across the room like a rag doll. Marshawn stood and lunged at Gage. Gage shot him twice, once in the right shoulder and once in the left thigh. Marshawn fell backward and landed awkwardly across the theater chairs. He was conscious, in pain, and unable to move.

"What the fuck is wrong with you?" Evan screamed at Gage as she rose from the ground in a great deal of pain. "Why would you throw me down like that?"

"Be glad I didn't put a bullet in your ass for letting a nigga eat your pussy."

"He went down on me! What was I supposed to do?"

"Hold him the fuck off until I come in, not lie back like a slut."

"I give the fuck up," Evan shouted. "I'm done with this shit and I'm done with you. That shit you keep putting up your nose is turning you into a paranoid idiot."

Gage rushed at Evan, wrapped his hand around her neck, and slammed her against the wall. "Ain't nothing over and done until I say it." He squeezed her throat. "Do you understand me, bitch?" Evan nodded as much as she could with a hand around her throat. With a hard thrust, Gage released Evan. "Go round that paper up so we can get the hell outta here."

Holding her neck, Evan limped away, her entire body aching terribly. *Gage is out his damn mind if he thinks we gon' be together. I'm getting away from his ass by any means.* Evan went up to the second floor study where she believed Marshawn kept his money.

Evan rummaged through the massive wooden desk in the study. In one drawer, she came across a chrome P-90 Ruger and a set of small keys. Evan zoomed in on the custom-built entertainment wall. There were four ceiling-to-floor bookshelves along that wall. At the bottom of each bookshelf were two wide and deep drawers with built-in locks. The keys look like they would be a perfect fit. Evan picked up the keys and went over to the wall. The first key she tried worked. This was no surprise to her. Over the four years she'd been doing stickups, Evan had come across so many men who kept keys to safe or lock boxes in the same room. She never understood the logic in that.

Evan opened the drawer. Inside were five medium cardboard file boxes. She lifted the lid off a box. There were at least twenty different stacks of tightly banded hundred dollar bills. Evan picked up a few of the stacks and thumbed through them. Each of the stacks appeared to contain a hundred each. If each stack amounted to $10,000 that box alone had $200,000 in it.

Evan looked in the other four boxes; they all were identical to the first box she opened. After opening the other seven drawers and finding the same setup, she knew that they'd hit the jackpot. If the numbers were what she thought they were, there was between $5 million and $8 million dollars in that room: enough money to keep her straight for a long time. Standing in front of all that money, she tried to think of a way to get half of it out without Gage knowing. He was under the assumption that there would only be like $500,000 there.

I could take three boxes down and double back later. That's too risky.

"What the fuck is taking you so long?" Gage roared from downstairs.

Evan hated the sound of his voice. She hated him. And here she stood with two issues both involving Gage. Evan didn't want to share that money with him nor did she want to be with him.

Over the last year, he had become a compulsive gambler and cocaine addict. The more money he lost gambling the more cocaine he did and the more aggressive he became toward her.

"Bitch," Gage yelled, "I know you hear me!"

Evan ran over to the desk, grabbed the gun, and began yelling, "Help me. Gage, help please."

Although Marshawn was severely injured, Gage bound his arms to the chair with a pair of flex-cuffs before going to rescue Evan. Following the sounds of Evan's screams, Gage sprinted up the stairs. Evan stood very still with her back against the wall next to the door with the gun raised. When Gage crossed the threshold, Evan fired the gun three times, shooting him once in the head and twice in the neck. His body slammed to the ground. Gage never knew what hit him.

Evan exhaled and stepped over Gage as if she never cared for him. In her mind, his murder was a necessary means to an end, because he would have never let her go.

Marshawn was barely conscious when Evan returned to the theater room. His pain was too great for him to talk, but when he saw Evan approaching, gun in hand, his eyes begged her for mercy.

"I'm sorry," Evan spoke, "but there is no doubt in my mind that if I let you live you will find me and kill me."

Grimacing in pain, he shook his head in disagreement.

Evan closed her eyes and shot him four times. When she opened her eyes there were four gaping holes in his chest. His eyes were wide open and blood poured from his mouth. She got her purse and ran back to the study.

Evan tried to figure out how she was going to get the money out the house. She also had to figure out how she was going to get her Mercedes and Gage's Navigator off the property. Both cars were registered to her. Evan looked down at her dress; it was covered in blood splatter. After thinking for a few seconds she knew exactly who to call. She took out her phone and made a call. "Come on, pick up, pick up."

"Where in the hell are you, Miss College Graduate?" Joey asked. "We're ready to party!"

"I'm in trouble, Jo," Evan said somberly.

"What's wrong, Evan? What happened?"

"I need you and Cee to meet me. I need some jeans or sweats and a T-shirt."

"I'll bring some clothes," Joey assured her. "Where are you?"

Evan gave her the directions to the house. As soon as she hung up, Evan got busy moving the file boxes to the first floor. It took close to twenty trips. Once she had all the boxes downstairs, she backed the Navigator into one of the five empty garage spaces. Evan loaded the boxes into the rear of the truck. Just as she placed the last box in and closed the lift gate, Joey pulled up outside the garage and blew the horn tree times, as Evan had instructed her to.

Evan opened the garage slot next to the Navigator and Joey pulled in. Joey barely had her feet out of the car when she began to question Evan. "What the hell going on and whose house is this?"

"I'll explain all that later. Did you bring the clothes?"

"Yes," Joey replied.

Cee exited the car with a bag of clothes in her hand. "Here." She gave the bag to Evan.

Evan slipped off the dress and put on the jeans and shirt. "Gage is dead," she announced nonchalantly.

Cee and Joey exchanged shocked looks. They didn't know what shocked them more: the news of his death or Evan's cavalier attitude. Joey placed her hands on Evan's shoulders. "Wait a minute. Stop, stop, stop, what do you mean he's dead? How did he die and where is he at?"

"He got shot. He's in the house."

"In this house!" Cee exclaimed.

"Yes."

"Did you call for help?" Cee ran toward the door. "How do you know he's dead?"

Evan caught Cee by the arm and yanked her back. "Trust me, he's dead; and he's not the only one in there who's dead. No, I didn't call for help. This was a drug deal that went all the way left." Evan handed Cee the keys to her Mercedes. "I need you to drive my car and stay in front of me."

The talk of dead bodies and drug deals gone wrong scared the shit out of Cee. She snatched the keys from Evan. "Y'all get in them cars and let's go. I'm not with none of this shit. I got three babies at home who need me," Cee said. "I tell you what, by the time I get that car started y'all better be pulling out that garage or I'm out." Cee ran out of the garage to the car.

Staring silently at Evan, Joey thought about the conversation she'd had with Zay six months earlier and wondered if this was really a robbery gone wrong.

Evan put her dress and shoes in the bag and gave it to Joey. "Put this in the car with you." She turned to get in the Navigator.

"Un-uh," Joey said, "not so fast." She looked Evan in the eye. "You don't have to do it tonight or tomorrow, but soon you will sit down and tell me everything that happened here. You owe me that because you called me here and I refuse to get caught up in something that I know nothing about."

Chapter Three

The Monday following the Luxe Enclave's grand opening was the first official day of business in their new offices. Evan decided to go in early in order to catch up on her work. She had put quite a few clients and events on the back burner in the weeks leading to the grand opening. Now, she not only needed to catch up, but get ahead in her work. The last thing she needed at this point was a blow to her reputation as a hard worker.

Evan arrived at the Enclave at seven o'clock a.m. but their offices didn't open until nine. The parking lot was empty. She pulled into her reserved space in front of the L Room. Dressed in a superbly tailored charcoal Chanel pantsuit, Louis bag on her shoulder, and Louis briefcase in her hand, she walked proudly toward the building that she owned. When she got up to the door, she realized that her keys were in the bottom of her purse. Evan bent down; she set her Starbucks cup and briefcase on the cement. When Evan stood upright, she became cloaked in fear when she saw the reflection of a masked man in the mirrored glass doors standing directly behind her.

The masked man placed her in a chokehold and shoved a chloroform-soaked towel over her nose and mouth. Evan tried to get out of his grasp but everything slowly faded to black.

I'm alive, Evan thought as she came to. *Thank God.* As she struggled to open her eyes she felt someone's hands on her arms and chest. Through blurred vision, Evan could see six figures hovering over her. Panicked, she came up swinging.

"Get off of me," she yelled. Suddenly she was pinned to the ground by her wrists.

"Ma'am, please calm down," she heard a strange voice say. She continued to squirm and scream.

"Evan, be still. They are trying to help you," Joey said.

Upon hearing her friend's voice Evan stopped moving. She squeezed her eyes tight then began blinking rapidly until her vision became clear. Evan was relieved to see that the people holding her down were two male paramedics. Joey, Cee, and two employees from the spa were standing behind the paramedics.

"Ma'am, can you tell me what happened to you?" the paramedic asked as he fastened the blood pressure monitor sleeve around her left arm.

Evan touched her throbbing head while thinking of a lie to tell. "I think I may have passed out because I didn't have anything to eat yesterday. I planned to grab a bite once I got here. When I got to the door I felt sick and dizzy then everything went black."

Joey eyed Evan suspiciously.

"Your blood pressure looks good," the paramedic told Evan, removing the sleeve. "We're going to lift you onto the stretcher now."

"For what?" Evan spat.

"To go to the emergency room," he replied.

"I don't need to go to the hospital. I just need to eat some food."

"Ma'am, you should get checked out in case it's something more serious. Not to mention you could have a concussion if you hit your head when you fell to the pavement."

"I'll make a sick appointment with my doctor this afternoon."

"Evan," Cee interjected, "what will it hurt for you to go on to the hospital right now?" Evan shot her a "mind your business" look. "Whatever." Cee waved her hand at her dismissively. "That's your silly ass if you fall out dead somewhere."

The paramedics helped Evan to her feet. After signing a waiver refusing treatment Evan went into the L Room. Joey and Cee followed, carrying her things. Much like her home Evan's office was decorated expensively in light pastels.

"My head is killing me." Evan opened the mini stainless steel refrigerator behind her glass desk and retrieved a glass bottle of Acqua Panna water. She popped two pills into her mouth and drank the water down.

"I have to get over to the spa." Cee set Evan's things down. "Are you going to be okay?"

"I'm better than okay," Evan said. "Go on. I know you've got clients waiting."

"I'll be back to check on you and to make sure you've made an appointment with your doctor," Cee assured her as she left.

"And I know you will," Evan mumbled, knowing that Cee was innately nurturing.

Joey was leaning against the file cabinet with a slight frown on her face. "I want to know what the hell is really going on, Evan," she stated.

"Nothing," Evan replied, rifling through her purse, pretending to look for something in order to avoid eye contact with Joey.

"You a damn liar." Joey crossed the room and tossed a folded piece of paper onto Evan's desk.

"What is this?" Evan asked.

"The note that was on top of you when I found your ass laid out. I assume whoever knocked you over the head left it for you."

Evan unfolded the paper and read it:

*It's way too easy to get at you. Thought that you
would at least make it fun. I decided to give you a
pass and let you live today. Next time you might not
be so lucky.*

Angrily Evan ripped the paper to pieces.

Joey sat in a mint green leather chair in front of Evan's
desk. "Now, do you want to tell me the truth?"

"It's nothing for you to worry about. This is a private
matter and I'm going to take care of it."

"No; wrong answer. It is not a private matter when
someone comes to our place of business and knocks you
over the fucking head."

This is the last thing I need. Evan inhaled deeply.
Exhaling, she said, "It's a guy I used to date. He's been
stalking me. I have a court date next week to get a
restraining order. Once we go to court, I know that he'll
back off. Until then I'll have to be extra cautious."

Joey didn't believe Evan's story but for now she would
act as if she did. "Well, until you get this thing straight-
ened out, whenever you're going to come in early have
one of the guys from security come in early to meet you."

"I will," Evan agreed.

"Finding you like that scared the shit out of me. I
thought you were dead. Be glad that I came in early. If
Cee would've found that note she would still be in here
losing her mind." Joey stood up to leave. "I'll be up in the
Penthouse if you need me."

"All right. And can we keep this stalking thing between
us? I don't need Cee driving me crazy."

"You already know I'm not saying one word to Cee,"
Joey said, heading toward the door. She turned back to
Evan. "What's his name?"

"Who?"

"The person who's stalking you."

"Oh, um," Evan stammered. "His name is, um, Tonio."

She is definitely lying. Joey shook her head with a small "gotcha" grin. "I think you should give the security team his name and a picture so they can be on the lookout for him." Joey turned and left the room.

Evan was so glad to see her go. Finally, she could process the situation. She was very unnerved by the defenseless attack that had taken place. The game that this person was playing had just surpassed psychotic. Evan was well aware that she could've easily been killed. She'd never felt so helpless in her life. It was time for this game to end and Evan had every intention of ending it on her terms.

First, she needed to find out this person's identity. She cut on her computer and began her search for a private investigator. Once she came across a nationally top-ranked private investigation firm in the area, Evan turned her search to security.

"What am I thinking?" Evan retrieved her BlackBerry from her purse. She scrolled through the contacts and found the number that she needed. *This silly nigga will do anything for extra money,* she thought as she waited for an answer. *He'll probably do it for free just to be around me.* Evan laughed. A man answered the phone.

"Hello, Rhamel, this is Evan. I have a proposition for you."

"Joey," Bev called out as she exited her burgundy 745i. Entering the headquarters building Joey stopped and waited for Bev.

"I just saw the ambulance leaving," Bev said, approaching the door. "What happened?"

Joey replied, "When I got here I found Evan passed out in front of the L Room."

"Oh, my God." Bev gasped with her hand on her chest. "Is she all right?"

"Yeah." Joey rolled her eyes. "I guess."

"What hospital are they taking her to?"

"Evan didn't go to the hospital. She's in her office."

"Why didn't she go to the hospital?"

"Because she is full of shit," Joey hissed, stepping onto the elevator. She slid a black card into a small slot then pressed a long button marked PENTHOUSE.

Bev sensed that something was bothering Joey. "What makes you say that?"

"I don't know." Joey shrugged. She rarely discussed Evan with anyone other than Cee or Zay. At the moment, Joey couldn't go to either one of them. Joey knew that these types of things scared the complete shit out of Cee. There was absolutely no way in hell Joey was going to Zay with anything negative about Evan. Zay would make an extra big deal out of the situation, since he already thought that she was shady.

Not only was Bev Joey's mentor, she was also a good friend. Therefore, Joey decided to confide in her. "Evan didn't pass out. Someone knocked her out."

"Who would do that to her?"

"I don't have a clue. She swears that someone is stalking her, but I know she's lying."

"How do you know that?" Bev asked.

"Trust and believe if Evan was being stalked I would've heard about it as soon as it started."

"Well, Rhamel did mention something to me when I was closing Luxe the other night. I didn't say anything to you because I didn't want to overstep my boundaries coming to you about your best friend."

"Look, Bev, unless it is some petty 'he said, she said' mess you can come to me. So, what did Rhamel have to say?"

"Evan was sitting in her car in the parking lot. He said that when he walked up on her he scared her and that she had a gun on her lap."

Something is definitely up. Joey knew that Evan would never have her gun out unless she felt that she was in danger. Truly concerned about her friend, Joey wanted to know what was going on so that she could be there for Evan, especially since Evan didn't really have anyone else. Finding out would have to wait. Joey's only focus for the rest of the day was the grand opening of the Penthouse later that night. There was a lot of work to be done.

"That only adds to a long list of suspect shit Evan's been doing lately," Joey said as they stepped off the elevator into the Penthouse. "The lying is what really bothers me. It is what it is, though, and I have no time to get caught up in that chick's mess. Not today."

The Penthouse opening was a fabulous celebrity red carpet event. Over a dozen players from Charlotte's professional sports teams that held Penthouse memberships attended. More than a few of them brought teammates, pro athletes from other cities, or friends from the entertainment industry. In an effort to attract new members Joey and Bev went all out. The top shelf bar was open for the duration of the event. There were three food stations. The seafood station offered colossal shrimp, king crab legs, and two-pound lobster tails. At the meat station the choices were filet mignon, New York strip, and prime rib. Two esteemed Japanese chefs manned the third station, making sushi per the guests' orders. Stunning waitresses dressed in fitted, low-cut white blouses, black miniskirts, and four-inch heels served the crowd.

The club's luxury sports bar ambiance alone was enough to make most of the charter members pay for the pricy membership. A sprawling 7,000 square feet, the Penthouse was a rich sports fanatic's dream. Ten eighty-inch screens lined the walls. Oversized brown leather chairs were situated throughout for members to relax in while watching games, drinking, or just chilling. There were two gaming rooms: one for poker and the second for casino-style blackjack and roulette. A private room equipped with poles and a bar could be used for events such as bachelor or birthday parties.

For the lavish event Joey played it pretty low key in a white tank, light blue True Religion skinny jeans, and beige Charlotte Olympia peep-toe platform pumps that were embellished with metal spikes. In her element, Joey worked the room chatting, taking pictures with guests, and just taking in and enjoying the scene.

Zay was not at all thrilled when he arrived to see Dawhar Bradley, an NFL standout, talking to his wife. He was convinced that Dawhar had a thing for Joey. Zay went right over and placed his arm around her waist, greeted her with a tongue kiss, and then smoothly whisked her away.

"Every time that nigga come to something he always up in your face."

"Zay, don't start with this again. Dawhar is not thinking about me; besides, he has a wife."

"That doesn't mean shit."

"You should know," Joey retorted.

"Oh, so you wanna take a low blow at me about some old shit, because I'm telling you that I don't like the way another dude getting at you?"

"Yes, because I'm tired of you constantly hurling accusations at me about this. I'm not the one who cheated in this marriage and I'm tired of getting treated like I did."

Joey stormed off. She got a few feet away then came back. "I've never done you wrong, so respect me and, most of all, respect my place of business."

***

"We're not going to be here long," Cee told her husband, Petey, while checking her hair and makeup in the visor mirror. "I just want to show my face for like an hour. I need to get some rest. My first client is at seven thirty in the morning."

"I'm cool with that, baby," he replied, wheeling the cream Escalade into the Enclave parking lot. As Petey drove by the L Room, he noticed a dark figure moving along the side of the building. He stopped and reversed the truck. "Who is that?"

"Where?"

Petey pointed. "Right there."

"I don't see anybody."

"It's somebody over there." He shifted the gear to drive then pulled down to the valet stand. "You go on in. I'm going to walk over to the L Room to make sure everything is okay."

"Oh, no, you not! That's the security team's job. Tell them to go check it out."

"All right," Petey conceded, knowing how easily frightened his wife could get.

"That's fine." She leaned over and gave him a kiss. "See you inside."

Cee got out of the truck and walked toward the building. The attendant gave Petey a valet ticket. Petey tipped him then set off to find Enclave's security.

"Hey, love." Cee greeted Joey with a hug.

Joey returned the hug. "What's up, mama? I'm glad you made it back. I know you're tired. Y'all got slammed at the spa today."

"Yes, we did! But, I'm not complaining." Cee smiled, rubbing her thumb and fingertips together like she had money between them.

"I know that's right."

"It looks really good in here. How's it going?"

"Great. We've even sold some memberships."

"That's what's up! Where is Zay?"

"He probably somewhere pouting."

"About what?"

"When he came in I was talking with Dawhar. A few of his people had just signed up for memberships. So now he back on the same shit about Dawhar in my face."

"Zay ain't tripping at all," Cee said. "Dawhar does flirt with you a lot."

"But I don't flirt with him. That man has a ten thousand dollar platinum membership to this club and he's gotten his teammates and friends to join. It is strictly business between us."

Cee held up her palms. "Hey, you don't have to convince me. Trust me, I understand that; but you need to check Dawhar. He needs to respect your marriage. That's all I'm going to say about it." Cee scanned the room. "Where is Evan?"

"Hell if I know." Joey sighed. "She came in earlier to make sure the serving stations were set up correctly. Said she was going home to change clothes and she'd be back."

"I hope she isn't somewhere passed out. That chick didn't even go see her doctor today."

"That doesn't shock me," Joey mumbled.

Zay was angry at the way Joey had handled him. He wanted to flip the fuck out on her and Dawhar, but he would never disrespect her place of business in that manner. The two double shots of Hennessy he'd just knocked down were beginning to cloud his judgment. If he had one more double shot he was going to forget that he was at his wife's business. Therefore, he decided to leave. He walked up behind Joey and said in her ear, "Yo, I'm out."

Joey turned to face him. "But you just got here."

"And why you worried? You don't want me here. Dawhar will keep you company."

"I need you here," she said, embracing him by the waist. "I'm sorry about the way I came at you. It has been a crazy day and I was a little on edge. Please forgive me and stay awhile."

Zay was a little apprehensive, but since Joey did apologize, he hugged her and agreed to hang around a little longer.

Bobby, one of the Enclave's security guards, rushed into the Penthouse and ran over to Cee, Joey, and Zay. "We need you outside now," he said, distressed. "Something bad happened."

"Bad like what?" Joey asked.

Cee noticed that the Bobby had dark red wet spots on his shirt. Suddenly she realized that Petey had not come inside. "Did you see my husband out there?"

"Yes," he said, unable to look her in the eye.

"Is he okay?"

He shook his head. "No."

Cee ran past the elevators to the stairs. She hurried down the stairs, followed by Bobby, Zay, and Joey. Outside, smoke was flowing into the night sky. It was hard to tell if it was coming from the L Room or Luxurious. Cee grabbed the security guard's shirt. "Where is my husband?"

"Come." He guided her to the side of the L Room. She became horrified at the sight of her husband, unconscious out on the ground, bleeding profusely. Rich, a security guard, lay next to him lifeless and covered in blood. Cee went over to Petey. "Noooooo," she screamed madly then dropped to her knees beside her husband and cradled his head in her arms. "Oh, baby, what happened to you?" Tears filled her eyes. Cee could hear the ambulance and fire truck sirens approaching. She knew that they were close, only seconds away, but it felt like forever.

Joey was in shock; the scene was overwhelming and upsetting on so many levels for her. Petey, her friend since high school, and Rich, her employee, lay severely wounded if not dead. To add insult to injury the Luxe Enclave had just opened for business. The publicity was going to be horrible but, at the time, bad publicity was the least of her worries with two human lives possibly lost.

Zay ran out to the parking lot then came back with four paramedics. Firefighters stormed the L Room with a water hose. Suddenly the grounds were swarming with Charlotte police. They immediately pulled Bobby and two other guards to the side to find out what was happening. Joey went over and listened intently as Bobby gave the police a rundown.

Bobby told the police, "Petey told Rich and me that he saw someone on the side of the building. When he took us over to the spot, there was a man with three lit Molotovs. He tossed one through the window. We all yelled out, 'Yo, stop,' and he started shooting at us. I ran. I thought that Rich and Petey were behind me."

Nothing could be done for Rich. He was dead when the paramedics got to him. Petey was loaded onto an ambulance and transported to Carolina's Medical Center with Cee by his side. Joey wanted to go to the hospital to be there for her friends but she had to hang around to handle things with the police and fire investigators.

The fire chief told Joey, "Damage to the structure is mostly water and it's one small area. Your sprinkler system did a good job smothering the flame before it could spread out of control."

That news was of little relief to her, as she watched Rich being carried away in body bag. The building could be restored; his life could not.

About forty-five minutes later Joey was sitting in the passenger seat of Zay's black Dodge Challenger. He was about to drive her to the hospital when she spotted Evan's car pulling into the parking lot. Rhamel was driving and Evan was sitting in the back. "What the fuck?" Joey questioned aloud. From the time Bobby informed them until now, everything had been so chaotic that she hadn't even thought about Evan. Something about Evan in the car with Rhamel didn't sit right with Joey. Instantly she felt that the incident had something to with Evan's drama.

"Hold up a minute," she told Zay, then got out of the car. Joey quickly made her way to Evan's car. When Evan saw Joey coming, she had Rhamel stop the car and she got out.

"What happened?" she asked Joey. "Why are the police and firemen here?"

Joey snapped. She grabbed Evan by the neck and slammed her against the top of the trunk. "Petey and Rich got shot trying to stop somebody from setting the L on fire. I know it has something to do with you." Joey squeezed her neck. "No more fucking games, bitch. You better start talking or I swear on my kids I will kill your sneaky ass."

Zay pulled Joey off of Evan. Gasping for air, Evan didn't know what to say or do; her next move had to be her best move. What would her next move be? Would she keep it one hundred and come clean with Joey? Or would she pack up and run from the past that was chasing her?

Chapter Four

Sitting in the family waiting room at CMC main hospital, Joey tapped her right foot rapidly, causing her knee to bounce furiously. It was a nervous habit that she had since childhood. Zay placed his hand on her knee and said, "Baby, I know your nerves are on edge, and so are mine, but that tapping is going to drive me up the wall." Joey stared blankly across the room at Cee. Joey couldn't begin to fathom feeling the hurt that was displayed on her best friend's face.

Wedged between her mother and her mother-in-law, Cee sobbed softly. Her makeup was stained with tears. The pale yellow cotton Von Furstenburg wrap dress she wore was splattered in big brown spots of Pete's dry blood. Her head began to throb painfully from all of the thoughts racing through her mind. Cee's chest tightened; she began to feel like her breath was leaving her body, and that the room was closing in on her. Suddenly she bolted from the chair and sprinted toward the exit.

Leaping from her seat Joey chased Cee. As Cee crossed the threshold of the door she bumped into Evan. Instantly Evan threw her arms around Cee. "I'm so sorry that this has happened to Petey," she said, crying.

Blood boiling, Joey stared at Evan icily. Their heated parking lot confrontation was cut short by the police, who had questions for Evan. Therefore, Joey didn't get the answers that she was seeking. Still, without blinking, Joey would bet her life that this entire incident was somehow connected to Evan.

Cee rested her head on Evan's shoulder. "This is so insane, Ev. I don't know what I'm going to do. How will I explain this to our kids?"

"Everything is going to be okay," Evan replied, stroking Cee's hair. "And you already know Joey and I are here for you."

Shaking her head, Joey sighed loudly, and rolled her eyes. *I should slap this bitch for fronting.* Evan shot her a mean frown. To Joey, Evan's presence was the equivalent of a killer showing up to his victim's funeral and giving condolences to the unknowing family.

"Mrs. Grayson," a doctor called out from behind.

"Yes, yes." Cee pulled out of Evan's embrace and ran over to him. "Is my husband going to be okay?" The more than two dozen family and friends in attendance gathered around to hear the doctor.

"I have to be honest," the doctor spoke frankly, "I don't like to give false hope, but at the same time I don't like to come across as cruel. To put it in simple terms, Mr. Grayson is in the highest level of critical condition. He has an enormous amount of irreparable damage to some of his major organs. He is on life support and if we were to take him off he would not survive."

"Lord, noooo," Petey's mother screamed as she crashed to the floor. A few of the males rushed to her aid. They lifted her from the ground and placed her on a couch as she continued to cry out loudly to God.

The doctor carried on without breaking his stride: "We will be monitoring for any signs of progress. Hopefully he will make some improvements, at the least, and we can go from there."

"Okay," Cee agreed, nodding but not at all okay with what she'd just heard. "When can I see him?"

"In about thirty minutes. He's just been set up in the intensive care unit. A nurse will come get you." With a nod to the family he left the waiting room.

Cee turned to Joey. "Since the kids are already at your house can they stay over? I don't want to leave Petey."

"They can stay as long as you need them to."

"All right." Cee inhaled deeply, trying to ward off a flood of tears.

Joey hugged her. "It's going to be fine, Cee. Call me if you need anything, no matter how small it is, or if you want me to come back."

On the ride home there was no music or conversation, just silence. Shock and confusion were heavy on both Joey's and Zay's minds. As Joey peered out the passenger's window she wondered if the shooting was really related to Evan's issues or if she'd jump to conclusions. Meanwhile, Zay was trying to figure out what was going on with his wife. Even in the most turbulent situations, Joey would normally be talking. She was big on theories. Therefore, Zay wondered why she wasn't tossing out at him any theories about the night's events. This led him to believe that she was trying not to divulge something. Joey had the uncanny ability of being quiet when she wanted to avoid letting something slip out. The most alarming clue for Zay was Joey's actions toward Evan.

Reaching over, Zay grabbed Joey's hand, intertwined his fingers with hers, and kissed the back of it. "You okay, baby?" he asked.

"That depends on what you call okay. This all is so surreal."

"Yes, it is. What's your beef with Evan?"

"Um, nothing really. I was just pissed at her for not being there," she lied.

"That is not why you jumped on that girl like that."

"What else do you think it could be then, Zay?"

"I don't know, but I know you and I know that you're not telling me something. You need to talk to me 'cause, remember, that could be me lying in ICU shot up."

"Don't you think I know this?" Shaking her head, a tear crept out of her eyes. "I feel guilty for being glad that it wasn't you."

Joey's inclination that the shooting was linked to Evan was strong, but there was no way that she could tell Zay. Not just yet. She knew that if she let him in on her suspicions he would confront Evan and not in a nice way. Before telling him anything she had to be absolutely sure about it.

"There is no doubt in my mind that you feel that way," Zay said, keeping his eyes glued to the road. "You need to keep it real with me and stop protecting ol' girl."

"How am I protecting her?"

"You're covering up something, Joey. Whatever it is got one person killed and your best friend's husband fighting for his life. Not to mention the heat that could be coming my way; heat that I don't need."

"Tell me how a shooting at my business is going to bring heat to you."

"Stop playing, Joey. You are not naïve."

Her face twisted in confusion. Joey replied, "I really don't understand how this affects you."

"Two people were shot. One has died! As one of the business owners you and everyone around you will be under investigation." Zay was being persistent on the subject because he'd come a long way in the world of narcotics.

Zay was the third of four boys. He was raised by his widowed mother in one of the most notorious sections of the city, North Charlotte. A mixture of houses, apartments, and housing projects, the neighborhoods in the area were crime ridden and teetered on the poverty line. His mom, Dorenda, cleaned house in Myers Park during the day and worked third shift at the Lance factory at night. She made just enough money to get by, enough to keep a roof over the family's head, and keep them clothed and fed.

By the time Zay's two older brothers, Tony and Rico, made it to high school they decided that they wanted more than what their mother's combined salaries could afford. So they began to hustle weed and crack. When they started out they were happy with being able to buy the latest sneakers and freshest clothes. Being good big brothers, Zay and their youngest brother, Jason, reaped the benefits of their older brother's gains. Tony and Rico were natural hustlers and they began to pull in more money than was needed for clothes and shoes. With the boys' mother working and exhausted all the time she didn't really notice what was going on in the beginning. A few odd happenings did catch her attention. For instance she kept finding money in her purse or work uniform. She thought it was one of the men from the factory who was always asking her out. But things got a bit stranger. Groceries began to appear on her doorstep. For two months straight when she went to pay the power and water, both bills had already been paid. When she mentioned the occurrences to her sons they acted as if these were miracles or lucky coincidences. Dorenda didn't believe in coincidences.

While on her on winter vacation Dorenda took the time to thoroughly clean and reorganize the apartment. In her boys' rooms she noticed that all four boys had nice clothing and they were not the hand-me-downs that she brought home from the houses that she cleaned. She snooped through the older boys' things a little more and came across close to $12,000 in cash. She didn't find any drugs, because the boys were smart enough to keep the work at the homes of their girlfriends. Even though there was no evidence of drugs, Dorenda knew that it was drug money.

Upon finding the money she was furious with her two older sons. While waiting for them to come in from school, the more she thought about it, the more she realized things had been running considerably smoothly.

Dorenda contemplated not telling them that she knew what was going on. But there was no way that she could do that.

That evening when Tony and Rico arrived home she was sitting at the table in the tiny kitchen with the money in front of her. The boys froze in fear at the sight. With a burning Newport lodged between her right forefinger and middle finger, she asked, "Where did this come from?"

The boys exchanged nervous glances, then Tony, the oldest, spoke: "We made it."

"How did you make it? I don't recall either of you clocking in at high-paying jobs."

"We've been selling a li'l weed here and there," Rico chimed in.

Dorenda rolled her eyes to the sky. "Boy, your daddy, God rest his soul, hustled a li'l weed." She held up the money. "This and the clothes I found ain't come from selling a li'l weed. I may be green but I'm far from stupid."

Tony sat down diagonally from his mother. "Ma, we are dabbling in more than weed. We're doing it 'cause we're tired of you slaving in those white people houses and killing yourself in that factory at night. And then the money still is barely enough to cover the bills."

Dorenda hated that her children were even worrying about bills. She couldn't help but think of her girlfriends from the factory who were able to quit their jobs after their sons or boyfriends began dealing drugs. She wouldn't dream of quitting her job; in fact, she had a better plan. So she asked Tony, "Do you know what you're doing?"

"We know enough."

"You have to know more than enough! And don't think for one second that I'm condoning this. But I was thinking I have a small amount of money saved and if I

work some overtime we could move out of this horrible neighborhood."

"You don't have to work no overtime," Rico assured her, "or go in your savings. Just find where you want to move and let us know how much it's going to cost."

Guilt plagued Dorenda for even having this conversation with her children. Instead of talking about moving she should've been cursing them out and telling them how wrong they were.

Tony could see that his mother was struggling with her decision and he scooted closer to her. "Mama, we're just trying to get this family ahead. We're not trying to make a career out of this."

"Promise me that you'll watch out for your brother." She nodded toward Rico, who she knew to be her hot-headed wild child. "Don't let him do anything crazy. More importantly keep this away from Zay and Jason."

A month later the family relocated to a midsized four-bedroom one-story rental in a middle-class neighborhood. The brothers did more than help the family get ahead. Within a year they helped their mother purchase a new five-bedroom home in an upper middle-class area. They also bought her a brand new car and themselves one each. Their hustle had turned into the career that they said it wouldn't. They did keep their promise and didn't let their younger brother get involved in drug dealing. That didn't matter much though; Zay and Jason had grown up around the action and absorbed the game. So when Tony and Rico caught eighteen-year federal bids, Zay and Jason stepped right into their shoes.

Zay was a natural hustler and he'd proven himself to be the best out of the four. He'd used his brothers' fortunes and misfortunes as his blueprint for the game. Thus far it had worked out very well for him. He was nearly eighteen years deep in the game. In those years he'd avoided any major run-ins with the law. Over the *last five years he'd flown quietly under the radar as one of the biggest heroin distributors in the Southeast. In doing so Zay had amassed great wealth. Wealth that his wife didn't even know existed.*

Joey knew that her husband dealt narcotics, but she didn't know he was dealing on the level that he was. At this point he had enough money to set his older brothers up properly upon their return home from prison in a few short months. There was enough money that, if handled properly, his children and future grandchildren would have enough to live off of. Zay was nearing the end of what he considered a magnificent run in the drug game. He didn't need any unnecessary bullshit hindering him from accomplishing his goal. He was not at all selfish in his thoughts, for his heart felt for the loss of life and the harm that Petey had suffered. His thoughts were with them first and foremost.

Whipping the car into the driveway of their luxury home in the Palisades neighborhood, Zay told Joey, "For now I'm going to play dumb and give you the benefit of the doubt about what you know. Soon, you better decide what's important and where your loyalties lie: with your family or with your shady-ass friend."

The sun was up and shining by the time Joey's head touched the pillow. She had been asleep for only two hours when her cell began to blast loudly in her ear. Joey sat straight up. Exhausted and discombobulated she didn't even remember falling asleep or the previous night's events. Once she saw Cee's name displayed on the screen of her iPhone everything that had happened came crashing into her mind.

"Hey, Cee," she answered in a raspy whisper. She cleared her throat. "Hey, Cee, how's Petey?"

"He's dead," Cee wailed. "He's dead. My husband is dead!"

In the days following Petey's death, life became very hectic for the ladies and their immediate circle. Just as

Zay predicted the police looked deeply into the personal and business lives of Cee, Joey, and Evan. They were ruled out early on as having any involvement. From the start of the investigation the police focused their sights on a serial arsonist who'd been setting buildings ablaze across the city for over a year. Since Molotov cocktails were the arsonist's signature flame starter, detectives assumed that it was he who attempted to set the L Room on fire and shot Petey and the security guard. The police did inform the families and The Luxe Group of their arsonist theory and assured them that they were doing everything to catch the suspect.

The Luxe Group paid for the security guard's funeral and burial expenses. Joey had also placed a sizable personal check in a condolence card to his family.

Petey's family had raised him in an Apostolic denomination faith church; they didn't believe in sad funerals. They preferred celebration of life services with upbeat music, Holy Ghost preaching, and shouting. A week after his death Petey's homegoing celebration was held on a sunny Monday afternoon. Petey's immediate and extended family wore white for the funeral as a symbol to show that they were celebrating instead of mourning. Petey's body lay in a stainless steel casket, top of the line, that was adorned with white roses. Dozens of wreaths sent from around the country surrounded the altar. He was loved by so many.

Everything about the service was upbeat; even Petey's mother was in good spirits. Cee couldn't get with it, though. Sitting in the first row between Evan and Joey she was inconsolable, at times sobbing loudly. It was heartbreaking. Cee's children held up very well considering the circumstances. The trips were composed and poised as they comforted the two younger children. The atmosphere at the cemetery after the funeral was drastically different from the church service. It was awfully sad, a lot of wailing and fainting among the family. The realization that this was the last stop with Petey in the physical world was too much for them to bear.

Cee sat staring stoically at the coffin that was parked in front of a stone mausoleum, with a steady stream of tears flowing from her eyes. As the graveside service came to an end and everyone was preparing to leave Cee whispered to Joey, "I'm not ready to go. I want to be alone with my husband for little while. Can you stay with me?"

"Of course I will, sweetie. You stay right here. I'll let them know to go ahead without us."

Joey caught up to Evan as she was getting in one of the family limos with Cee's children. "Hey, listen, Cee wants to hang back for a little while. We'll ride to the repast with Zay."

"Are you sure?" Evan asked, looking over Joey's shoulder at Cee who was still seated in front of the casket. "The staff has the repast ready for the family's arrival. I can wait with you guys."

"No. We're good," Joey stated directly.

"Well, all righty then."

The exchange was quite awkward. In the days leading up to the funeral, conversation between the two friends had been at a minimum. If and when they did talk it was only pertaining to business matters or the planning of Petey's repast that was being held at the L Room.

"Guess I'll see you guys at the repast," Evan said, feeling ever so slighted by her long time bestie as she turned to head for the car. She knew that she was the cause of the tension. Knowing what had to be done to clear the air she turned around. "Ay, Joe, you wanna get together tonight for drinks and have that talk?"

"I sure do," Joey replied matter-of-factly before walking away.

After the last car exited the cemetery, Cee walked up to her husband's casket, flung her upper body onto it, and began to sob loudly. Seated on a bench about fifty feet away Joey and Zay watched quietly. Resting on the casket, she continued to cry for five to ten minutes. Out of nowhere she began banging the casket and screaming, "Why, why, why, Petey?"

Joey stood to go console her. Zay put his arm out, blocking her path. "Chill, Joe, let her get this out."

As badly as Joey wanted to run over to Cee, hug her up, and let her know that it was going to be all right, she followed Zay's advice.

"Why did you have to go back there? I asked you not to!" Cee screamed at the casket. "Now what am I supposed to do? Who's going to teach our son to be a man? Who's going to walk our daughters down the aisle? Who's going to hold me down?" The anger that she was feeling subsided and the hurt from the overwhelming pain set in. Her angry screams turned to soft whimpers. In a voice barely above a whisper she started to pour out her heart to her slain love.

"Petey, I love you so much. I don't know how to go on without you. My heart is shattered and I don't think I'll be able to pick up the pieces without you. I know that you would want me to be strong and I'm going to try to be strong, for the kids. I don't know if you knew it, but you were my world, you and the kids. I'd give up everything that I've accomplished just to have you back. It means nothing if you're not here."

Cee's shoulders heaved up and her body shook violently as the tears began to flow even faster. "I don't want to leave you. I swear I don't. Everyone who loves you is waiting on me at a repast in your honor." She sobbed. "So I must go now. I will always love you and I promise you that no one will ever take your place. You are and always will be my only husband." Cee kissed Petey's casket. "Farewell, my love." She motioned for a cemetery worker to come over.

"Are you ready for us to put the casket in the vault, ma'am?" the worker asked.

Cee closed her eyes and nodded up and down. Three more cemetery workers came over. Two men on each side, they began to wheel the casket into the stone mausoleum. Unable to watch Petey being put into his final resting place, Cee turned and strolled over to Joey and Zay. "I need to get out here," she said, falling into Joey's waiting arms. "I can't see him go in there knowing he'll never come out."

During the repast Cee wore a brave face, mainly for her kids, as people laughed, cried, ate, and shared their fondest memories of Pete. Of course it was hard for Cee, but the fact that it was being held inside the very building that Petey died outside of made it twenty times harder. Not to mention this was Cee's first time being back on the premises since that fatal night. Though it was tough for her being there it was somewhat comforting to be in the last place that she saw Petey alive, the place that they'd shared their last kiss ever, and it was as if she could still feel his spirit there.

Cee's appetite was pretty much nonexistent. Food wasn't high on the menu for her, but gin and tonics were. The drinks helped her get through the repast. They also cleared her head enough for her to notice that there was some type of tension between Joey and Evan. It wasn't hard to notice in such a setting. Whenever Evan came into Joey's presence, Joey would remove herself. Then there were the times that Cee caught Joey unconsciously scowling at Evan. Cee made a mental to note to ask Joey, whom she was closer to, what was going on between the two.

The repast wound down about seven that evening. On the way out, Joey came across Evan as she was instructing her staff on the cleanup duties for the night. Joey waited for her to finish then said, "I hope you still want to get together for drinks and that long overdue talk?"

"Ain't nothing changed," Evan replied, smug and a little fed up with the shade that Joey was throwing.

"Okay. So where and when?"

"Vinnie's at eleven."

The only thing that Joey really wanted to do was pick up her kids from her mother-in-law's house, go home, and chill with them. With the chaos of opening the Luxe Group followed by the shooting, it had been weeks since she'd gotten to spend quality time with her three sons—Braden, nine; Chaz, seven; Axle, six—and her three-year-old daughter, McKinley. *Fuck Evan. I'm going to get my kids,* she thought during the drive.

Thinking of the importance of getting the truth, she pushed that thought out of her mind and mashed down on the Range Rover's gas pedal, speeding all the way home.

An unusual silence for a Tuesday evening greeted her as she entered her opulent residence. Absent were the sounds of the boys roughhousing, cartoons and video games blaring from the televisions. The quietness reinforced Joey's longing for her children. With no time to get caught up in her emotions, she shook her feelings off. She went straight to her master bath and began to undress.

At 765 square feet this wasn't any normal master bath. Joey helped to design it and it easily rivaled spa baths in some of the most luxurious mansions across the country. With light brown and beige marble walls and Chanel flooring, a sunken, jetted bathtub large enough for six people was located in the middle of the room. A glass shower/steam room ran the length of the back bathroom wall. It had four large showerheads, one on each end, two that hung from the ceiling, a marble bench and steam vents. A forty-two-inch flat screen was mounted on the wall above the vanity styled like a celebrity's dressing room. This was one of Joey's favorite rooms in the house. Whenever she felt overwhelmed she would escape to her master bathroom for a long soak in the tub while the sound of her favorite R&B tunes poured from the surround speakers enclosed in the walls. She could easily spend hours in this bathroom.

With time ticking closer to eleven p.m. there was no time for a nice, extended soak. Joey turned the shower on, disrobed, and stepped in. Standing beneath the ceiling-hung showerhead she allowed the steaming hot water to drench her perfectly coifed hair. She poured a good amount of shampoo into her palms then began to wash her hair. As she scrubbed her scalp with her fingertips she wondered what the secret was that Evan had been keeping. Joey knew that it must've been pretty serious or embarrassing for Evan not to share it with her. As far as Joey was concerned they knew each other's deepest and darkest secrets.

After a twenty-minute hair and body cleansing, Joey thoroughly dried her hair and pinned it up in a neat bun atop of her head. Once done, she slipped on a pink and chrome jogging suit and a pair of deep chocolate Vuitton sneakers.

When Joey got down to the four-car garage she started to get back in her Range, then decided against it. Instead she opted to drive her brand new toy, a Porsche Panamera that had been delivered the day after the shooting that had taken Petey's life. She felt that it would've been inappropriate to pull it out in the immediate days following the incident. The custom car was definitely the hardest car in the city. It was black, with a black interior, and it sat on twenty-two-inch black rims. Joey nicknamed it Black Beauty. "I might as well take you for a spin," she said, admiring the car, "'cause if my business doesn't recover from this craziness I may have to sell you."

Pulling into the parking lot of Vinnie's Raw Bar, Joey spotted Evan conversing with a scruffy, gray-haired, bearded older white man with whom she seemed very familiar. Rhamel was sitting in the driver's seat of

Evan's Jag looking on. Joey backed into a parking space that faced where Evan and the man stood. She watched as the man handed Evan a large manila envelope then went on his way. To Joey this was certainly weird by all appearances. The sound of Joey's ringing cell filled the car, and when she saw her husband's face flash onto the screen she quickly answered, "What up, babe?"

"What up, babe," he shot back sarcastically. "Where the hell you at?"

"I'm at Vinnie's. I came to meet Evan for drinks and to talk."

"What happened to us going to get drinks?"

"We still can; meet me up here."

Zay scoffed at his wife's suggestion. "One, I don't want to be around phony-ass Evan; she's your people. Two, I wanted to go in one car. And why you take your new car just to meet Evan?"

"I drove the car 'cause it's mines and I wanted to drive it at least once in case I have to sell it."

"Why would you have to sell your car?"

"What if my business doesn't recover from what has happened?"

"Man, go ahead with that. Luxe is straight and as long as I'm straight you don't have to sell shit. You got me?"

"I got you." She smiled to herself, loving the surety that her husband brought to her life.

"So how long are you going to be at Vinnie's?"

"I just got here, but this shouldn't take longer than an hour. I have to rap with Evan for a minute."

"Make it fast or I'm out." With that he ended the call.

Joey entered Vinnie's and found Evan sitting at the rear of the bar. "What's good, lady?" she greeted her, taking a seat opposite Evan at the table.

"Nothing much," she responded while scouring over the contents of the manila envelope. "I already order two rounds of martinis."

"Un-huh, this shit must be real serious you got drinks on deck."

A perky blonde in the bar's uniform, a barely there tank and cutoff denim booty shorts, came over. "Here you go." She set four martinis down before them.

"I see you ordered my favorite," Joey said, lifting the martini glass filled with olives stuffed with blue cheese.

"Can I get you anything else?" the waitress asked.

"Yes," Evan said, "a bucket of oysters with hollandaise sauce, and you can put in for another round of drinks."

"Sure thing." The waitress smiled before prancing away.

Evan continued to study the papers. Joey took a sip of her drink then asked, "Who was the old white dude you were talking to outside?"

"Hmm. I didn't know you saw that," Evan replied, laying the papers down on the table. She took a sip from her glass. "That was a private investigator I hired to find out who's been stalking me."

"So you are being stalked?"

"Yes, but by who I don't know. At first I thought it might be the girlfriend or a wife of someone I had dated. Now, I think it's much deeper than that."

"What do you mean?" Joey quizzed her.

Evan gulped the rest of her drink down and placed the glass back on the table. "When I was in college, over those four years I worked with Gage to set up a good number of drug dealers; and I'm not talking regular drug dealers. I'm talking about dudes who were getting major paper, upper hundred thousands to millions."

Joey shook her head in disbelief while listening to her friend talk. She suddenly felt pissed at herself for not listening to Zay all those years ago. Quietly drinking martini after martini and eating oysters for more than an hour Joey listened as Evan recounted her secret life with Gage. Although Evan came clean about many things, she didn't tell the complete truth about the final robbery.

Evan did admit that it was a robbery gone wrong versus a drug deal gone wrong, as she had told Joey and Cee when they came to get her. She also failed to tell Joey that she had actually killed both men that night. Nor did she reveal the amount of money that she received that night.

At the end of her bold revelations Evan held up the envelope. "This is information on the dealers I robbed. Not surprised most of them are dead. The others are dopefiends or cracked out. But, there are three I believe are very capable of stalking me." Evan looked to Joey for a response. Sitting tightlipped with a poker face, Joey gave none. "All righty then," Evan quipped. "I'm flying out in the morning to see them. I'll be gone for two days. Three days max." She studied Joey's face once more to catch a glimpse of emotion, to no avail. "Don't have anything to say?"

"Oh, I have a lot to say." Joey chuckled. "But I'm going to keep it short and sweet, for now. First, do you think your stalker is the shooter?"

Evan shrugged. "Honestly I don't know."

"Well, I do and I also think that you're the most selfish, self-serving, manipulative bitch I've ever known." Joey got up, pulled some cash out of her bag, and tossed it on the table. "Years ago I was warned about you! I defended you over and over and now I feel like a fucking fool." Joey walked away angrily.

Evan pulled out what she knew was more than enough to cover the bill and tip. Tossing it on the table she chased Joey, catching her in the parking lot. "Ay, Joe, wait."

"Leave me alone, Evan," Joey said over her shoulder.

"No, wait a minute." Evan caught up and grabbed Joey by the shoulder.

Joey turned around and swatted her arm away. "Didn't I say leave me the fuck alone?"

"I'm not leaving you alone! You wanted to have this conversation and now you running!"

"Bitch, ain't nobody running. I'm trying hard not to punch you in your fucking face. So I'ma keep it moving 'til I sober up and calm down."

"Punch me for what? Admitting that I made some dumb decisions over a decade ago?"

Completely disgusted, Joey looked Evan square in the eyes. "I'm angry at you for so many reasons that I can't even think clearly." She took a deep breath to collect herself. "I'm mad that you called us to a robbery, lied about it, and then kept us in the black about it all these years. I'm mad that you didn't come to me weeks ago when the stalking started. But you couldn't without revealing the truth. I'm mad that your so-called dumb decisions ten years ago more than likely cost our best friend's husband and our employee their lives."

Joey got right in Evan's face. "Most of all I'm mad that you're not the person I believed you to be. I'm about to black out so I suggest you talk to me when you get back from doing what you need to do." Joey got into her car and peeled away leaving a stunned Evan standing in the middle of the parking lot.

Watching through high-powered binoculars from a few blocks away, Evan's stalker saw the confrontation between the two best friends. He didn't know what had been said but he was pretty certain that the chain of events he'd set off was causing the rift between them. The discovery of the rift also confirmed his belief that Joey was tied to Evan's robbery schemes back in the day. Since he now had that confirmation it was time for Joey to catch some of the wrath that had been previously reserved for Evan, although with Joey he had no plans on wasting time with mind games. Everything with Evan was personal because she had played him. Since he felt that Joey had benefited from his money, it was time for her to pay up plus interest. And he knew just how to get it.

Cruising down I-77 South Joey was unable to think straight. She was having a really hard time putting the things that Evan had confessed to in perspective. Needing to talk she dialed Zay's number, even though she knew that she was facing a huge "I told you so." Joey called three times before reaching him.

"Yo," Zay answered above the loud music in his background.

Joey frowned at her phone. "Where are you?"

"I'm at Jason's bar."

"I thought you were going to wait for me at the house."

"You said that you would be home in an hour. That was two hours ago so I bounced. Meet me over here. I rode with Jason."

"I'm almost home. I'm buzzed, I'm tired, and I don't feel like driving all the way back across town. I do need to talk to you though. How long do you are going to be?"

"As soon as Jason closes up I'll be home."

At home Joey made herself a grape martini then she went into Zay's smoke stash. She retrieved a Swisher Sweet cigarillo and two small buds of Kush. Joey split the Swisher down the middle, emptied the contents, ground up the buds between her fingertips, and sprinkled the fragrant weed over the cigarillo paper then twisted it up. Joey was an occasional smoker. She'd smoked from time to time with Zay, on vacation, or on days like this when she needed to elevate her thinking.

With a martini in one hand and a blunt in the other Joey got comfortable on the couch in the family room. For the sake of having some noise in the house she powered the television on. Different parts of Evan's story played out vividly in Joey's mind as she smoked and sipped. Joey even began to question her own judgment especially since she'd always fancied herself a good judge of character. The liquor, weed, and the nonstop television running began to come down on her and she soon dozed off into a sound sleep.

At about seven thirty the next morning Zay lightly shook his sleeping wife's body. Stirring out of her deep sleep Joey rubbed her eyes with the back of her hand. She looked at her husband then at her watch and back at her husband. From his appearance Joey knew that he had just gotten in. "I know you didn't break day," she said sitting up.

"I called you to let you know that some important business came up. You didn't answer so I texted you. When you didn't reply I figured that you were knocked out."

Joey peeked at her phone and saw the missed calls and the text message. "I smoked some of your Kush. It put me on my ass. I was out before I knew it."

"You back on your smoking shit now?"

"You know how I do," she replied smiling coyly.

"Since you smoking," Zay said, and pulled her close and began kissing her on the neck, "smoke one with me."

After eleven years his kisses still made her body shake. "Okay," she purred.

"Go upstairs and put something sexy on for me. I'm going to twist up a few and make sure Jason is good."

"Jason's here?"

"He's in the guest room lying down until it's time for his flight to leave."

"Where is he going?"

"Out West. Go ahead and get right. I wanna get up in that for the next couple of hours before we pick up the kids."

Obliging her husband Joey retreated to their bedroom. After a quick shower, she covered herself in shimmering lotion and generously sprayed Bvlgari, Zay's favorite, on her body. Joey smiled at her reflection. She looked damn good in a lace sheer deep purple bra and matching V-string lace thong, especially for a woman who had given birth to four kids. She applied a light gloss to her lips and entered the bedroom. Dressed only in oversized basketball shorts Zay sat on the California king bed with his feet up leaning back against the upholstered, tufted headboard, puffing on a blunt. A carafe of mimosa that was prepared, two champagne flutes, and a plate of tropical fruits were on the nightstand next to the bed. Joey picked up the carafe, filled both glasses, and handed one to Zay. Simultaneously he passed the blunt to her. Joey hit it a few times, passed it back, picked her glass up, and downed the mimosa causing a sensual, euphoric feeling to come down over her. Sexily she stretched out across the center of the bed.

Zay slid down next to her. Using his hands he navigated her body, simply touching some parts, squeezing and massaging others. Through the sheer material he gently bit, sucked, and licked her stiff nipples. As his hands neared her throbbing middle she spread her thighs wide giving him great access. Intertwining their tongues they kissed passionately. With his fingertips Zay massaged her clit in a circular motion making her completely melt and moan in pleasure. Her inner walls tightened as her juices began to drip down. Just as she was about to cum the conversation with Evan from the prior night flashed into mind. *Damn. I need to tell Zay, but this feels too good. There is no way I'm ruining it.* Pushing the thoughts out of her mind she exploded all over Zay's hand.

Flipping Joey onto her stomach, Zay palmed her round ass, and opened her cheeks. Repeatedly he stroked from her clit to her anus with his tongue, as bad as he wanted to stick his swollen rod in that mouth that he absolutely loved. But, he couldn't resist going in the warm, pink and cream-coated hole that was poking up at him. He eased just the head in then pulled it out. Zay dipped it in and out a few more times. This little trick sent shivers down

Joey's spine and as much as she liked it she wanted all of him inside of her.

"Stop teasing," she panted over his shoulder, "and put it in."

"How bad you want me up in that?"

"Bad."

"How bad?" he toyed.

"Very bad," she whimpered as he continued to tease her by tracing her wet folds with the tip of his dick.

Zay unhooked her bra. It fell onto the bed beneath her body. Cupping her breasts he entered her behind.

"Yessss, baby," Joey gushed squeezing him tight with her vaginal muscles.

Reaching down with his hand he played with her clit while stroking her forcefully. With each stroke, Joey's cream cascaded over his shaft. The hot, moist flesh had Zay ready to erupt, but he held it because he wanted to feel her cum while he was inside of her. Knowing what to do he began nibbling on the crease between her neck and shoulder. Flicking his tongue back and sucking on that spot, he could feel her walls contracting in and out followed by an explosion of creamy liquid.

"Awwwww," Joey gasped pleasured by the intense orgasm that she was experiencing. The pulsating walls thumping against his dick sent waves of ecstasy through Zay's body as he released an overwhelmingly satisfying nut inside of Joey. They spent the following two hours making aggressive yet passionate love. When they were finished Zay went off to shower and Joey remained in bed checking and returning numerous e-mails. She'd decided to tell him about her meeting with Evan once he was done showering.

The constant vibrating of Zay's iPhone on the night-stand was distracting Joey from what she was doing. Joey picked up the phone to turn the vibrate feature off when the text on the screen caught her eye: Baby, I think I caught your cold.

Blood boiling, she called the number back. There was no answer or personal message on the voice mail, just the standard automated greeting. Buck-naked, Joey stormed in the bathroom like a Category 4 hurricane. "Who is this bitch you fucking with now?" she angrily demanded to know.

"What are you talking about?"

"This." Joey shoved the phone in his face.

Zay snatched the phone from her hand, and looking over the message he responded, "Man, you flipping over nothing. This is a broad I do business with."

"Yeah, fucking right, Zay. I don't even know you right now, 'cause you on some bullshit."

"Why are you going through my phone after we just had a good morning?"

"Fuck you! I wasn't going through your phone. I was trying to stop it from vibrating. And if I was going through it so the fuck what?" she said pushing past him to turn the shower water on.

"I don't go through your phones."

"Yes, you do and don't try to flip this around on me because you got caught." Joey stepped into the shower shutting the glass shower door so hard a small crack inched across middle of it.

After the shower she dressed in simple turquoise halter maxi dress, accessorizing it with huge flat gold hoops, multiple size gold bangles, and gold thong gladiator flat sandals. Grabbing her beige Artsy bag, she headed out for some quality fun time with her kids.

On Joey's way to the garage she passed through the kitchen, where Zay and his brother Jason were sitting at the island eating. They were also discussing the trip that Jason was about to depart for.

"What up, Joey?" Jason spoke.

"Hi, J," she responded dryly as she grabbed a juice from the refrigerator. Joey could feel Zay's eyes watching her. She refused to acknowledge him as she headed for the garage.

"Ayo," Zay hollered. "Where are you going?"

With one foot out the door she inhaled deeply, and turning around full of attitude she replied, "I'm going to check on Cee; then I'm going to get my kids, and take them out for an afternoon of fun."

"I thought that we were going to do that together."

Smiling coldly she suggested, "Go do something with that bitch you gave your cold to." She slammed the door behind her.

"Oooh, sister-in-law is pissed. What was that all about?" Jason asked.

"Some complete bullshit. Remember that stripper Trini I was fucking with a few years ago?"

"Yeah."

"I don't know if you saw her last night, but she was in the bar. She was all pressed as usual, trying to be nice. I blew her off by telling her I wasn't there to party." Zay got up to get some more food from the oven. "I'm like 'I got a cold; I just came through to see my brother.' That's when I came back and posted up in your office. Then this morning that bitch texts me talking about 'Baby, I think I caught your cold' and Joey saw it."

Laughing, Jason shook his head. "That's not good. I'm surprised she didn't take your head off."

"I'm surprised she didn't either! She cursed me out lightly and let it go." Zay wondered why his wife didn't make a much bigger deal about it. He did know that the less a woman said the less she cared, and the less she cared the more likely it was that there was someone else. *Not my wife,* Zay reasoned with himself. "Anyway, back to business. Is the money lined up?"

"Yeah. Harper has the certified checks and she's going to meet me at the airport. When we get there I'm going to meet up with Asaad Nyfeed make sure that shipments go out and we'll be back in the air."

The plans for Zay's second-last shipment of heroin were coming together perfectly. Following the shipment after the next one he would be out of the drug distribution business for good. He knew nothing was perfect until the product touched down, hit the streets, and the profit had been made. Zay tried to have faith that everything was going to go according to plan, but there was an eeriness in the air that he couldn't put his finger on.

Getting up to rake his plate Jason asked his brother, "Zay, did you give any thought to what we rapped about the other day?"

"About you taking over the operation?"

"Yes."

Zay smiled at his younger brother. He loved Jason with all his heart. Although they were just a year and a half apart, watching Jason through the years was like watching a son grow and use the skills that he'd ingrained into him. Like Zay, Jason had the ambition, intelligence, and hustle to thrive in the treacherous game of drug distribution, although Jason did possess a few flaws that could be detrimental in his line of work. At times he could be hot tempered, a cowboy, and obsessed with money.

Zay wiped his mouth with a cloth napkin. "I don't understand why you can't be happy with the money that you've made. You're sitting on millions stacked on millions. Why are you pressed to take over this operation when you can get out of this game with your life and your freedom?"

"I hear you, bruh, but you are about to stop the operation when there is still hundreds of millions to be made. Like Asaad said it's going to be an open market out here and he'll have no one to send the work to. And if he does find someone who knows the lay of the land, it will take years for them to build what he has built with you."

"No, it will take years for whoever he finds to be able to pay cash for the work like us, instead of getting it on consignment. Asaad is only concerned with the money that he'll be missing. We are only one of the regions that he sends work to and we've made millions so you know that he's easily made billions. His greed for more money is going to be his downfall." Zay took a deep breath then continued, "Our brothers are coming home and Mama will have all of us here for the first time in eighteen years."

Jason threw his hands in the air. "Come on, man, you know I could get on that plane today and die in a crash. Ain't no guarantees in this life that says if we leave the game behind something else won't kill us. Besides, if I take over you'll still get a cut of the profit."

"I don't want a cut." Seeing that he was getting nowhere with his line of reasoning Zay conceded, "If this is what you really want, you have my blessing. I really respect that you didn't cut my throat and partner up with Asaad on your own."

"Never that, big bruh," Jason grinned. "You know I live by the motto 'Family is everything; loyalty is priceless.'"

Chapter Five

Evan chartered a luxury jet to fly her to three cities in forty-eight hours. Out of the crop of drug dealers she'd robbed who were still alive, she chose three of the most likely candidates to go visit. The three former kingpins had been the richest and most powerful and vengeful out of the living and free she had to choose from. For her security she had Rhamel tag along.

The first stop on Evan's three-city tour was Detroit, Michigan, the home of Timmy Lloyd. In the nineties Lloyd was one of the biggest cocaine dealers in the state. Back then he was known for his long bob, expensive gators, and his fleet of foreign cars. Through the investigator Evan learned that Lloyd now worked at a youth center earning a meager income and he lived with his sister and elderly mother. The investigator did not consider him a credible threat. From what Evan remembered of him he was vicious and ran his empire with an iron fist. If anyone in his organization stepped out of line or was suspected of being a snitch, their death certificate was guaranteed to be signed.

Therefore no "working with kids for pennies" story could make him a nonthreatening figure in her mind. Evan needed to see him with her own eyes. What she saw completely changed her disposition. Encountering Lloyd from a distance at the youth rec center that he ran, Evan found him to be a sullen, downtrodden, and paralyzed from the waist down, a shell of his former self. After observing him for an hour or so she was certain that he was not the person after her.

The next stop on her itinerary was Baltimore, Maryland, to see Vontrez Mitchell, once a major player in Baltimore's infamous heroin trade. With his elite hustling skills, strong leadership, and charismatic charm he was one of the best "get money" hustlers the city had ever seen. The investigator had labeled him at best a minor threat, since Mitchell was now a pastor and gospel singer. Mitchell's change of life didn't deter Evan's thoughts of him. She'd seen her fair share of criminals who used the cloth as a shield.

After sitting in on Mitchell's evening service at his megachurch on the outskirts of Baltimore, Evan deemed him to be sincere in his new life. Now bordering on obesity Mitchell was still charismatic, but he now used his charms to spread God's Word to his massive flock. Not only was he a serious pastor, he was also a renowned Stellar Award–winning gospel recording artist.

The following day she landed in Hartford, Connecticut, to visit with a very credible threat, Reza Townson. His current residence was a federal halfway house. He'd been released from prison three months earlier right around the time that the stalking had begun. Evan went to the construction site where he was working just as his shift ended. She followed him to a nearby small family diner.

Sitting alone in a booth, Reza was reading the sport's page of the local paper when Evan approached. Staring at him up close briefly she noticed that he looked as if he hadn't aged a day and he was still very handsome, even with the Philly-style Muslim beard that he was donning. "Do you mind if I sit?" she asked.

Looking up from the paper, Reza eyeballed the exquisitely dressed, beautiful woman standing before him. There was a familiarity about her that he couldn't immediately place. He could tell that she had money.

She reeked of it in her Karl Lagerfeld dress, Zanotti pumps, flawless diamond accessories, YSL shades, and a Balenciaga bag, just a handful of the designers that he'd laced quite a few women with during his heyday. Never one to turn down the company of pretty woman, Reza told her, "I don't mind if you sit at all."

"Thank you," Evan replied sliding into the booth.

"You're welcome, but I have to ask why do you want to sit with me? Do we know each other?"

"I thought that my face was one that'd you'd never forget." She pushed her designer shades from over eyes to the top of her head.

One glance of her eyes was all that it took and he knew exactly who she was,."Mika."

"That's who you knew me as, but I'm quite sure you know that my name is Evan."

"No, I only know you as Mika. Why would I know any different?"

Evan set her bag on the seat next to her. "I'm not going to tiptoe around the issue. We both know what I did to you."

"Hmm, how could I forget?"

"Look I was a different person back then. I was young and easily manipulated by an older, streetwise, and abusive boyfriend. I'm so, so sorry for robbing you."

"How did you find me?"

"An expensive private investigator tracked you down for me."

"So, you paid good money just to apologize to me?"

"No."

"I thought not." He laid his paper to the side to make room for the plate and coffee that the waitress was placing before him.

The waitress turned to Evan. "Would you like anything?"

"No, I'm good. On second thought I'll take a ginger ale."

"I'll be right back," the waitress replied walking away.

Digging into his plate, Reza asked, "What actually brings you here?"

"Someone has been stalking me and I thought that someone could be you." She sighed. "If it is you I want to know what I have to do, well I mean pay, to make it stop."

Reza chuckled. "Listen, sis, the same way that you've changed, so have I. I got out of prison three months ago and I'm still not really home. I'm in a halfway house and once I'm done there in a few weeks I still have five years of federal probation over my head. I'm keeping my nose clean just so I don't go back." He put his fork down and took a drink of his tea. "Most importantly while I was on the inside I found Islam."

Cocking her head to the side Evan twisted her lips to the side. "You know how many niggas I know come home claiming to have found religion in prison then be on some other shit after they've been home for a while?"

"Hold up, baby girl, I don't owe you an explanation. You wronged me! I'm just trying to let you know that I'm at peace with my past. You didn't even need to apologize to me. I already forgave you a long time ago."

Stunned by his admission, Evan looked at him weirdly.

"Yes, I said that I already forgave you." He flashed his pretty teeth. "I've forgiven anyone I felt wronged me or I was holding grudges toward. You and your man robbing me was one of the crazy things that happened to me around the same time that eventually led to my downfall. Right before the feds picked me up my son took a bullet that was meant for me."

"Oh God. I'm so sorry to hear that."

"Don't be. I've made peace with that, too. It was part of my path just as prison was. That's why I'm not bitter about any of my past, because I now have a peace that I would have never been able to attain if I remained on the streets." He picked his fork up. "With that said, sweetheart, I have no interest in stalking you, attacking you, or disrupting your life in any way."

There was an authenticity and sincerity in his eyes and words that made her believe him. *If not him then who?* she silently questioned herself as she slid out the booth and stood up. "I'm happy that you've changed your life for the better and again I'm truly sorry for what I did to you." Going in her bag she pulled out $20,000 in neatly stacked ones that were covered in smooth black wrapping paper. Placing the stack on the table she slid it over to him. "It's not much or what I took from you, but I think that it will help you get situated." She wrote her cell number down on a napkin. "If you ever need anything, give me a call."

"I'll take this," he said accepting the napkin from her, "but I don't want this." He slid the money to her.

Evan shot him a puzzled look.

"I'm good on that." He nodded toward the money. "I'll keep this." Reza held up the napkin. "If it's okay I'd like to get to know the real you this time around. I was really digging you before you beat me. I think that you was digging me too; that's why you didn't let that nigga kill me."

Chapter Six

"Once again I would like to say thank you," Joey said addressing The Luxe Group's managerial staff and department supervisors from the head of a long glass rectangular table at the end of their biweekly conference meeting. "I really appreciate all of your hard work following the very unfortunate events that took place here the week before last." Joey carefully chose her words, since Cee, who was supposed to be on bereavement leave, was sitting to her right. Joey had no clue that Cee would be in attendance when she prepared her notes for the meeting. Not wanting to be cruel or insensitive to her best friend, Joey refrained from mentioning that she was delighted that Luxe and the L Room hadn't lost any bookings and were still scheduling future events.

"Those of you working the Penthouse event I'll see you tonight and if there are no more issues that need to be addressed this meeting is hereby adjourned."

All of the employees came over to Cee greeting her with hugs, and welcoming her back from her short two-week break. After the room cleared out Joey asked Cee, "What in the hell are you doing here? I thought you were going to take at least a month off."

"Joe, if I don't get out that house I'm going to lose it." Cee twisted her face trying to stop the water that was filling her eyes from escaping. "Everything reminds me of Petey. The only time I don't think of him so much is when I'm working."

On the verge of tears Joey managed to crack a smile at Cee. "Well, since you so hell bent on working can you tighten me up with a roller set and a blow out for tonight?" She raised her eyebrows hoping to lighten Cee's mood.

"Yeah, girl." Cee forced a weak smile. "Come on before my next client gets here."

On the walk over to the spa the best friends chatted about small things, mostly pertaining to Luxe and Luxurious, along with things that occurred in Cee's absence. Joey led the conversation keeping it light in an attempt to keep Cee's mind off of Petey. Joey received a personal shampoo from Cee instead of one of Cee's three assistants, a perk of being Cee's bestie and business partner. While rolling Joey's hair Cee asked, "Where's Evan? Why wasn't she at the meeting?"

"She had to go out of town to take care of a few things. I think she'll be back tonight or first thing in the morning."

"Oh. Where did she go?"

"Ummm," Joey stammered, "I think New York."

"What was up with you two at the repast? You were throwing a nice bit of shade at Ev."

"Girl, you know how Evan can be," Joey lied. "She was doing stuff to piss me off all week and by the time we got to the repast I'd had enough of her." Joey was not about to unload all of Evan's bullshit on to Cee.

"Yeah, if anyone knows how that Evan can be it's me," Cee said placing the clip in the last roller. She pulled off Joey's plastic styling cape and replaced with a cloth one. "Go get under the dryer." Cee spun the styling chair around and pointed her finger at Joey. "And don't you come out until you are all the way dry." Suddenly Cee's face twitched involuntarily. It was very noticeable.

Joey jumped out of the chair. "Are you okay?"

"I'm fine; that's just a side effect from the nerve pills my doctor prescribed me. He said that it will pass, especially since he lowered my dosage."

"You scared me for a minute." Joey picked up her purse and headed for the dryer room.

Cee closed the door to her private styling suite and locked it. She pulled a small YSL compact mirror from her purse. She opened the compact and retrieved a small clear blue Baggie filled with two grams of cocaine. Laying the open compact flat on her styling station she poured a tiny pile of powder onto the compact's mirror. Using a straight razor she raked and separated the powder into three lines. Hovering over the mirror, she held her left nostril down with her left index finger, and with a tightly rolled hundred-dollar bill inserted in her right nostril she vacuumed the three lines up swiftly.

This self-prescribed medication was all that she needed in the days following Petey's death. Her decision to self-medicate wasn't intentional. While gathering Petey's clothing for him to be buried in she'd come across a vial of cocaine in his sock drawer. When he was alive, they would dabble in coke a little every now and then to enhance their sex life. Neither had an addiction or problems stemming from their infrequent use.

Now that Petey was gone, Cee found that cocaine gave her the pick-me-up that she needed to get through the day. She told herself time and time again, *I won't get hooked*. It was a foolish notion that she and so many before her had fallen victim to. Putting everything back in its place, Cee looked in the mirror, and checked her nose for any traces of residue. Satisfied with her appearance and feeling good she opened her door and invited her next client in.

***

Zay watched from an office window as ten commercial box trucks left an appliance warehouse across the street. Each truck carried various appliances such as washers, dryers, refrigerators, and dishwashers. The interior of the appliances were lined with kilos of heroin. Those trucks plus five that had left earlier in the day were all headed to multiple cities in different states to distribute the work. Once the last truck was out of sight, he let out a small sigh of relief. He hadn't been this nervous or paranoid about a shipment since the first time he'd gotten a big shipment from Asaad five years earlier. The heightened sense of nervousness could be attributed to his anticipation of getting out of the heroin trade and his brothers coming home in a matter of weeks after eighteen years in prison. Late for an important brunch, Zay rushed out of the building and drove to his mother's house.

Jason and Zay pulled up to their mother's Dilworth ranch-style brick home at the same time. "What up, bruh?" Jason dapped Zay and embraced him tightly in the middle of their mother's immaculately manicured yard.

"Not shit. Just got back from making sure the trucks went off without any problems. Everything good with the spots around here?"

"Oh, yeah," Jason assured him, nodding. "I was done stocking them before nine."

Zay rang the bell, although both brothers had keys to their mother's home. Dorenda answered the door with a wide, warm, welcoming smile that could always be expected. She was a timeless beauty, with a slender build, smooth cappuccino skin, and caramel dyed hair. Dressed casually but elegantly she donned a cream V-neck knit three-quarter-length sweater, cream silk slacks, and a few pieces of subtle fine gold jewelry that her sons had gotten her over the years. As they entered she hugged both of them tightly and kissed their cheeks.

"Where's my girl?" Dorenda asked Zay shutting the door.

"I don't think Joey is going to make it, Ma. She has one of those membership drive things at the Penthouse tonight."

"She's been so busy; the only time I get to see her is when she's picking up the kids. I thought we'd get to catch up today."

"I know, Ma. She wanted to come too," he fibbed. Zay knew that his wife wasn't there because she was still upset over the text message and she preferred not to be in his presence more than she had to be.

"Daddy, Daddy!" came children's voices as six kids rushed the living room. It was Zay's four kids along with Jason's two daughters: Keeba, who was twelve, and Mariah, who was ten. Joey's and Zay's kids were there for spring break, while Jason's daughters were permanent residents. Dorenda had taken the girls in when their mother became strung out on oxytocin among other prescription and designer pills.

Relishing her role as grandmother, Dorenda adored her grandbabies and during any holidays or school breaks she made sure that they were with her. "Okay, boys, I have the table on the deck set up. The kids can go out and play; they've already eaten."

The kids raced out the back door and down onto the lush green grass over to the enormous swing, slide, and playhouse set; they had a private playground at Grandma's house.

The brothers took a seat at the table on the high deck overlooking the backyard. Beaming with fatherly pride they smiled as they watched their kids, both feeling that their kids were their greatest accomplishments. Dorenda came out carrying a large round tray of hot platters. Jason jumped up and grabbed the heavy tray. "Ma, why didn't you tell us to help you bring the food out?"

"Boy, please, I have lunches and dinners out here all the time when y'all are not around and bring this same tray out," she replied. Well known as stubbornly independent, Dorenda preferred to do things for herself. Even though her sons paid all of her bills she started her own custom cake business specializing in wedding cakes from home ten years earlier. What started as a little side business grew by leaps and bounds in a few short years forcing Dorenda to lease a storefront and employ bakers.

The constant mother, Dorenda prepared her sons' plates, served them, and then took her seat. Spreading a peach cloth napkin across her lap she asked, "So what was is so important that I needed to whip up this brunch?"

"We got something special for you." Jason cheesed from ear to ear.

"What did I tell you boys about buying me stuff? I have way more than I need already. If you wanna do something for me donate to charity or the church in my name or your children's names. Teach them about giving."

"Calm down, Ma," Zay interrupted her respectfully with a light chuckle. He went into his back pocket and pulled out a medium-sized white envelope wrapped in a magenta ribbon tied in a neat bow. He handed it to his mother.

"What is this?"

"Open it," they replied simultaneously.

Dorenda opened the envelope, took out the folded papers, and read them. Her mouth fell wide open; she covered it with her free hand. Big, juicy tears rolled down her face as she read the deed to her home. She'd used the money from the sale of her first home for the deposit on her current home. Zay promised Dorenda when she put the money down on her Dilworth home that he would pay her mortgage every month; therefore, the monthly statement came directly to him.

Five years earlier the brothers decided that while the money was flowing good they'd quadruple the scheduled monthly payment in an effort to pay Dorenda's mortgage off early. The twenty-year home loan had been paid off in a little under ten years. "I can't believe you boys did this for me." Dorenda got up and embraced Zay tightly. "Thank you, son."

"You're welcome Ma."

She hugged Jason. "Thank you, baby."

"I live to see you smile, Mama," Jason said as a tear fell from his eye.

Taking her seat she kept shaking her head unable to believe that she was the sole owner of her home free and clear of the bank. Staring at the deed Dorenda beamed. "This is so amazing and with my two oldest boys coming home I feel so blessed."

Jason reached across the table and squeezed her hand. "You deserve every blessing you get, Mama, and then some."

"Well speaking of your brothers coming home . . ." Dorenda looked into Jason's eyes and then into Zay's.

"What's up, Ma?" Zay questioned knowing full well the direction that she was taking the conversation.

"One thing you two know about me is I'm not dumb and I don't claim to be a saint. I know what you do has afforded this family a wonderful life yet it has also taken eighteen years of your brothers' lives. You two have successful businesses that continue to do well, but you can keep one foot in the door at your companies and the other in the streets." Pausing for a second, she inhaled, exhaled, and continued. "I don't want your brothers coming home and one or both of you going to prison or even worse me having to bury you."

At two different times over the eighteen-year period three of Dorenda's sons were incarcerated at the same time. Fifteen years earlier Zay did a stint for a year and a half in state prison and when he got out Jason went in for a two-year bid. Dorenda just wanted all four of sons home at the same time.

Zay looked his mother square in the face. "Ma, I'm pretty much done and by the time Tony and Rico get home I'll be completely done."

"I'm so happy to hear that," Dorenda exclaimed, then turned to look at her youngest son. "And what about you?"

"I can't give you an exact retirement date, Ma, but I'm working on one."

"Well, while you're working on it think of those two little girls." She pointed at Keeba and Mariah playing in the yard.

"I do think of them; they're the reason I put my life on the line."

"When your brothers went away their children were toddlers and now they will be coming home to adults. Do you want to go through the same thing?"

Not wanting such a happy brunch to be marred by the escalating conversation, Zay interjected, "Don't worry about him, Ma. I'll work on him. Now let's enjoy all this good food you cooked."

Agreeing, Dorenda reluctantly moved onto another topic while thinking, *We will finish this conversation, maybe not today, tomorrow, or next week, but we will finish.*

The evening's event at the Penthouse was yet another membership building drive. It wasn't as over the top as the grand opening, but it was still luxurious and upscale. Even in Evan's absence her staff did a magnificent job on the food service end with an array of fabulous choices. Bev had the bar, the waitresses, and the gambling areas moving like a well-oiled machine. The only thing left for Joey to do was charm the nonmembers into buying a membership.

Joey worked the room in an orange backless wide-legged YSL halter jumpsuit and a pair of green snakeskin Lorenzi platform pumps. Many of the night's guests loved her and she had them eating out of her palms. It was a packed house and memberships were selling quite well. Dawhar was there along with some of his teammates from the league. Joey was elated when she approached their poker table and Dawhar told her, "My people love the spot." He was smiling widely feeling every bit of the liquor coursing through his system.

"I'm glad to hear that." She gave them a winning smile while shaking their hands as Dawhar introduced each of them.

"They love it so much," Dawhar slurred, "they all want to join."

"How excellent!" She clasped her hands together and bowed over in excitement. "What are y'all drinking?" She waved over the head member service hostess and a waitress.

"Patrón," Dawhar replied trying to divert his eyes from her body.

Joey's pretty face, tanned skin, and dangerous curves increased his attraction for her every time he saw her. He'd wanted her since first laying eyes on her two years earlier. His wife was a nonfactor in decisions regarding where he stuck his dick. He definitely didn't care about Joey's husband although he should've.

"Whatcha need, boss lady?" the sinfully curved thick waitress asked.

"Bring these gentlemen a bottle of Patrón and Ace. Charge it to my account."

As the waitress left to fill the order, the head membership hostess, Isadora, approached the poker table. An absolute chocolate beauty, Isadora rocked an expertly cut chin-length blue-black bob. She was perfection in a peach and lavender Herve Leger Bodycon dress. The six-inch Fendi slingbacks elongated her well-toned long legs. Drool was nearly dripping from the men's mouths as they ogled her.

Joey smiled at the men's reaction to Isadora whose official job title was assistant manager of the Luxe nightlife. Hailing from Atlanta she'd helped run some of Atlanta's most exclusive night spots. She was second in line to Bev, but Joey pulled her from behind the scenes thinking it would be hard for a man to say no to a woman as beautiful as Isadora. "All of these gentlemen would like to get a membership," Joey told Isadora. "Can you take care of them for me?"

"Of course." Isadora flashed a million-watt smile with her iPad in her hand as she went around the table explaining the member levels, gathering info, and swiping their credit cards through the magnetic reader affixed to the top of the tablet. Once done Isadora returned to Joey, who was chatting with Dawhar about nothing much. "Okay, Joey, I sold one gold, two platinum, and one black elite membership. I've taken their payments but we are completely out of membership cards on the floor."

"That is not a problem. I'll grab some from my office."

"I'll go with you," Dawhar offered, jumping at the opportunity to be alone with her.

"That's okay. It will only take a moment."

"I wanna go; plus, you never gave me the full tour," he insisted.

"If you insist." Joey shrugged. She had no qualms about letting someone who'd brought in more than $60,000 in membership take a stroll to her office.

Dawhar was a jovial drunk, joking and laughing while they were on the elevator ride down to the headquarters floor. Joey slid her access key down the slot next to doorknob, opened the door, and flipped the light switch up. "This shit is fresh." Dawhar marveled at the luxuriously decorated and furnished modern space. "This don't even look like an office."

"Thank you," Joey said taking a seat behind her desk. "This will only take a sec." She unlocked the middle drawer on the right desk panel and took out a long cardboard box. She counted out fifteen cards for each level of membership. Only a limited amount of the unregistered coveted cards were allowed on the floor at one time. The rest were under lock and key at all times. Joey dropped the box back into the drawer and locked it. "I'm ready." She swiveled her chair to the right to stand, but was startled by Dawhar's midsection that was only inches from her nose. In utter shock she blurted, "Dawhar, what in the hell are you doing?"

"You are so sexy. I've been wanting you for so long." He caressed the left side of her face.

Joey slapped his hand away. "Ayo, what the fuck is wrong with you, yo!"

"Cut it out. You know that you want me too. I see the way you look at me." He leaned to kiss her.

Pushing back in the chair, she mushed his face back. "Get out of my office right now!" she demanded loudly. "You're drunk and you need to leave." She pointed at the door.

Leering at her, an evil scowl spread across Dawhar's face. He closed his hand into a tight fist. In that instant Joey felt in emanate danger. Dawhar backhanded her, knocking her out of the chair and onto the floor face first. He grabbed her hair. "Bitch, get up." He pulled her up to her knees and ripped the top of her jumpsuit. Using his free hand he fondled her bare chest. "Hmm they're softer than I imagined. Let's see if that mouth is as wet as it looks."

Dazed from the backhand Joey's vision was foggy, but she could see that he was unzipping his pants. Panicked, a jolt of adrenaline cleared her sight as she began clawing at the hand in an attempt to free herself from his tight grasp. "Let me go," she cried out while desperately trying to wiggle away.

"Be still, bitch." He slapped her. "Open your mouth," he growled, his stumpy, stiff, erect penis protruding from his pants.

Joey clenched her lips together firmly locking her jaws. She refused to open her mouth. Dawhar punched Joey striking her nose and mouth.

She slumped to the ground where she caught a quick glimpse of her purse beneath her desk. Once more he snatched her up by her hair and rubbed his genitals against her face. Squeezing her face he continued to try to force her mouth ajar. "Open up, bitch," he said, foam forming in the corners of his mouth.

Squirming she tried to keep his dick from touching her face as she fumbled through her purse with her left hand. *Come on, come on, where is it?* Tears began to fall as realized she was fighting a losing battle. Her fingertips grazed the item that she was searching for. *Thank God.* Joey snatched her hand from her purse producing a black stun gun. Sticking it firmly against Dawhar's outer thigh, and with the push of a button, she released 50,000 volts into his body. Dawhar collapsed onto his back shaking and convulsing horribly.

Panting hard, she held on to the desk, and pulled herself up. Joey picked up the receiver and dialed Bev's extension.

Recognizing the extension Bev answered quickly, "Hey, Joey, what do you need?"

"Come to my office. Bring security."

"Are you okay?"

"No. Please hurry!" Joey placed the receiver on the hook. She looked at Dawhar in a semiconscious state as he moaned and gurgled. Anger filled Joey's body; she picked up the heavy multiline phone and slammed it down onto his head.

"You perverted muthafucka." She kicked and stomped him with the one shoe that she still had on. Losing her footing, she slipped and landed on her ass. Falling made her angrier. On her knees she scrambled to his head; swinging madly she hammered his face and chest with her fist and forearms.

Bev burst through the door. "Joey," she shrieked. Slipping out of her blazer Bev rushed over, wrapped the blazer around Joey's shoulders, and dragged her away from Dawhar. Seconds later four security guards stormed the room only to be flabbergasted by the sight of the NFL star stretched out on the floor. Taking notice of Joey's blood-smeared and swelling face, Bev asked, "Sweetheart, what happened in here?"

Trembling, Joey stammered, "He . . ." She struggled to get the words out. "He tried to rape me." She buried her face into Bev's chest so that the guards would not see her crying.

"Get him outta here," Bev ordered. The starstruck guards were slow to move. "What are you standing there for! I said get him out of here now!" she roared. With some pep they each took hold of a limb and carried him out. "I'll call the police," she said and reached for the phone clipped to her waistband.

"No police," Joey told her. "We've had enough bad publicity."

Bev knew that it wasn't just about the bad publicity. She came from a family and neighborhood that didn't believe in running to the police. They solved their own problems. "At some point you should report this; he doesn't need to get away with this. Do you want me to call Zay?"

"Not yet. I have to get my head together first. I have to tell him my way or else he will kill that man." Joey was telling the truth; though Zay wasn't menacingly violent he was in a line of work that could call for violence at the drop of a dime. On more than one occasion Zay had to resort to violence. In the beginning of their relationship Joey had borne witness to her husband killing a man. Therefore, she knew exactly what he was capable of. "The only thing that I want is Dawhar off the property and for you to keep the event going smoothly."

"Are you sure? I don't think you should be alone right now."

"Yes. I'm okay to hide out in here until closing."

"All right. I'll be back to check on you shortly." Bev moved for the door.

"Bev," Joey called out to her.

"Yes?" She looked back.

"Thank you."

"There is nothing to thank me for. But you are welcome."

Joey went into her office bathroom, and when she saw her reflection in the mirror she was mortified. Not only was she swelling up, she could see the onset of purple bruises. Unable to stand her appearance she turned from the mirror and started the shower. Over and over she washed her face scrubbing it hard. It was excruciating but she just wanted to get any trace of his nasty-ass genitals off of her skin.

How could I let this happen? She couldn't begin to wrap her mind around the violation that she experienced.

Crushed and humiliated she leaned against the shower wall, slid down to the floor, curled up in the fetal position, and cried like a baby. After a while she pulled herself off the floor and got out of the shower. She went into the closet inside the bathroom and put on a white V-neck and a pair of jeans. When she exited the bathroom Joey found her two best friends sitting on the white leather couch talking.

"Oh my God!" Cee jumped up. "What happened to your face?"

Evan stood up. "Aww, sweetie." She moved in for a closer look.

"What are y'all doing here?" Joey asked relieved to see them; and she didn't care about the rift between her and Evan. At the moment she needed a friend and was grateful to have her two best friends at her side.

"Bev called me," Cee replied. "She said that you had an emergency."

"I just got back into town," Evan mentioned still staring at Joey's face in disbelief. "I came to see how the event was going. That's enough about us; what the fuck happened to you?"

"Dawhar Bradley happened to me." Joey plopped down on the couch.

There was a knock at the door. "I got it," Evan said and opened it.

Isadora was standing there with a tray containing a bucket of ice, a bottle of coconut Cîroc, and a carafe of pineapple juice. "Bev sent this up for Joey and I still need the membership cards from Joey."

"Okay," Evan said dryly, taking the tray. She wasn't too fond of Isadora; Evan didn't like the way Isadora looked at her. It wasn't just the looks. There was something about Isadora that she couldn't place her finger on. "Wait right here." She pushed the door closed with her foot. Evan set the tray down. "Joey, where do you keep the member cards?"

"Oh, um, there should be some that I took out on top of my desk."

Evan picked them up and went back to the door. She opened it and handed the cards to Isadora.

"Thank—" She was cut off by Evan closing the door.

Evan fixed everyone a drink before taking a seat. Joey guzzled hers down right away, and then tearfully told her friends what transpired in her office an hour earlier.

"That's some ol' bullshit," Cee announced when Joey finished speaking. "Where is Zay? Did you call him?"

"No, this isn't something that I can tell him over the phone. You know Zay he will flip out, find Dawhar, and kill him."

"And Dawhar deserves it," Evan added.

"Evan, no one can get away with killing someone that high profiled. Either way he's going to spaz as soon as he sees my face. At least if we're face to face I can calm him down and get him to be rational. I feel like a fool." Joey sobbed.

"Don't," Cee stopped her. "You better not dare blame yourself for what that sick perv did to you. If Zay don't get him, I will."

"Whoa." Joey dabbed the tears from her eyes with a piece of tissue. "I know that you got a lot of pent-up aggression because of what you're going through but I did get him pretty good myself. I don't want anyone, especially you, getting in trouble. Your kids have already lost one parent."

"I know and speaking of Petey, right before Bev called me one of the detectives on his case called me. They caught the arsonist."

"They did!" Evan and Joey exclaimed in unison.

"That's great," Evan chimed breathing a sigh of relief.

"Not exactly," Cee responded. "He's not the person who shot Petey."

"Are they sure?" Joey questioned.

"Yes, they are very sure; he was locked up in Durham that night."

Shaking her head Joey peered in Evan's direction. Refusing to meet Joey's blaming eyes Evan focused on Cee asking, "Do they have any other suspects?"

"Nope, not at all, but they assured me that they will keep looking."

The friends sat for two hours drinking and talking. In the middle of their girlfriend reunion, Cee received a call from her daughter, Talia. The news on the on the other end was disturbing. After conversing briefly Cee hung up the phone and told Joey, "Come on we need to get you out of here. Shit is about to hit the fan."

"Who was that?"

"It was Talia, and she said TMP and Wahoo Sports are reporting that Dawhar was just released from the hospital. They're saying that he was there because he was beaten by Luxe bouncers after refusing your advances."

Deeply appalled Joey scoffed, "The fucking nerve!" The humiliation took a back seat to the rage that was gripping her. "That's okay, because I'll give the gossip sites something to blog about. I do have to get out of here and get to Zay before the news does."

The trio traveled down the building's service elevator in order to avoid partygoers. As they neared Joey's parking space, headlights shined brightly at them as a speeding vehicle veered toward them slamming to a stop less than a foot from their bodies. The driver's side front and rear doors flew open, and out jumped Dawhar's trophy wife, Leska, along with the wife of another Tigers player.

Charging at Joey, Leska screamed, "You fucking slut whore, what kinda of shit are you on? My husband doesn't want your Raggedy Ann–looking ass so you get your rental cops to jump him?"

"Back your prissy mix-breed ass the fuck up out my face before I stomp a hole in it. Your creep of a husband tried to rape me and he got what was called for by me and not my security team."

"He tried to rape you?" Leska mocked with a cackle. "Dawhar doesn't have to rape you. He has me and he could have any woman he wants."

"That's the problem; he ran into one he couldn't have."

Emerging from the car, Dawhar shouted, "Ain't nobody try to rape you, ho. You was throwing that pussy at me."

Joey was flabbergasted by Dawhar. Prior to opening the Luxe she'd promoted events and parties for him over the last four years. In doing business she'd never picked up on his sociopathic traits. "You have to be the foulest nigga walking," Joey seethed at Dawhar then said to Leska, "He's lying about this rape, the same way he lies about those two little boys he has by that young girl on the south side."

Rumors of Dawhar's illegitimate kids were an extreme sore spot for Leska, for the obvious reasons but even more because she was barren. The mere mention of those kids made her manic. Leska drew back and swung at Joey. Cee caught Leska's arm midair, bent it behind her back, and whaled on her.

"Oh, hell no." Leska's friend stepped up to intervene.

Joey scooped her up and slammed her down. Grabbing her back she rolled around crying, and groaning. Joey shook her head. *This silly bitch running up and don't even want it.*

Dawhar marched over to rescue his wife, but he froze when Evan pulled her gun and aimed it at him. "Don't even try it. I already want to put something in you for that shit you tried to pull on Joey."

Yes, he was bigger and stronger than all of them put together but he wasn't made of Teflon. "Just get your girl off of my wife; that's all I want. She doesn't deserve that. She doesn't have anything to do with this."

"Oh, well she shouldn't have brought her punk ass up here," Evan said coolly keeping the gun aimed at him.

The thrashing that Cee was doling out was cringe worthy. Growing up Joey, Cee, and Evan were known for their fist game. Among them, Cee was known to be the better fighter. Evan and Joey had seen Cee deliver some beat downs over the years but none this harsh. Leska's efforts to fight back were futile. Cee's punches were coming at Leska at what felt like one hundred miles per hour. Joey and Evan attributed Cee's ruthlessness to pent-up frustrations stemming from Petey's death. Little did they know the extra strength was from the powder she snorted during a trip to the restroom.

"Cee, that's enough." Joey wrapped her arms around Cee's midsection and tried to tug her away. "Chill, Cee." Using all her strength Joey yanked hard and pulled Cee off.

Dawhar moved in fast to check on his wife as flashing blue lit the darkness. Sirens rang out as a black unmarked car followed by four squad cars converged on the parking lot and pulled right up on them. One of the detectives, a short black man sporting a pot belly in a cheap suit, went over to Dawhar.

"What are you doing here? I told you to go straight home and we would handle this," he fussed. "What happened to your wife?" He pointed at Leska's freshly battered face.

"That dumb-ass black bitch," Dawhar shouted nodding at Cee. "She beat her up."

"Dumb bitch?" Cee frowned. "You fucking faggot-ass rapist."

"Do you wanna press charges?" the detective asked Dawhar and Leska.

"They can't press shit." Cee rolled her neck. "This is our property. I was defending myself and my business partners."

"Hey," a thin-nosed white detective yelled, "everybody be quiet." He looked over at his partner. "Sanders, we can handle that later." The white detective was becoming annoyed by his partner's blatant ass-kissing of the NFL star. Through his wireframe glasses he scanned the faces before him. Pausing on Joey's face, he said, "Joell Tappens."

A raised brow and her anti-authority attitude in effect, Joey responded, "Yes?"

"I'm Detective Blankenship and this is my partner, Detective Sanders. We're going to need you and your security team to come downtown."

"In regards to what?"

"The attack on Dawhar Bradley."

"So he really went to five-o with that wack-ass lie?" Joey chuckled softly in disbelief. "What if I told you that I had proof that he's lying."

Blankenship's ears perked up; he'd found Dawhar's version account of the events hard to believe. He knew that the only reason his colleagues were so quick to gobble up Dawhar's story was because of his celebrity status. A woman having a man beaten because he rebuffed her advances was too farfetched for the seasoned detective. Blankenship saw it exactly for what it was: a man trying to save face with his wife. Being that it was his job he had to investigate the allegations. Placing a hand on Joey's upper arm, Blankenship eased her off to the side out of earshot of his partner and Dawhar. "What kind of proof do you have?"

Joey hated that she was even talking to the police. She didn't like the police and, although she was the victim, Joey felt like she was snitching. Looking at Dawhar's smug face she realized that the only way she could defend herself against his insulting lies was to share her proof with the law. "The security feed from my office," Joey replied.

"What's on the footage?"

Joey saw Dawhar and the other police aiding Leska to her feet like she was the one who had been violated. "How about we all go watch it together."

Cee, Joey, Evan, the two detectives, three uniform officers, Dawhar, Leska, and the other football wife all gathered in Joey's spacious office. Holding the remote in her clammy hand, Joey was a little apprehensive about showing the footage in front of everyone. She was about to relive the pain, humiliation, and embarrassment in front of everyone. Joey knew that Dawhar should be the one wearing the shame so she released her anxiety and pressed play.

Cold beads of sweat popped on her forehead as the footage began with him and Joey entering the office. While the situation unfolded on camera Joey kept her eyes locked on Dawhar. Leska gasped loudly when she saw the assault on Joey begin. Every officer glanced angrily at Dawhar then turned their attention back to the screen.

As the worst moment of her Joey's life continued to play out, Zay and Jason stepped into the room. Joey's heart dropped to the pit of her stomach. Catching wind of what was circulating online, Zay came to confront his wife. The sight of Joey's face horrified him, but not as much as what he saw on the screen. At first he thought that he had to be having a nightmare. *This can't be real.* Frozen by shock, Zay stared watching his wife being brutally violated.

Sickened by what she was witnessing Leska gagged hard, and she covered her mouth to keep the vomit from rushing out. She bolted from the office with the football wife chasing her.

Zay's shock quickly thawed and his anger erupted as he barreled toward Dawhar with Jason right by his side. The police jumped between the men breaking up anything before it could even begin. "Cuff him," Blankenship said, and pointed at Dawhar, "and get him out of here." One officer placed Dawhar under arrest while the other three blocked Jason's and Zay's access to him. Zay yelled at Dawhar, "You know what it is when I see you, pussy-ass nigga!"

"Fuck you and that bitch," Dawhar shot back.

"You a dead man walking and that's on my kids, nigga!"

The arresting officer hurried Dawhar out the office. The remaining uniforms stood by the door to ensure that the brothers remained inside until Dawhar had been taken off the property. Zay went to his wife; lifting her chin with his finger he examined her bruised and swollen face. He had to bite down on the inside of his cheek to keep from exploding again.

"I'm okay," Joey said softly.

"Don't lie to me."

"Mrs. Tappens," Detective Blankenship said, "I need to get a copy of that footage and for you to come downtown to give a formal statement."

"I can download you a copy," she replied, "but I don't want to press charges."

Completely taken aback, he asked, "Why not? After all we just saw?"

"And you also saw me get him back. I'm good. If he hadn't come to you with his lies, I would've never have told you."

"Well," the detective said, and sighed, "that footage alone is enough for the state to bring charges without your statement." He reached into his interior jacket pocket. "Here's my card if you change your mind."

"Okay." Joey took the card with no intention of ever using it. "And one of my partners," she said, and thumbed over her shoulder at Evan and Cee, "can get that footage downloaded for you."

"We'll go do it now," Cee said walking out with Evan.

Turning his attention to Zay, Blankenship said, "Sir, I know that you are very upset, but please don't do anything stupid once this guy is freed on bond. If anything, encourage your wife to press charges and let us do our job."

Zay responded with a nod, but the veteran detective knew that he only did it to appease him. The fire burning in Zay's eyes told Blankenship that there was going to be some sort of retaliation. On the way out Blankenship said to a younger uniformed officer, "If I saw my wife on that tape I wouldn't give a damn about this badge. I'd kill the scumbag with my bare hands."

Once the police cleared out, Zay asked Joey, "What was Dawhar doing in your office?"

Tearfully she responded, "Baby, I swear to you nothing shady was going on at all. I promise I'll explain to you. I just want to get out here." Although Zay was a little suspicious about why his wife was alone with Dawhar, it pained Zay deeply to see her in this condition.

He tossed his keys to his brother. "Take my car." He wrapped his arms around his wife's shoulder, and said, "Let's go home."

At the house Joey watched as Zay paced the floor furiously expressing his anger. "I should've got at his disrespectful ass a long time ago when I saw that he was checking for you. The way he looked at you, I told you to watch yourself around him. Now look what happened."

"You're blaming me?" Joey squealed then sobbed uncontrollably.

"No, not at all." Zay sat next to her on the couch and pulled her head into his chest. She curled up and rested her body against his. "Stop crying, Joey, I didn't mean it like that." He kissed the top of her head. "Dawhar always had lust in his eyes when he looked at you. I knew if given the chance he would try you. I didn't think he would rape you, but he is one of those entitled niggas. That's okay. I just hope he feels entitled to the bullets that I'm going to put in him."

Joey sat up and faced him. "You can't kill him."

"Why not? He bleeds just like the next nigga."

"If you thought the shooting at the L Room brought heat your way, imagine if Dawhar ends up dead. Our lives will be under a microscope."

"I can handle whatever comes my way; and he is going to get dealt with, though, just to let the next nigga know ain't shit sweet over here."

"Is killing him about him hurting me or protecting your rep?"

"It is all about you." Zay raised his voice. "And our family. If I let this shit slide some young robber on the come up may think he can get some cash from me by grabbing you or the kids and I won't do nothing. That's why I'm going to shut that shit down right now."

Aware that her husband's anger was too fresh for compromise, Joey decided to fall back. She picked up the remote and powered on the TV to watch the six a.m. news that she watched every morning. "Oh my God." Her mouth fell wide open from the shock of seeing an Eyewitness News reporter standing in front of the Luxe Enclave. The border across the bottom of the screen read: NFL STAR CHARGED WITH SEXUAL ASSAULT.

Joey turned the volume up as the reporter began to speak: "Good morning, this is Natalie Ramon reporting live from the Luxe Enclave where the upscale Penthouse sports bar is located. It is at this exclusive members-only club that Tigers star cornerback Dawhar Bradley allegedly sexually assaulted a female employee. Due to the nature of the crime, police are not releasing her name or position. CMPD did release this fifteen-second snippet of the assault. The victim's image has been completely blurred out. I must warn you the footage is very graphic."

Joey winced when the most horrific incident of her life flashed across the screen. Zay snatched the remote from her and cut the TV off.

Shaking her head Joey mumbled, "This is getting worse and worse."

"The local news is nothing; ESPN will have Rachel Nichols out there by lunchtime today."

"Uggggggggggh," Joey groaned. "I can't deal with this shit right now. I wish I could just get away."

"That's exactly what you should do. You know what? That is what you're going to do."

"I can't just up and leave. Who's going to run the clubs?"

"Bev and Isadora," he answered. "Your managers have been doing a great job. It's a perfect time to get away. The kids' spring break starts Friday."

"Yes, it would be nice to spend some quality time with the kids."

"We'll take them to Atlantis, bring them back home, then go to Miami for a few days before the gala and chill on one of the yachts; just me and you."

"I'm cool with that, but our last trip with the kids was in the Bahamas."

"I didn't say the Bahamas."

"You just said Atlantis."

"Yeah, Atlantis in Dubai."

Chapter Seven

"Mom, who is that you're texting with?" Taleah asked.

"None of ya business, little girl." Cee smirked sitting at the table in Del Frisco's Double Eagle steakhouse with her triplets. Cee's younger children were in Dubai with Joey and her family. To show her appreciation for the terrific help that the triplets had been with the younger kids, Cee had treated them to a shopping spree earlier in the day.

After Petey's passing the girls moved back home, commuting an hour each way daily to Winston-Salem for their classes at Wake Forest. The trips helped their younger siblings with homework, cooked for them, and drove them to their extracurricular activities.

"Let me find out Mommy got a boyfriend," Talia teased.

"Chiiiild Boo." Cee rolled her eyes. "That ain't even happening."

The girls laughed then Tanine said, "Mom, you do plan to date again? I'm not talking about in the near future or even the next six months."

"Tanine." Cee sighed. "I don't know. That's not something that even crosses my mind."

"I know that Dad wouldn't want you to be lonely or alone for the rest of your life."

"Note taken." Cee winked. "I'm more concerned with your little brother and sister for the next five years than some affairs of the heart."

"Speaking of PJ and Shelby," Talia chimed in, "we've decided to move home and transfer to Davidson this coming fall to help with them."

"No, you will not." Cee placed her phone flat on the table. "I can handle them and when I need help I can call on your grandmothers."

"We know that, Mommy," Taleah responded, "but they're our brother and sister. I believe that they would much rather have us around."

"Listen, girls, you have helped in ways beyond what I could've hoped for and I'm so grateful. I know that you were grieving too."

"Yes," Tanine interrupted, "but being here with you and them has helped with our grieving process."

"I understand that. I just cannot allow you girls to leave the school that you love. Besides in a few weeks you'll be on summer break and by the time the fall semester starts I will have a system in place."

"Dang, Mom," Talia spouted. "We thought that you'd be happy."

"I know, right." Taleah frowned.

"Sorry, Mommy," added Tanine. "You're going to be mad because it's a done deal. We've already been accepted at Davidson and signed the transfer papers."

"What?" Cee squawked. Before the girls could respond, Cee's phone went off. She read the text, stood up, and said, "I'm going outside for a minute. We'll finish this when I come back."

Exiting the restaurant Cee spotted a white 2013 Lexus GS sitting on twenty-two-inch chrome wheels, with black tinted limousine windows and Jeezy blasting not far from the valet stand. *This nigga might as well have 'drug dealer' stamped on his plates,* Cee thought walking toward the car.

Sitting behind the wheel Stacey watched Cee lasciviously as she made her way down the concrete steps. He couldn't take his eyes off her thighs, which were tightly wrapped in a pair of gray J Brand wax jeans.

"This bitch is sexy as shit," he said aloud checking Cee out from her exquisitely cut hair to her five-inch heels.

"Looking real good this evening," he greeted Cee as she slid into the passenger's seat.

"Um, thanks," Cee replied with a half smile immediately blinded by all the sparkling diamonds from his grill to his wrist.

"You know that you don't have to pay for this." He waved a clear Baggie of cocaine in front of her face. "Not if you hang out with me." His eyes were coated in carnality.

Rolling her eyes Cee replied, "Try being more respectful of my husband who passed not too long ago. I do not whore myself out for coke."

She hated having to deal with Stacey. His flirting disgusted her but he had the best nose candy in the city. Therefore dealing with his crudeness for five minutes was well worth it. Stacey didn't miss the shade; he dismissed it. He'd seen plenty of arrogant, rich bitches talk fly to him while their paper was stacked. Then after their money dried up he'd have them snorting lines off his dick.

Cee counted out nine crisp hundred dollar bills and five tens. "Here." She handed him the money. "Nine fifty."

"You got two hundred more?" he asked.

"For what? You said nine hundred and fifty for ten grams."

"When you called I was out already. I had this half ounce made up for somebody else. Folks didn't meet me when they said they would so I bounced on 'em. I don't have a scale with me to take out the extra four grams. Look just give me a hundred fifty and you can have it."

"A'ight." She pulled out eight twenties. "Here's one hundred sixty. I don't have any change."

A black Denali pulled ahead of Stacey's car. The valet attendant ran out, opened the door, and the driver stepped out. When Cee recognized him she snatched the cocaine, and shoved it in her bra. "I'm out." She hopped out of the car.

Stacey tapped his horn and rolled down his window. "Yo, Jason! What up, my nigga?" He threw his hands up.

Jason looked at the driver with his eye squinted and realized that it was Stacey. Out of the corner of his eye he caught a glimpse of Cee. *What the fuck is this?* "What up, Stacey?" he spoke approaching the driver's window. He extended his hand and dapped Stacey up. He looked over the roof of the car. "What's going on with you, Cee?" Jason asked peeping the situation.

"Oh, nothing," she stammered. "I'm having dinner with the trips. I stepped out here to speak with Stacey for a sec."

Stacey had major respect for Jason and didn't want to rub him the wrong way. "Jason, I didn't know she was ya peoples, but it ain't even like that though. This was strictly 'bout business."

"You good, playboy, she's not my lady or anything like that. Our families are good friends." He glanced over at Cee who was walking away.

"Stacey, I'm going to catch you later and take some of ya money at the poker table."

"I don't know about taking my money." Stacey chuckled. "I'm on the way to the spot off of Tyvola right now to play a little bit."

"A'ight. I might check it out later on," Jason said crossing the front of the car. Jogging lightly he caught up to Cee and hugged her. "How are you doing?"

Nervously she replied, "I'm doing well."

"You sure?"

"Everything is day to day."

"I feel ya; but what were you doing with ol' boy?"

"He was squaring up the bill for his girl's hair."

"I'm not trying to be up in your business, but you know that I know better than that right?"

"What do you mean?"

There was no getting one over on Jason. From years in the streets and a cokehead baby mother, he knew a user when he saw one. "I wanna talk to you. Got time for a drink?"

Cee looked at her watch hesitantly and replied, "I guess I have a little time. Let me let the girls know."

Cee went over to her daughters. "I'm going to have a drink with Jason." She nodded her head in his direction. The trips waved happily at him.

"Were you texting Uncle Jason?" Taleah grinned.

"No, I was not!"

"Sure, Mom." Tanine giggled.

"Anyway when the waitress brings the check send it over to the bar."

Cee joined Jason at the bar as he was placing a takeout order. Once he finished she asked, "So what's up?"

"Like I said, I'm not trying to get in ya business, but I know you was copping powder from that li'l nigga."

"Yeah, but it's not what you think. I'm not an addict. I don't use like that; only a bump here and there to keep me sa—"

"Before you even go there," he said, cutting her off, "I can tell that you're using more than a li'l bit."

"You got me, but I'm not strung out or nothing."

"Not yet."

"I know how to stop when I want to. Pete and I used to get right from time to time and I never got hooked."

"Yeah, but you was using on your own terms for fun. Now, you need it to numb the pain and each time you're going to need a li'l more."

"I know what you went through with your daughter's mother and her addiction but I'm not her."

"True, but the two of you are more alike than you know. Like you she had a successful career and like you she used coke to numb something painful." He paused while the bartender served their beverages. "I'm not going to pretend that I know the pain of having a spouse killed. I do know that you don't have to go this route."

A single tear slid down her right cheek. "Right now I don't know another route. All I know is my husband was snatched from me like this." She snapped her fingers. "A li'l coke helps ease the stress and the pain."

"Cee, I'm begging you, please don't do this to yourself. Petey is gone but you still have your kids and a great career." He meant every word that he said, too. A true dichotomy, he sold the most addictive narcotic known to man. Yet, he was preaching against the use of hardcore drugs. "Have you been talking to anyone about what you're going through?"

"I don't feel like being pitied upon; plus, people have their own problems. I don't want to get people down with mines."

"You can't get me down. If you need someone to talk to or lean on you can call me, and I'm not coming at you sideways either." He would never push up on her at such a vulnerable point. Jason wasn't close friends with Petey, but through Zay they were really cool. "I'm here for you and the kids, especially PJ."

"When I start blowing you up don't duck me." She laughed wiping tears from her face.

"Never that."

"Could you please not mention my little affair with the white girl to your brother or Joey?"

"For now I won't but if it ever gets to the point that you need help, I will talk to Joey."

That bitch ain't shit either, John Doe thought watching Jason and Cee from a table in a low lit corner of Del Frisco's. *The dirt on her husband's grave is still fresh and she up in this nigga face.* Feeling that Joey owed him also, John Doe figured he'd get it out of Zay's lucrative operation. He'd been trailing Zay for days before discovering that Zay wasn't really hands-on with the work or the cash. Through his research he learned that Jason worked more closely with the money and the dope. Therefore, John Doe had been following Jason pretty closely.

At this point he'd obtained all of the information that he needed to make a move. Tired of playing silly mind games with Evan, John Doe decided that it was time to get serious, collect the paper that was rightfully his, and exact the appropriate revenge on Evan.

"What does one woman need with all this space?" Reza asked Evan following Evan out of the dining room. During his kingpin reign he'd lived in some of the finest homes but nothing as opulent as Evan's.

The pair had just finished a chef-prepared dinner that Evan arranged for Reza's arrival. He'd flown in that day for a two-week visit. Since returning from her trip to Connecticut, Evan and Reza had spoken every day. At times they would talk for hours on end genuinely getting to know one another this time around.

Evan found him to be wiser, humbled, and truly intro-spective. Day after day she looked forward to his calls, as did he. Soon the long-distance conversations were not enough. With a busy wedding season starting, it was impossible for Evan to return to Connecticut. Longing to be in one another's presence physically they agreed that it would be best for him to visit her.

"This is my dream house," Evan stated while removing a bottle of Ace from the wine refrigerator behind the bar. She grabbed two champagne flutes from above the bar. "I wanted to live in it with all of this white furniture and carpet. I knew I had to do it before I had kids."

"Ohh, so you do want to have kids?" Reza inquired.

Evan shrugged. "I'm not really sure. Every now and then I get baby fever, especially when I see my two best friends with their kids." She twisted the cork of the cham-pagne bottle until it popped off. "If I do have kids it will be when I slow down. I want to be a hands-on mother, the same way my mom was with me."

"I can't believe you don't have a man coming through here," Reza said exploring the room.

"As you know," she said, and gave him a flute of champagne, "I have a history of choosing Mr. Wrong. So, I fell back from serious dating for a while. It's cool though, between a cold bottle of this," she said, and held up the bottle of Ace, "and my toys I'm good."

"Your toys?" He raised his eyebrows. "I would like to see you play with your toys."

"I bet you would, but it's kind of a solo act."

"It doesn't have to be."

"Maybe later." She blushed. "We have to get dressed for the party. The driver will be here in an hour and a half."

"That's plenty of time." He eased up on her smiling coyly.

Everything about him was better than she remembered. His body was tight, his face was beautiful, and her resistance for him was low. Reza grazed her cheek with his lips and his tongue along her earlobe. "Hmm," she moaned, her vagina jumping.

"You know how bad I want you?" He palmed her ass giving it a firm squeeze. "We got unfinished business to take care of." He kissed her bare shoulder.

"Yes, we do," she said, "but, if I'm going to put on a show for you I'm going to need a much stronger drink."

"I have something better than a drink to loosen you up."

"What?"

Reza pulled out a clear Baggie of beige translucent crystals.

"What the fuck?" Evan squealed. "I don't fuck with meth, nigga."

Reza laughed. "Neither do I. This isn't meth; it's molly."

"And what the hell is that? Because it sure looks like meth to me."

"It's MDMA, pure ecstasy. No cocaine, heroin, or other chemicals."

"Does it have you jacked up for hours like X? That's what I hated about X pills when I used to pop them."

"Nah, this is a real subtle high."

Evan gave it a little thought. It had been a long time since she'd really let her hair down. "Okay, I'm game."

Reza pinched a few small crystals out of the bag and placed them in the palm of her hand. Evan tossed them in her mouth, took a swig of water, and scowled from the bitter taste. "Eww that shit is nasty just like X."

Reza popped some and chased it down with champagne and pulled out a blunt of Kush.

"How long does it take to kick in?" Evan asked.

"About twenty minutes. If you take a shot of something strong and hit this," he said, and held up the blunt, "you'll feel it sooner than that."

Evan poured a double shot of Patrón and tossed it back. After hitting the blunt a few times she went to her room and retrieved her favorite toy. On the way back to the parlor, euphoria descended over her from the top of her head to the soles of her feet. "Whew!" She swayed side to side.

"What is that little thing supposed to do?" Reza pointed at the small vibrator. "My dick is bigger than that."

"This," she said, and held up the lavender vibrator by its slim handle, "is an eight hundred dollar premium toy. The motor is very powerful, yet it is quieter than a church mouse. It's the best on the market."

"Word? Well, show me how well it works."

The molly had Evan feeling extremely uninhibited; she reached behind her neck and pulled the tie to her halter dress loose. It fell to the floor revealing her bare breasts and a soft pink thong. Taking a seat on the edge of a 1920s-inspired stark white chaise, she was spread eagle. Her stomach fluttered as Reza took a seat directly in front of the chaise for a view up close.

Evan pushed her thong to the side, licked the tips of her fingers, and moistened her clit with the saliva. She powered on the vibrator to the medium setting. She stroked her vagina lips with the round silicon head a few times to entice herself. Her clit throbbed as if it were begging to be touched by the vibrator. Placing the vibrator on the tip of her clit she massaged the vibrator against it. A wave of pleasure like she never experienced electrified her body. "Oh God," she screamed locking eyes with Reza. She knew that he was turned on and that turned her on even more.

Reza moved over to the chaise and slid behind her. Cupping her breast he licked and sucked her neck and shoulders. Evan turned the vibrator on high. Leaning back against him, her ass rose slightly above the chaise, as she gyrated and wound her waist rhythmically. The pleasure became more intense with each stroke of the vibrator, and each touch, kiss, or lick from Reza.

In a sexy voice barely a notch above a whisper, Reza spoke into Evan's ear, "Tell me how it feels."

"Wonderful. Ahhhh. Better than it has ever felt before. Ooooh, baby." Trembling, her body stiffened, and water slipped from the outer corner of her eyes. Evan's walls contracted hard as cream tumbled down them and exploded all over the white chaise. Enjoying the mind-blowing orgasm she continued to rub her clit with the vibrator leading to multiple orgasms back to back. After the last nut she cut off the toy and tossed it to the side. She wanted to feel Reza inside of her.

Turning around Evan tried to ease him back and mount him. Holding her off by the shoulders, Reza asked, "What are you doing?"

"I want to ride you."

"There is no time for that. I told you I only wanted to watch and remember. We can't be late for your friend's dinner."

"We can be late; we're only going for drinks and dessert since we already had dinner." High and horny Evan pleaded, "We can do it one time."

"Nah, 'cause once we start we're not going to stop."

"All right," she caved. "Let's get dressed. I'm ready to get back home and we haven't even left."

Evan retreated to her bedroom, while Reza went into a guest room to get dressed. After a steaming hot shower, quick hair and makeup Evan emerged from her bedroom in a cream cotton tank, cream linen cuffed short shorts, and gold strappy four-inch Jimmy Choo heels. Still floating from the molly she strutted into the parlor with more confidence than usual. Reza was sitting next to the bar drinking a tumbler of Rémy XO.

Immediately Evan sized him up. "Givenchy tee, Balmain jeans, and McQueen sneakers. Boy, you sure are stunt 101 for a construction worker just coming home from a ten-year bid."

"I was fly when you met me."

"Yes, you were," she agreed grinning.

"I'm going to always be that way, too."

"I guess construction pays better than I thought," she said eyeing the black diamond bezel Audemars and black diamond bracelet affixed to his wrist.

"Construction does pay more decently than I imagined." He looked down at himself. "But construction didn't pay for any of this." Reza waved his hand over his body. "This is that 1995 blow money, sweetheart." He stated freely something he never would've had he not been high. "Yeah, they put a nigga down for a decade, but they didn't find the money I buried in my grandma's backyard."

A coded knock on an interior door on the side of the parlor interrupted them.

"I thought we were alone," a startled Reza said.

"We are in the house, but this door leads to the private apartment above the garage. Rhamel, the head of security at the Enclave, is staying up there. He's been providing personal security for me since all this madness started getting more and more out of control." She unlocked the door's deadbolt, and opened it.

Rhamel entered the room; he paused in the doorway momentarily at the sight of Reza.

"Come on in, Rhamel. This is my friend Reza and, Reza, this is Rhamel."

The two men exchanged half-ass nods.

"Evan, the car service is here," Rhamel announced.

"Let's roll," she replied leading the way out. "Rhamel, Reza will be here for the next two weeks and after tonight I will not be moving around too much at night. Unless we're at the Enclave you can pretty much have your evenings to yourself."

"Okay, boss lady," he responded, jealous of and dismayed by Reza's presence. Over the course of providing Evan with personal security Rhamel had built a rapport with her through talking, joking, and laughing. They'd even had some personal conversations, but never inappropriate or intimate. Foolishly he thought that they were on the verge of something more. *How does she know he isn't her stalker? Ol' slick ass,* Rhamel thought, eyeing him suspiciously.

A black Maybach 67 was idling in Evan's circular driveway. The driver, Curtis, a middle-aged black gentleman, was holding the rear passenger door open for Evan and Reza to enter. Rhamel took his place in the front passenger's seat.

"Miss Evan, would you like the partition up?" Curtis asked.

"Yes, please."

Once the partition was up Reza said, "Let me find out this cornbread-fed nigga is your boyfriend."

Evan burst into an uncontrollable fit of laughter. "You must never tell that joke again."

"I'm not joking. I peeped how dude was looking at me."

"That Kush and molly got you tripping." Evan leaned forward and grabbed the bottle of Clicquot rosé from the bucket of ice. She poured a glass, passed it to Reza, and poured one for herself. She raised her glass. "To us this time around."

"To us." He tapped his glass against hers.

"You the only dude I got my sights on." Evan kissed him, slipping her tongue in and out of his mouth and sucking his bottom lip reassuringly.

By the time they arrived at Chima Brazilian Steakhouse the birthday girl and her guest were filing out. The party wasn't over though; Evan and Reza followed the crowd to Diamonds Gentlemen's club where they partied in a large VIP section reserved for the birthday party guests. Evan and Reza popped more molly, consumed monstrous amounts of liquor, and tossed racks upon racks of ones.

Evan danced seductively on Reza. The strippers and the sexual tension were at a fever pitch. Standing against the wall on security duty, an irked Rhamel tried not to watch. It was impossible. His dick swelled with Evan's every shake and pop. At one point he'd gotten so into it he started unconsciously squeezing his dick and Reza saw him. Snapping out of his trance, Rhamel realized what he was doing and quickly tucked his hands in his pockets. Looking around to make sure no one saw him, he locked eyes with Reza.

Laughing Reza shook his head. *Fucking pervert-ass clown.* Smirking, he winked at Rhamel then pulled Evan close, fondling her breasts and inner thighs. He licked her neck and mouthed at Rhamel, "Nigga, you know what it is."

Steamed Rhamel left the VIP section talking to himself. "Taking shit from some fuck boy is not part of my job description." Outside, he thought about calling a cab to leave; then he saw Curtis standing outside the Maybach smoking. Rhamel joined him. After a few smokes and chatting about the NBA finals Rhamel calmed down. He decided that he wasn't going to let Reza get in the way of the excellent pay that he was receiving from Evan.

Opening the door to reenter the club he bumped into Evan and Reza. Greatly intoxicated, Evan wore a wide grin and sang, "Hey, Rhaaaaa, we ready to blow this joint."

"Okay, boss lady," he replied holding the door for them.

Inside the car Evan and Reza popped more molly and got off into each other real heavy. Evan knelt before him and pleasured him orally for ten minutes. When she finished he propped her up in the seat, yanked her shorts off forcefully, pushed her legs back parting them wide, and dove in tongue first. Using his mouth he made love to her tender mouth for the duration of the ride.

Arriving back at Evan's, Rhamel entered the apartment through the garage entrance. Evan and Reza had barely made it through door when they started ripping each other's clothes off. They were unable to contain themselves and started fucking on the floor of the foyer. Once they finished, they moved into the parlor and got it in on her vintage white couch. Five positions and thirty minutes later in much need of hydration they went into the kitchen, refueled on liquids, then had another round of sex on the center island.

With plenty of juice and water in hand they finally made their way to Evan's bedroom. They continued to go at it like wild beasts on the floor, in the bed, in the shower, and then back in the bed. By the time they finished the sun was up and the birds were chirping. Totally exhausted they fell into a deep slumber until late afternoon.

Chapter Eight

On her sixth and last full day in Dubai, Joey returned to the Atlantis resort from a massive shopping spree from the BurJuman and Wafi Malls. She had so many bags from Chanel, Escada, Saks, Louis Vuitton, and Bugatti B More that the bellhops had to load them onto two carts and follow her to the suite.

"My Lord!" Dorenda gasped when Joey entered the suit with the bellhops in tow. "What did you do, buy the entire mall out?"

"I know that it's a lot, but I need all of these things for Miami. I won't have time to do anything in Charlotte. When we land there tomorrow Zay and I are only staying a few hours and then we'll be back in the air."

She rifled through her purse in search of dirhams to tip the bellhops. In a matter of seconds they'd unloaded both carts and organized the shopping bags from smallest to largest in four neat rows. "Thank you," Joey said handing them seventy-three dirhams apiece. Joey closed the door behind them and flopped down on the chair opposite Dorenda. "Mommy, I am worn out."

"I bet you are, toting all them bags around and it's hotter than Hades out there."

"You know if you would've come with me, there would be three times more bags than that."

"After shopping at that ridiculously huge mall and the street markets. I didn't think that there was any more shopping to be done."

"Listen, BurJuman and Wafi is the truth! If I would've gone to that mall first I wouldn't have bought anything at that Dubai mall for myself."

"It was that nice?"

"Yes, ma'am, it was."

"Well." Dorenda sighed. "If I ever get to come back I will check them out."

"What do you mean if?" Joey smiled with a raised brow. "We're coming for an adult-only trip, so we can take part in all that this city has to offer for people older than four through ten."

Joey and Dorenda were close, like mother and bio-logical daughter. It hadn't always been that way. In the beginning, Dorenda was highly skeptical of Joey, whom she'd pegged as just another pretty face and gold digger like all the others Zay kept around. Even seven months into their relationship, when Zay made it known that Joey wasn't just another fling, Dorenda still wasn't feeling her. About six months down the road Joey's grandmother died. It was then that Dorenda learned that Joey was raised by her, due to the absence of Joey's mentally unstable mother. That endeared Dorenda to her, but it was Joey's self-sufficiency and independence that earned her respect. From there they formed the type of bond that would survive even if Joey and Zay's relationship didn't.

Joey was elated to have Dorenda in Dubai along with Zay and the kids.

In addition, Nija, Zay's twenty-two-year-old niece and the daughter of his oldest brother, Jason's daughters, and Cee's children were there. Just being with her loved ones gratified Joey. All of the kids were having a ball, tak-ing advantage of every fun activity that the resort had to offer. The resort had an amazing water park that included a hands-on experience with dolphins and a mega arcade.

They also had plenty of fun outside the resort. For Joey, seeing the smiles on Cee's kids' faces after what they had been through made the trip worthwhile.

Although most of the activities revolved around the kids, Joey and Zay stole some some time for themselves. They went on an early morning desert safari, hung out at an authentic hookah lounge, and cruised the Dubai Lake Canal. On this day Joey made sure that she got some time alone to do the things that she wanted. Noticing how quiet the suite was Joey asked, "Where is everybody?"

"Zay and the boys are at the arcade and Nija took the girls to the beach."

"Good," Joey leapt up. "I'm going to shower real quick. You and I have a spa appointment. We're going to get out of here before the kids come up in here trying to slow us down."

"This is the best mani pedi I've ever had in my life," Joey exclaimed lying nude on a massage table. She was covered by a white sheet with a manicurist on her hands and a pedicurist on her feet.

"I feel the same way," Dorenda replied from the table next to her getting the four-star treatment as well. "I felt like I was walking on air when I left here the other day."

"I'm going to get Cee to get this Bastien Gonzalez line for the Luxe spa."

"How is Cee doing?" Dorenda inquired.

"I believe she's doing well considering . . . you know. She may never get over losing Petey, but she'll get through it."

"That's the truth. I definitely got past the death of my husband. I had to; I had four boys to raise. I sure as hell never got over it."

The main reason of the trip to Dubai was to get Joey away from all the uproar surrounding the incident with

Dawhar. Thus far the unfortunate event had barely been mentioned. In the days following the attempted rape there had been some major revelations about Dawhar. He had a penchant for rough and violent sex. After the video of him attacking Joey went viral, five women came forward with accusations of rape including the seventeen-year-old he'd secretly fathered two sons with. Most of the women were young, fairly poor, and easily intimidated by his star power. Besides buying their silence with cash, Dawhar also made them believe that no one would believe them over him.

Dorenda and Joey had yet to discuss the assault. By all appearances, Joey seemed to be doing well, but Dorenda wanted to gage how well she was doing emotionally.

"Joey, I know you probably don't want to talk about the assault, but I want to know how you are doing and I want the truth."

Joey contemplated this for a moment then spoke: "Right after it happened I kept bouncing between sadness, embarrassment, and anger. I was miserable, but then those girls he actually raped came forward. One of them said if he had not been caught on tape attacking me, she would have never come forward." Joey shook her head. "That poor girl said her own mom didn't believe her. She said her mom told her that he has beautiful women throwing themselves at him so why would he need to rape her." Tears began leaking from Joey's eyes as she went on. "Baby girl was only fifteen when he raped her and she said if her mother didn't believe her she knew that the police wouldn't. Ohhhh, that broke my heart." The manicurist dabbed Joey's face with a piece of tissue.

Joey smiled at her. "Thank you."

"That is just terrible," Dorenda replied. "Some women should have never been allowed to have children."

"After hearing that I stopped pitying myself. Those young girls did get raped and as hard as he tried he couldn't rape me."

"I tell you this: God works in mysterious ways and everything happens for a reason. Dawhar came up against a woman he couldn't intimidate and he got exposed for what he truly is. The attack on you made it possible for those babies to come forward. Now they will be able to get the justice they deserve."

During his twelve years in the league Dawhar had been a celebrated wide receiver with unlimited talent comparable to the likes of Darrelle Revis. At thirty-six he was faster and better than half the league's young corners. A charismatic guy, fans across the nation loved Dawhar; therefore, companies lined up to give him endorsement deals. Following the assault on Joey and the allegations from the other women, he was suspended from the league indefinitely. All of the endorsement deals he garnered over the years were snatched away, and players around the league, including his friends, disassociated themselves from him, and his wife hardly said two words to him.

Once the city's most beloved star, Dawhar used to frequent the finest bars and restaurants. A lot of times he didn't even have to take his wallet out. The red carpet that had been laid out for him at those establishments was now rolled up for good. He was no longer welcome. The only place he could visit were holes in the wall, dives, much like the east-side bar that he was in on this particular night drowning his issues in cheap cognac. It was filled with old cokeheads, prostitutes past their prime, and downtrodden alcoholics. Dawhar didn't mind the bar's patrons; unlike everyone else in Charlotte they were not giving him dirty looks or heckling him with vulgar remarks.

Sitting at the far end of the bar, slumped down with his forearms resting on the bar top, Dawhar had just knocked down his fifth double shot when an edgy young beauty breezed through the door. Fair skinned with wild, wavy blond hair, the petite chick had on extra-tight blue skinny jeans, a red sequined tank, and six-inch Bakers heels. From just a glimpse Dawhar sat at attention. He watched as she switched to the middle of the bar and slid onto a barstool.

"Ay, barkeep," he called out waving the bartender over. "Give me another double and whatever she's drinking." He pointed at the girl. "I'm paying." With all the trouble that he was in Dawhar still couldn't help himself.

The bartender went over and talked to the girl then returned to the end of the bar with Dawhar's double shot. "She wants you to sit with her."

Dawhar hopped off the stool and staggered over to her and took a seat on the stool next to her. In a Spanish-coated accent she said, "Thank you for my drink."

"You are very welcome and beautiful." He garbled his words. "What are you?"

"I'm black, silly." She giggled.

"With that accent?"

"I'm a black Dominican."

"Okay, okay, I'm D. What's your name?"

"I'm Mya."

"Mya, what is your fine ass doing in a nasty joint like this?"

"I come here for the strong martinis."

Drooling and disrobing her with his eyes Dawhar said, "I know somewhere much nicer than this with better martinis."

"And where is that?"

"The Ritz. I can get a room. We can order up some food and all the martinis you want."

"Sure."

"For real?" He couldn't believe she agreed so easily.

"Yeah."

Dawhar threw some money on the bar. "Let's go." With his blood alcohol level triple the legal limit he swayed and wobbled out the door.

"Would you like for me to drive?" she asked, expressing concern for his ability to drive in his condition.

"Why not?" He tossed her the keys without warning. "Have you ever driven a Bentley before?"

"No."

"I don't know why I even asked you that. Looking at those cheap-ass shoes you ain't never been close to a Bentley or inside one." He doubled over in a fit of laughter.

Stupid idiot, Mya thought not amused.

"Damn, baby, don't be mad. You rolling with a rich nigga. Enjoy. Shit, you suck this dick good I'll change your life."

A black cargo van with blacked-out windows pulled up behind Dawhar. The sliding door opened suddenly. Dawhar turned and came face to face with three masked men. He twisted his body to run but his efforts were thwarted by a black hood that one of the men slipped over his head. A long syringe was plunged into Dawhar's neck, and the fluid from the needle knocked him out instantly. The men tossed his body into the van and sped away.

"Pendejo bastardo," Mya muttered. *"Tonto del culo."* She laughed as she slid comfortably into the Bentley driver's seat. Starting the engine, she operated the luxury vehicle with ease. She owned two. "I hate cheap shit." She kicked off the shoes and tossed them onto the back seat.

The name Mya was an alias; her real name was Dorca and she belonged to well-structured hit squad out of southern Florida. Dorca wheeled the Bentley to the parking lot's exit, waited for a tractor trailer to pass, and made a right out of the parking lot. The mechanical rear door of the tractor's enclosed trailer raised up, a silver metal ramp descended onto the street, and Dorca drove the Bentley into the trailer. The ramp retracted, the door went down, and the tractor disappeared into the night.

Chapter Nine

"Ooh, my face is beat to death," Joey raved peering into the floor-length mirror in the living room of an extravagant three-bedroom yacht that belonged to a yacht rental company that Zay owned. She had just received a flawless makeup job from M. Latrice, Miami's top makeup artist and the head of makeup at King of Diamonds.

"I'm glad that you like it," M. said scurrying around the room packing her makeup case.

"I know that Charlotte doesn't compare to Miami, but there has to be something I can do to steal you from KOD's," Joey joked. "No, but for real I want to at least fly you in for my big events."

"Now that is something that can be arranged, but aren't the artists at the Luxe spa really good?"

"Not as good as you. I mean I can do what they do."

"I could come up and do some hands-on training classes with them."

"That is a wonderful idea!"

"Before you leave Miami let's sit down and work out the details."

"Okay," Joey said rummaging through her purse for cash. "M., did Cee pay you?"

"No, I almost forgot. She told me to call her when I was done with you."

"I'm paying for the both of us." Joey handed her four crisp hundred dollar bills.

"Thank you, Joey. I'm sorry that I have to rush. I really wanted to see you in your gown, but it's one of our busiest nights at KOD. I have to get there early. Are you guys still coming through after your event?"

"Yes, we'll be there. The section is already reserved," she replied escorting M. off the yacht.

"See you tonight and I want to see plenty of pictures."

"All right, see you later." Joey returned to the main salon. "Cee, I'm ready."

Chatting and laughing among themselves in an intimate manner Cee and Jason entered the salon. Homing in on their body language, Joey thought, *Are they flirting?*

"Jo, do you want me to do your hair in here or in the bathroom?" Cee asked.

"The bathroom is fine," she responded eyeing the pair suspiciously.

"Give me five minutes to set up." Cee left the room.

When she was out of earshot, Joey questioned her brother-in-law. "What's going with you two?"

"What do you mean what's going on?"

Cocking her head to the side, Joey twisted her lips. "You know exactly what I mean. Ever since y'all got down y'all been real chummy, chatty, and touchy-feely."

"It ain't like that. Cee good peoples and she needs someone in her corner right now. She don't wanna burden you and Ev too much."

"Yeah, right!" Joey scoffed with one hand on her hip. She pointed at him. "Jason, don't be taking advantage of my friend while she is grieving."

"I'm looking out for your friend. If her two best friends were on their job . . ." He stopped short before spilling the beans about Cee's coke habit. "Look, sis, you the last person I thought would be coming at me like that. You know I don't get down like a creep."

"Mmm-hmm," she said surveying his army green tee and fatigues cargo shorts. "Why are you not dressed and where is Zay?"

"Right here." Zay entered the room in a dark beige tee and beige fatigues pants.

Joey looked at her watch. "When are y'all going to start getting ready? The car is going to be here in less than an hour."

"I changed the pickup time; the car will be here in two and a half hours."

"Why did you do that?"

"I have something important to take care of." Zay kissed her softly slipping her a little tongue. "We'll be back."

Zay and Jason left the yacht, walked down the marina, and boarded a speed boat with two dark-skinned Cuban men. The driver appeared to be in his late sixties and the younger Cuban couldn't have been more than nineteen years old. The boat sped away and didn't slow down until they were deep into the Glades. The younger Cuban went below deck and returned with a man whose head was covered by a black sack. The man's wrists were tied so tight they were deeply bruised and covered in dry blood. The young Cuban flung the hooded man onto the tarp-covered floor. Zay reached down and snatched the hood from the man's head.

Dawhar opened his eyes but couldn't make the shadowy figures against the purplish-orange sun setting in the sky. He blinked rapidly to gain focus. When his vision cleared, his eyes bulged when he recognized Zay. He immediately began pleading but it was just a bunch of muffled hums, because his mouth was covered in duct tape.

"Yeah, nigga." Zay grinned wickedly. "I'm guessing right about now you realizing you fucked with the wrong man's wife, huh? You probably thought I was some lame-ass dude."

Dawhar shook his head side to side hastily.

Not much for a lot of jaw jacking, Zay retrieved a four-teen-inch knuckle guard combat knife with a serrated blade and shoved it into Dawhar's abdomen repeatedly at least ten times then dropped the knife next to his near-lifeless body. The Cubans picked up Dawhar's limp body and tossed him into the water making a dull thud on contact. The sound attracted two massively humungous alligators lurking nearby.

Creeping over to the body, the gators positioned them-selves at opposite ends of Dawhar. As if coordinated, they simultaneously opened wide, and sunk their teeth deep into his flesh. Twisting and pulling Dawhar like a rag doll, the gators ripped him apart at the midsection.

Zay stared in silence as the alligators devoured their human meal. It felt good to avenge the attack on his wife. He wasn't happy that he'd had to kill again. Zay didn't take pleasure in killing because for him murder was a necessary means to an end when there was no other remedy. When someone harmed his family in the manner Dawhar had, murder was the only solution.

An approaching airboat took Zay's attention away from the horrific scene in the water. Zay looked down at the older Cuban who was rolling up the blood-soaked tarp. "Ay, my man, someone's coming."

Without looking up he replied, "That's your ride back. Take your clothes off."

"Huh?"

He nodded at Zay's clothes.

Zay looked down; his shirt and shorts were covered in blood. Hurriedly he began to remove his clothes.

The younger Cuban opened a metal insulated box affixed to the deck. Steam rose from the box. He dipped his hand in and pulled out two scalding hot damp towels. He gave the towels to Zay. "Use these to clean your skin while I get your clothes."

Jason leaned over to Zay and muttered, "Damn these muhfuckas is thorough."

The younger Cuban came back with a set of clothes identical to what Jason and Zay were wearing.

"I'm good," Jason said, "I don't have any blood on me."

"You must clean up and change too," the older Cuban spoke. "Little spots that the eye can't see could be on you."

Asaad Nyfeed's annual gala was an extravagant fund-raising event that he held every spring in Miami. The $1,000-a-plate affair was a mix of old money, new money, politicians, socialites, A-listers, and kingpin-level dealers. The proceeds from the yearly event went to the campaign funds and personal pockets. All of the politicians in attendance were in Asaad's pocket.

Asaad's heroin entered the country through three major port areas: California, Florida, and Louisiana. In each state he had high-ranking police officials, judges, mayors, senators, and congressmen he took good care of financially. In return through their connections the politicians made sure that the heroin made it into the country without interruption.

Joey spared no expense when it came to dressing for the gala, because the women who attended the gala were couture types. Joey was astonishing in a $7,000 lilac, one-shoulder chiffon Marchesa gown. The gown's strap was wide and embellished with Swarovski crystals. Fitted at the waist it flowed eloquently from her torso to the floor.

Cee was equally impressive in a black lace cap-sleeve Marchesa gown, a gift from Joey, who'd begged her to come with her. She thought that it would be good for Cee to get away and to keep her company while Zay and Jason wandered the room networking. Usually she'd be stuck with a dingy vixen Jason brought as a date. To Joey's surprise this year Jason didn't bring a date but judging by the way Cee and Jason were playing one another closely she understood why.

During the cocktail hour Joey and Cee watched people while playing fashion police. The friends giggled at a middle-aged woman displaying a horrible set of legs in an outrageously short, tight dress.

"Who told her that would be okay with that horrible shape?" Joey joked.

"I don't know, but um, um," Cee stuttered, distracted by something over Joey's shoulder. "Who is that chick with all that ass in Zay's face?"

Joey turned to see a female with infinite curves in an emerald green lace and silk Versace gown that hugged her like a second skin. A young Joey would've flown over and said, "What the fuck is this?" Now older and refined she didn't even flinch; the woman could easily be a business associate, and Joey wouldn't dare embarrass Zay or herself by flipping out like a first-rate hood rat. She was no fool though; from a distance she monitored the situation carefully. Zay and the sexy mystery woman's interaction seemed to be harmless, but if it veered toward flirty lane Joey would most definitely check the situation. A familiar man soon approached the woman and Zay.

"Isn't that Sincere?" Cee asked Joey.

"Yeah, it sure is." The woman turned toward Sincere and from her side profile Joey realized that it was her good friend. "Oh my God, Cee, that's Kisa Kane."

The two women walked over just as Jason was walking over. Joey eased up behind Kisa with her index finger over her lips so that no one would alert Kisa to her presence. Disguising her voice in a deep bass tone, Joey leaned into Kisa's ear from behind and said, "All I want for my birthday is a big-booty ho." Then she squeezed Kisa's ample ass with both hands.

Kisa whipped around ready to spaz on the man who dared to try her. When she saw Joey's face a smile spread across her face. "Hey, baby girl," Kisa squealed excitedly wrapping her arms around Joey and hugging her tightly. "How are you?"

"I'm good." Joey beamed, just as excited.

"No, how are you really doing?" Kisa raised her brow. By Kisa's expression, Joey knew that she was referring to the Dawhar incident.

"I'm okay. Honestly I'm okay."

"We've been out of the country. As soon as we got back, I went to your house first then I went to the Luxe looking for you and Bev told me that you were in Dubai."

"Yes, girl, I had to go to Dubai and get away from all the chaos."

Kisa reached around Joey and grabbed Cee by the hand. "Damn, Cee, I didn't see you." Kisa embraced her. "I'm so sorry about Petey and that Sin and I were not able to make the funeral. We'd just left the country when he passed. Did you get the flowers?"

"Yes, Kane, I got the flowers, the cards, and the money, which was a bit much."

"The money was for the kids." Kisa winked. "How are you holding up?

"I have good days and a lot of bad days, but I'm making it."

"You already know if you need anything, and I mean anything, you better pick up the phone and call me."

"Man, don't hate 'cause you niggas are the second and third flyest dudes in the building," Sincere, Kisa's husband, teased Zay and Jason animatedly. He was spectacular in a beautiful Dolce & Gabbana tuxedo, with a white jacket with black lapels. Beneath it he wore a black shirt, black suspenders, black pants, black diamond cufflinks, and black Mauri ostrich and suede loafers.

"I guess your flashy Harlem ass supposed to be the flyest man in here," Zay said flashing his high-wattage pearly whites, incredibly handsome himself in a navy Tom Ford tuxedo.

"To show me a dude flyer you gotta put a mirror in front of me."

"You are still the slickest talking nigga I know." Jason shook his head smiling.

"Blame it on my old head." Sincere laughed. "I know one thing for sure the three baddest women in the building are standing right here."

"Always the charmer," Joey said.

Kisa rolled her eyes. "Always the flirt is more like it."

"You love it though." Sincere stroked his wife's face; he then looked at Cee. "I'm sorry for your loss and I apologize for missing the funeral, but—"

Cee cut him off. "Kane already explained." Cee attempted a smile but her face muscles fought against it. Tears coated her eyeballs and stung the corners of her lids. Most times when people extended their condolences it didn't bother her. Then there were the instances like this one when one expression of sorrow completely over-whelmed her. "Thank you," Cee said to Sincere. "Excuse me, everybody. I need to go the ladies' room." The tears fell as she turned to walk away.

"Oh, no." Joey proceeded to follow.

Jason grabbed her by the arm. "That's okay, Joe. I got her."

"Damn. I didn't mean to upset her," Sincere remarked.

"Don't worry, Sin," Joey reassured him. "It wasn't you. She's touch and go."

"She's doing a lot better than I would be doing if I were in her shoes," Kisa admitted.

"I know exactly what you mean," Joey replied. "Kane, I'm so glad that you're here. We really need to catch up. What table are y'all seated at?"

Kisa opened her beige Evening in Versailles clutch and peeked at her gala ticket. "We're at table twenty-five."

"Damn, we're at seventeen."

"Don't sweat them tickets," Zay told them. "Asaad will make sure we're at the same table."

"Okay, baby." Joey intertwined her arm with Kisa's. "Let's go take a peek at the auction items." Walking away from their husbands, Joey said again to Kisa, "Kane, you have no idea how glad I am to see you. I need to talk to somebody and you're the only one I can tell everything to."

"What's bothering you?"

"It's too much to go into here; we're going to KOD's after the gala. You guys should come with. We can talk over drinks before going."

"If I weren't so tired from all the overseas traveling I would go. I don't think I'm going to make it through this gala. After the auction I may be out. Where are y'all staying?"

"We're staying on one of the yachts. I would invite you over there, but I can't have this conversation anywhere around Zay or Cee. I need to talk to you about Evan—"

"Oh, yeah," Kisa interrupted, "I saw her two weeks ago at Diamonds of Charlotte with Reza LaCroix, a big-time coke dealer back in the day out of Hartford. He just came home from a ten-year bid."

"I remember him vaguely. Evan was with him?"

"More like all over him. We were in the same VIP section for Simone's birthday and she was so fucked up that she didn't even see me."

"Evan?"

"Yes. Evan."

"It's like she's living a double life. That's the same type of shit that's been going on for years that she's been keeping secret, the exact stuff that I need to talk to you about."

"Well, we're staying here at the Fontainebleau, why don't you come here and we could have lunch at LaCote around one?"

"Cool," Joey replied eyeing a rare purple crocodile Hermès Birkin bag encased in glass sitting atop a white post, valued at $85,000.

"This is what I want." Kisa peered into the security glass.

"Are you going to bid on it?"

"I sure am."

"What if the bid gets up to eighty racks or more?"

"Sincere is going to buy it! He owes me. He's been dragging me around the world with this import business he's started and I've been doing most of the footwork."

"I hear you." Joey sighed. "The bag is dumb nice, but imagine me telling Zay to buy it for me."

"He would get it," Kisa answered confidently. "Zay could buy you ten of these at eighty grand a pop and it wouldn't hurt him one bit."

"Kane, it isn't like that. I know Zay still got some money on the streets but most of his income is from his legitimate businesses now."

With a screwed face Kisa asked Joey, "Are you serious right now?"

"Yes."

Realizing that Joey wasn't playing coy Kisa said, "I know I schooled you to the game better than that. You do know what's going on in your house, don't you? Niggas don't rub elbows with Asaad because they have 'some' money on the streets. Zay got the East Coast streets locked with that boy."

"Boy? Fuck outta here. Zay don't fuck with that heroin."

"You really have no clue." Kisa shook her head.

"I guess I don't. You're here so do that mean Sincere is back in the game?"

"No, Sin is here because his family has ties to Asaad's family and Asaad is helping with this importing business. Let me be clear though: Asaad is getting something out of it, because any favor that Asaad gives he expects something in return."

Joey looked across the room at Sincere and Zay.

The two old buddies were in deep conversation when Asaad came up to them. "Ah, two of my favorite gentlemen," he announced with wide grin. He placed an arm on each of their shoulders. Asaad was draped in a wonderfully designed black Ralph Lauren Purple Label tuxedo, and patent leather Louis Vuitton dress shoes. He was a gorgeous specimen, an Afghanistan native; Asaad had smooth dark olive skin, jet raven curly hair, a full beard, black eyes, and teeth so beautiful that they looked like veneers. "What are you two guys up to?" He spoke with perfect English diction; not a trace of Middle Eastern dialect could be heard.

"Just catching up," Sincere replied.

"That's wonderful." Asaad beamed. "Haven't seen you two in the same room in so long I tend to forget that you know each other."

"I see you're in comedic mood tonight," Zay responded.

"Business is very good so life is good. Did Sincere tell you about his new venture into the import-export world?"

"Yes, he was just telling me all about it. It sounds like a good thing."

"It is a very good thing. It will enable us all to earn money from yet another avenue."

"I'm hoping so," Sincere said reading a text on his smart phone. "Excuse me for a minute. Butta and his fiancée are at the entrance and I have their invites." Sincere walked off.

"So," Asaad said, "did my people help you to take of your problem today?"

"Yes, they got it done."

"Without any problem?"

"It was completely smooth."

"I'm happy to hear that. This means we have a deal, correct?"

"Of course," Zay replied reassuringly. "I gave you my word and you know I don't break that."

"To be clear, you'll keep running the distribution for the next year and transition Jason in to take over for you when you step down."

"I'm clear on it."

Asaad extended his hand and Zay took it. The two men shook firmly cementing their deal.

In the dead of night, cloaked in black from head to soles, John Doe held his breath as he squatted behind a wide five-foot bush on the side of a suburban two-story home. It had been a busy night for him. He'd already hit two of Zay's stash houses. Between the two homes John Doe made out with five and a half kilos of heroin. Bricks of pure high-grade heroin would be a major come up for any robber, but John Doe wasn't out for a lick. There was a method to his madness.

Taking down the first two houses wasn't hard because they were occupied by females, whom John Doe took down easily. The house that he was currently sitting on wasn't going to be so easy to infiltrate. This house was the money spot. Four men rotated twelve-hour shifts; two of them were in the house at all times, unless one of them made a store or food run. Fortunately for John Doe, the two guys on the night shift were creatures of habit. They made their dinner run the same time every night. John Doe's intention was to catch one of them slipping when they were leaving but he'd gotten there after one of the men had left. Now he had to wait for him to return.

Continuing to wait on the side of the house, John Doe knew that he might have to scrap his plans to rob this spot. Timing was imperative and at any time one of the girls from the other houses could be discovered and alert the men at this home. Just as John was about to give up, headlights illuminated the house as a silver Challenger turned into the driveway.

Donavan, a six foot brown-skinned twenty-something dude, hopped out of the car with an Outback carryout bag while talking on an iPhone that he had cradled between his chin and shoulder. "Look, baby, you want me to fly you out here?"

Cutting across the grass he dug in his pockets for the house keys. "Ayo, shorty, it's a yes or no question," he barked into the phone. "You want me to fly you out here?" Annoyed by his inability to find his keys and frustrated by the female on the line, he snapped, "Ay, talk to you later."

He hung up the phone and dropped it into his back pocket. He set the bag on the second porch step and pulled all the items out of his pocket. "This is some real live bullshit. I know I got the keys off the table."

Donavan found the three house keys wedged between a stack of banded hundreds. Snatching the bag up he climbed the rest of the stairs, opened the screen door, and unlocked the two top bolt locks. He pushed the key into the knob lock and turned. Fear gripped him when he felt the barrel of the gun pressing against the back of his neck

Through clenched teeth, John Doe spoke. "You better not move." With his free hand John Doe pulled a pistol from the small of Donavan's back and tucked it in his waist. "You do any funny shit I'm going to blow your neck right off your shoulders. Now open that door real easy like."

Donavan followed John Doe's orders and they went through the door. With the bottom of his foot, John pushed the door shut.

Isaac, the other man on shift, yelled out, "Gad damn, boy, 'bout time you got back. I'm hungrier than a muh-fucka."

Keeping the gun on Donavan's neck, John Doe spoke in a low but authoritative voice. "Put your hands behind your back and clamp your fingers together." Completely shaken, Donavan did as he was told. John Doe slid a zip tie over his hands onto his wrists, and tightened it to the point of almost cutting his circulation off. "Move." John Doe nudged Donavan with the gun.

He walked helplessly through the hall as sweat excreted from every pore on his body.

Perched on the edge of the couch, with $350,000 or more on the coffee table in front of him, Isaac placed stacks of green bills into a money counter and organized them as they came out. "Yo, Don, it took you forever to get back; now you taking damn near as long to bring me my food. You better not be texting that bitch begging her to come see you and—" Isaac went silent when Donavan appeared with John Doe holding the toolie on him.

John Doe pulled the gun that he'd taken from Donavan and aimed it at Isaac. "Don't do no dumb shit and you'll keep breathing." He looked at the table. Eyeballing the money, John Doe could tell that it was a few hundred thousand. "Bag that paper up. Use that." He pointed the gun at the soft leather duffle next to Isaac's feet.

Coldly staring at John Doe, Isaac slowly reached for the duffle. "Hurry the fuck up," John Doe hollered.

Isaac grabbed it, opened it wide, and using his forearm he raked the cash into the bag. Rushing, he knocked quite a bit of the money onto the floor angering John Doe.

"Pick that bread up," John Doe barked, "and don't let any more hit the fucking floor either."

Isaac squatted down and picked up two of the stacks that had fallen to the floor. He reached down to grab some more money and instead wrapped his hand around the handle of a P-89, jumped up, and took aim.

John Doe squeezed his gun's lever, firing off three rapid shots. Two of the bullets tore gaping holes into Isaac's abdomen, and the third ripped through the right side of his chest. His body fell back backward between the couch and the table.

John Doe gripped Donavan by the collar then slung him to the floor. "Don't try shit!" He grimaced. "I will kill your ass too." John Doe got the duffle and loaded the remaining stacks into the bag. He looked down at Isaac and shook his head. *Silly muhfuckas always down to die for shit that don't even belong to them.* With all the cash in the bag, he moved around the first floor checking the cabinets, drawers, and closets for additional cash. Pretty sure that the neighbors heard the gunshots and called the police, he settled for what he had.

On his way out, John Doe knelt down next to Donavan, who was shivering uncontrollably from fright. He pointed the gun at Donavan's temple. "Tell ya boss I'm going to keep hitting his spots until his wife and Evan pay me what they took from me."

At three a.m. Evan was stirred awake from her sleep by a freshly showered Reza slipping beneath the covers. He pulled Evan's nude body toward him and kissed her.

"Where have you been all night?" she asked.

"I hit a few bars and the strip club with Rhamel."

"You two have been hanging pretty tight since having that come to Jesus talk."

Tired of the constant verbal jabbing between Reza and Rhamel, Evan sat them down and made it clear that Rhamel was going to be her security and Reza was going to be around. Therefore, she forced them to converse until they came to some type of understanding. The little sit-down went better than any of them could've expected. From that point on when Evan was at the L or tucked safely in the house, Rhamel and Reza would hit the streets.

"Rhamel is a cool dude," Reza stated. "He has his corny moments, but he isn't too bad to chill with, especially since you don't have time to chill with me."

"Sorry." Evan raised her hands. Making air quotes with her index and middle fingers she said, "I don't have time to 'turn up' every night because I have a demanding career. Not to mention I hung out every night your first week here."

"Hey, I was only joking; I don't wanna party every night either. I'm just enjoying this vacay, because when I go back to CT it's going to be all work."

"What if you didn't go back to Connecticut?"

"Huh?"

"I like having you around so I was thinking . . ."

"I heard what you asked and I like being with you too, but my job that I have to keep to stay in compliance with my federal probation is in Connecticut."

"You could get a job here."

"It's not that simple for me to get a job, Ev. People with no felonies can't get jobs right now. Me and my five felonies just can't up and get another job that fast. I went through a special program in Hartford to get that job."

"Getting a job won't be so hard if I own the company."

"Nah, un-uh, I couldn't."

Evan placed a finger over his mouth. Rising up, she straddled him. "In the midst of the madness I have going on around me, having you here has made me happy in a way that I haven't felt in a very, very, very long time." She leaned in and with the tip of her tongue she tickled his earlobe and gently nibbled on it. Grinding her wet, pulsating middle against his stiff main vein, she said, "I owe you. Let me make it up to you."

"Hmmmm shit," he moaned, "if you put it like that." Lifting Evan by her hips, Reza raised her up slightly, enough for her the tip of his rod to tap at her dripping wet entrance. "I just might have to stay, but it all depends on how well you're about to perform." Evan bucked her pelvis enveloping his dick inside of her warm pocket. She performed four times in a row and each time she gave the performance of a lifetime.

Chapter Ten

"I'm so glad y'all talked me into going to KOD's," Cee slurred standing on the yacht's upper deck. Barefoot, rosé bottle in hand, wearing a floral backless romper she swayed from side to side. "That was the first adult fun I've had since Petey died."

Extremely inebriated Zay, Jason, and Joey were chowing down on a small feast prepared by the yacht's staff in an attempt to soak up the mounds of liquor that they'd consumed. Joey tried not to laugh but her best friend was pure comedy in her drunken eyes. More than anything Joey and the guys were laughing from the joy of seeing their friend having a good time.

Cee raised the bottle to them. "This one's for you, my family: thanks for showing me a good time." Turning the bottle up she guzzled it down.

"You still drinking, Cee?" Joey questioned amazed that Cee was still going so hard.

"Like the peewee say, I'm turned up, heeeeeeeey."

"Bitch, it's five thirty in the damn morning. You need to turn all the way down before your ass get alcohol poisoning. You need to sit and eat some of this food so you don't get sick." Joey thought back as far as her intoxicated mind would allow. "You didn't eat lunch or at the gala. How are you been drinking all night with nothing on your stomach?"

Jason looked at Cee to catch her response. There was no doubt in his mind that she was high on cocaine and the drug was enabling her to drink like a fish without passing or vomiting.

"I dunno," Cee sobbed as tears cascaded down her face.

"Don't cry," Joey said bewildered by Cee's sudden mood shift. She picked up a white cloth napkin and drunkenly stumbled over to Cee. "I'm sorry. I won't say anything about you eating anymore. I was just worried."

"I could give two fucks about you saying something about it. I feel like a fool," Cee cried, looking to the sky.

"Why?"

"I'm out here," Cee said, waving the champagne bottle around, "screaming about the good time that I had and my husband is dead. He can't have any more fun. I don't deserve to have any more fun."

"Now you do sound foolish." Cradling Cee's face in her hand she told her, "If anyone deserves to have a good time it's you after all that you've been through in the last four months. Petey loved to have fun and the last thing that he would want for you to do is to stop enjoying life." Joey pressed her forehead against Cee's and stared into her eyes. "Do not beat yourself in the head or feel guilty over having a good time. Okay?"

"Okay." She hugged Joey. "I love you, Joe. I swear I do. You're always in my corner since we were kids. If no one else is there for me I know my bestest bitch is." Cee let out an infectious giggle that passed on to Joey. Their laughter filled the predawn air as they held on to one another swaying side to side until they fell onto the deck floor.

"It's time for y'all drunk asses to go to bed," Zay announced.

Jason came over to assist Cee up off the floor. "Come on. I'll help you to your room."

"And that's all you better do," Joey spouted sitting up. "I'm watching you, nigga." She pointed at her eyes with her index and middle finger then at Jason. "Don't be taking advantage of my friend because she's drunk."

"Whatever, Joe." He laughed, pulling Cee up by the waist.

"I ain't playing," Joey shouted behind them as they walked down the side of the deck and disappeared inside of the yacht. Joey got up and flopped down next to Zay.

"I don't know what you sat down for," he said. "I'm ready to go to bed so I can take advantage of you."

"The sun is about rise; that's why I wanted to eat out here." She picked up a blanket from the floor next to her feet. Kicking her feet up on the bench she stretched and rested her head in Zay's lap.

Zay looked down at her face. "I love you."

"Awwww, I love you too." She clasped his hand between hers.

"No. I mean really love you," he said in an emphatic tone.

"I know you do." Joey kissed the back of his hand.

"Every move that I make, right or wrong, is for you and the kids. I'm glad that you're my wife; more than that I'm happy that you're the mother of my kids."

"Let me find out that Henny Priv got you sappy."

"My mom always said a drunk heart speaks a sober mind. It's been a long time since we've gotten to spend time like we have on the trips the last two weeks."

He wanted so bad to tell her that he'd killed Dawhar for attacking her. As with his thriving heroin distribution business that he hid from her, Zay felt that it would be best to keep the murder a secret. He only hid these things from her so that she couldn't be hindered by the law if something ever happened. He caressed her face. "There is really nothing that I haven't done for you except die and you already know I'm down to die for you and our kids."

"Instead of dying for us, why don't you concentrate on living for us?"

"What does that mean?"

Joey usually didn't question Zay too much when it came to his street business. She was a little nervous to bring up what Kisa had told her, but the liquid courage inside of her gave her the push that she needed to mention it. "I kind of heard that you've been getting money on a level ten times beyond what I ever imagined." She stared at him to see his response, but there was none. Although he was plied with liquor, he had his poker face on. "Okay, let's talk hypothetically then. Hypothetically you're getting major kingpin money, plus the money from your trucking company and the yacht rental business. I know how much we have in the bank accounts and the safes that I have access to. You have more than enough to leave the streets behind."

"Hypothetically if what you're assuming is true, I was due to leave it all behind in the next few weeks, in time for my brothers' release. I was looking forward to it, too. Hypothetically speaking of course," he warned.

"Why did you say 'was'?"

"Because it can't happen like that now."

"Why not?"

"Someone that I love more than anything got into a bad situation. I had to call in a favor to correct the issue. Now to return that favor, I must continue to play my position for just a little while longer, hypothetically speaking."

In a stark white tank, blue denim hot pants, brown leather gladiator sandals, and eyes covered in oversized brown Chanel tortoise shades, Joey walked through the maze of tables at LaCote's outdoor beachside deck. The sun was shining, the temperature was a perfect balmy seventy-eight degrees, and the rolling blue ocean waves were pristine. Unfortunately, a banging headache and a gripping bout of nausea were keeping Joey from enjoying it. Kisa took one look at Joey as she approached the white linen-draped cabana and knew that she was hung over.

"Sunglasses and Advil last night must've been mad real," she teased Joey.

"Girl, I told God that if He stop the room from spinning for five minutes I would never ever drink again." Joey took a seat and was instantly repulsed by the foods that she normally adored. Occupying the center of the table was a chilled seafood platter of king crab legs, prawns, oysters, and clams next to a pitcher of Côtes de Provence rosé sangria. Joey covered her mouth and swallowed hard to keep from dry heaving.

A waiter appeared and asked Joey, "Would you like for me to pour you a glass of sangria?"

"No! I need a ginger ale and saltine crackers."

"That shit is not going to help." Kisa jumped in and took over: "Bring her a Bloody Mary; that will cure your hangover. And can you bring me a Lobster Thermidor please?"

"Yes," the waiter replied and turned his attention to Joey. "Would you like to place your order also?"

"Yeah, I need to get something on my stomach." She scanned the menu. "Let me get the vegetable pissaladière. My stomach can't take any seafood right now."

The old friends kicked it about their children, reminisced a little, and made plans to attend the upcoming fall fashion week in New York. After two Bloody Marys, some ginger ale, and food, Joey felt renewed so she moved on to the topic that she was there to discuss. Joey disclosed everything to Kisa from finding Evan passed out in front of the L Room to Evan revealing her former life as a robber.

Kisa was floored by what she'd heard. "I knew that Evan had some shit with her. Back in the day when we used to make little moves when she'd come through with the cocaine, I'd wonder if we got popped would she hold up or would she rat. Evan has that selfish type of energy sometimes. You couldn't have told me in a thousand years that this bitch was robbing niggas."

"Zay had a feeling that dude she was with back then was robbing or they both were robbing."

"What did he say when you told him that you found out she was robbing?"

"I haven't told him yet."

"Wait a minute, wait a minute, you haven't told him?"

"Kane, honest to God I was going to tell him the night that I found out, but then we fell out over a text message some bitch sent him. Then Dawhar attacked me and plus I really didn't want to say anything until Evan found out who was stalking her and if they were the person who killed Petey."

"From what you told me there is no question that the shooting at the L is tied to Evan's bullshit. Everyone around her is at risk until this shit gets resolved. That is so crazy that you haven't told Zay though. He could've had this shit handled."

"You're right." Joey sighed. "I can't even argue with you." Joey looked left and did a double take when she saw Cee speed walking toward her.

"Hey, Kane." Cee bent over out of breath.

"What's up, Cee? Why are you breathing so hard?"

Holding up her palm, Cee took a few moments to catch her breath. "I ran all the way from the valet stand at the front of the Fontainebleau to back here."

"Why?" Joey asked.

"Because, your husband is not too far behind me and he is on fire. I have never seen him this mad before. I mean his whole aura is red right now."

"Mad for what?"

"From what I could make out on the other side of the door he was hollering about a robbery, his cousin was shot, and then he said your name and Evan's."

Taking a deep breath, Joey exhaled. "Oh my God, it's always some shit."

Looking in her phone, Kisa picked up a pen, and wrote on a napkin. She folded the paper and slid it across the table. "This is a number for my people. She's good at tracking people." Kisa stood, leaned across the table, and whispered in Joey's ear, "The murder game is her thing, too."

"Uh-oh," Cee said, "here he comes."

A visibly angry Zay was headed straight at them. He didn't acknowledge anyone. He grabbed Joey's arm. "Get the fuck up, yo!"

Joey yanked her arm from his grasp. "Don't curse at me like that."

"Don't do that," he warned. "I'm so heated right now I can barely contain myself. Unless you want to be embarrassed in ways that you never been, I advise you to get your ass out so that we can leave."

Knowing he meant every word that he said, Joey got up, quickly hugged Kisa good-bye and left the restaurant.

The walk from LaCote to the front of the Fontainebleau was a bit lengthy to begin with, but at that time it felt endless for Joey. Not a word was exchanged among the trio until they reached the valet area. Jason was waiting in a chauffeured Mercedes S600. Joey followed Cee to the 600 and was about to get in when Zay yelled out, "Ayo, you riding with me." He got into a 2013 ice blue Lamborghini Aventador with cream interior. It belonged to a luxury vehicle rental company that his yachting business partnered with to provide vehicles to his yacht renters. Zay had borrowed the Lambo for a romantic excursion he'd planned to take Joey on later in the day. Those plans were out the window now.

Guiding the car out of the lot Zay said, "Make me understand why three of my stash spots got hit last night, my cousin was shot and nearly bled to death, and the cocksucka who did it is screaming you and shiesty-ass Evan owe him money!"

Perplexed Joey shrugged. "I don't know why anybody would say that I owe them anything. I don't have anything to do with that shit!"

"What shit, Joey?" Zay roared shifting gears and increasing the car's speed.

"I meant to tell you this a long time ago," Joey began nervously, "but then we fought about the text message, Dawhar attacked me, and I kinda wanted to wait until Evan found out."

"Yo," he yelled, "stop talking in fucking circles and tell me what the hell is going on."

"The night of the funeral Evan told me that her and Gage were sticking up drug dealers back in the day and not regular ones. Kingpin-type dudes. For a while now she has been getting stalked and she believes that it could be one of the people she robbed." For the second time that day, Joey recited what Evan told her.

Zay listened silently in gross disbelief for the twenty-minute ride. By the time they arrived at Kendall-Tamiami Airport, Joey was finished. He parked the car next to the awaiting ten-passenger luxury chartered jet. For five minutes he didn't speak; he just watched as the luggage was loaded onto the jet. Joey could tell by his throbbing jaw muscle that he was thirty-eight hot. She didn't dare to open her mouth until he indicated that he was ready for her talk.

Jason tapped on the driver's window. "You good, bruh?"

Staring straight ahead, Zay nodded his head up and down.

Jason looked over at Joey then back at Zay. "We're going to go ahead and get on the jet."

"We'll be on there in a minute," Zay said breaking his silence.

Walking away Jason wondered, *How in the hell did sis-in-law get tied up in this shit?*

Zay looked over at Joey and calmly stated, "You whack and you just as shady as Evan is. That's the real reason you didn't tell me about this bullshit."

"I just told you why I didn't tell you at first."

"Because a bitch texted me. You gon' ride with that excuse?"

"It ain't no excuse; it's the truth."

"I don't care if you caught me fucking a ho in our bed!" he exclaimed thunderously. "You don't keep no shit like this from me! That's how I know it's more to this story than you're telling and that's why you didn't tell me a long time ago."

"There is nothing that I'm not telling you," Joey screamed with tears spilling from her eyes.

"Why is this muhfucka saying you owe him?"

"I don't know!" she shouted.

"What the fuck ever, you lying-ass bitch!"

Anger overcame Joey. "I'm a liar? I'm grimy? Fuck you, Zay! This morning I was the best wife in the world when you were drunk! Now my word don't mean shit? Go fuck yourself." She got out of the car.

Zay hurried out and shot around to the front of the car and got in her face. Snarling less than an inch from her face he said, "Because you're my wife, I haven't wrapped my hands around your throat and choked your ass out. Isaac, my aunt's only child, almost died! The money and the work that was taken I have to replace! All because of some dumb shit you silly-ass hoes did."

"On my kids I swear to you, Zay," she pleaded, "I don't have anything to do with this."

Zay knew whenever Joey swore on their kids she was telling the absolute truth. Though he felt a twinge of relief that she didn't have anything to do with Evan's mess, he was still vexed that Joey hadn't told him what she'd learned about Evan.

"Okay, so maybe you didn't have anything to do with it, but you still kept something so serious from me and look what happened."

"I'm not wearing the blame for this," Joey spat. "This shit comes with the game! If it hadn't been this mutha-fucka who's stalking Evan it would have been a stick-up kid. If you can't take the bad consequences get out the game."

"Get out the game!" He exploded, "I was on my way out the game, but now I'm stuck in it another year all because of your hardheaded ass!"

"Because of me how?"

"You don't listen! I told you ten years ago that Evan wasn't straight. You didn't listen. I told you that Dawhar was lusting after you and you didn't listen." He mushed her forehead with his index finger. "You took the nigga in your office and he beat ya ass trying to take ya pussy."

The tears poured faster and harder as she tried to figure out how he could bring up one of the most painful experiences of her life and throw it in her face so callously.

"I had to deal with Dawhar because of you." He shoved his finger against her forehead again. "You never listen."

"What do you mean you dealt with him?" Joey whined.

This ain't for her, he reminded himself. *But she needs to know that what she does affects more than her.* Leaning close to Joey's ear he said, "I killed him and the only way I could do it right was to get help from Asaad. Now, I owe him another year of moving heroin." He walked away then came back. "Before you ever tell me to get out the game again, remember you're the reason that I can't, you simple-minded bitch."

After landing in Charlotte, Jason and Zay got into a waiting black Suburban driven by Donavan. They took off to check on Isaac; he was in the ICU at Carolina's medical center. From there, Zay wanted to assess the losses from the robberies. Joey and Cee got into Joey's Range Rover, which had been parked at the small private airport. Joey started the car, yanked it into gear, and sped out of the lot.

"What about the bags?" Cee asked Joey.

"They're going to deliver them to my house," Joey replied. Her eyes were red and puffy from crying during the entire flight.

"You didn't say a word on the jet. Can you tell me what's going now?" Cee asked, genuinely concerned.

"Our dear best friend and business partner, Evan Dooley, was playing foul when she was attending Clark. Her foul ways have caught up to her."

"What was she doing?"

"Evan and Gage were robbing major dealers."

"Shut up! You're lying."

"No, on the real they were. And now one of them is on her ass. Evan doesn't know who it is and because they think I owe them money too, they robbed Zay's stash houses last night. Stash houses that I didn't even know existed."

"Wow. That shit don't even sound real. I can't even picture Evan's snooty ass robbing anybody, let alone a drug dealer. When did she tell you this?"

"The night of Petey's funeral," Joey answered steering the truck onto I-277. "I could get past her hiding the robberies from us, but when her past starts affecting the present and us, it's a problem. Then there's the night that she called us to that house after her graduation. Do you remember that?"

"Hell yeah, that's the night that Gage got killed."

"That wasn't a drug deal; it was a robbery."

Goose bumps sprang up all over Cee's body. "We could've been killed if someone thought we were a part of it."

"Exactly." Arriving at the Luxe Enclave, Joey saw Evan's car in her assigned space by the L Room. "She's here." With Cee by her side Joey stormed into Evan's office like a typhoon, only to find that Evan wasn't there. "Where's Evan?" Joey asked a passing staff member.

"She went to a meeting."

"In here or the Luxe building?"

"The meeting is off the property," the staff member replied walking away.

"Call her, Joey," Cee urged.

"No. I don't want her to know I'm back until she gets here." Joey sat behind Evan's desk and put her feet up on it.

"You didn't have to walk me in." Evan's voice carried down the hallway as she walked toward her office hand in hand with Reza. "I'm only going to send a few e-mails, grab some files, and then I'll be on my way home."

"That's cool and I can wait. You can ride with me and Rhamel can bring the Jag to the crib."

"If you insist." Evan crossed her office threshold and flipped the light switch up. "Joey." She gulped, a little startled to find Joey behind her desk and Cee seated in front of it. "I didn't expect y'all back until later in the week. Is everything okay?"

"No, bitch," Joey replied. "Everything is not okay."

Reza squeezed Evan's hand. "Maybe I should wait outside."

"Maybe you should stick around," Joey offered, "and find out who you're truly dating."

Completely crossed and locked in a staring match with Joey, Evan mumbled to Reza, "Go ahead, babe. I'm sure this won't take long."

"Don't be so sure about that, babe," Joey spat.

Reza released her hand and backed out of the room. Evan slammed her bag on the middle of her desk. "What the hell, Joey?"

"Who is dude?"

"He's my dude."

Joey looked at Cee. "Did you know Evan had a dude?"

"Nope. Must be another secret." Cee smirked.

Evan turned to Cee and iced grilled her. With a dramatic roll of the eyes and neck she returned her attention to Joey. "Why are you in my office with your feet on my desk being disrespectful?"

"My husband's stash houses were robbed last night."

"And what does that have to do with me?"

"It's the same person who's after you and for some odd reason this jackass says that you and I owe him money."

"I don't have a clue as to why they would say you owe them."

"Well, you better get one." Joey leapt from the chair, advancing aggressively on Evan. "Instead of going home to get some dick you need to spend your every waking hour finding out who this person is."

"Whoa!" Evan threw her palm up to Joey's face. "You got the right to be mad, but you're not going to keep disrespecting me."

Joey slapped her hand down. Cee jumped between them before Evan could retaliate.

"The nerve of you." Joey pointed over Cee at Evan. "All this crazy shit that keeps happening around here falls directly on your shoulders. You better be thanking God I ain't drag ya ass around this bitch."

"Bitch, if you was feeling so froggy ya ass shoulda leapt."

Joey reached around Cee and popped her in the jaw with a right. Evan thrust Cee to the side and clocked Joey in the face with set of two pieces. Blocking the third combo Evan tried to land, Joey elbowed her in the neck, grabbed the back of Evan's head, and rammed her knee into Evan's face three times. Blood splattered from Evan's nose and mouth as she dropped to the floor. Joey brought her foot back to kick Evan, but Cee jumped in front of Evan.

"That's enough," Cee screamed. "We too tight for this. Y'all gotta find a better way to get to the bottom of this."

Winded from the light brawl, Joey panted, "You don't even get it, Cee. This isn't just about the robbery. It is about everything that has happened in the last four months. She," Joey said and pointed at Evan, "didn't pass out in front of the L Room. She got knocked out. That's why Rhamel is always with her and—"

"Don't," Evan interjected sensing the direction that Joey was going in. "Not like this and no one knows for sure."

Cee's face went blank as it began to dawn on her that her husband's murder was tied to all of the craziness that Joey was speaking of. Though she'd caught on, Cee needed to hear the words said aloud. "What are you saying, Joe?"

"The man didn't try to burn down your spa or the Luxe building. Only the L Room."

Cee felt her body temperature escalate; the sound of her own heartbeat filled her ears, and her head felt as if it were swelling. Closing her eyes, she inhaled deeply to try to calm herself; it usually did the trick. Not this time. Cee opened her eyes, and all she saw was blood. Glaring at Evan she spewed, "You grimy, grimy, bottom of the barrel, lowlife, selfish bitch. You knew from the start and you didn't say one fucking word!" she shrilled. "If my kids didn't have just me I would hop on your ass and beat you 'til you stop breathing!"

Wincing in pain Evan stood up. "I'm so sorry, Cee, I—"

"I don't want your pitiful apology. I want my husband! You can't give him back though. Unless you're coming to tell me the name of the bastard who killed my Petey, don't ever in your life again apologize. You too." She looked from Evan to Joey. "I'm done here. I don't want to be friends or business partners with either of you."

"What?" Joey squealed. "This is Evan's mess! I don't have anything to do with it."

"You had an idea and you said nothing. Nothing! Therefore, I have nothing to say to you!" Cee's words cut into Joey real deep.

Grabbing one handle of her unzipped yellow Celine Boston bag, she snatched it from Evan's desk. The contents of the purse flew through the air and her Chanel compact crashed onto the floor, popped open, and an ounce of cocaine dispersed into the air. Evan and Joey both zeroed in on the white powder. Together their eyes traveled up from the cocaine to Cee, who bent down collecting her items.

How could I not recognize all the signs? Joey asked herself.

Feeling their eyes, Cee looked up as she tossed the last item in her purse. "Guess the cat's out the bag! And I don't give a fuck; take your judgment and shove it up your big asses!"

Pulling into the Luxe Enclave parking lot Jason asked Donavan, "Does that look like the dude who stuck y'all?" He pointed to an unfamiliar man standing in front of the L Room.

"Nah, that ain't him."

"Are you sure?"

"Yeah. That don't look nothing like him and the nigga who hit us had a nasty scar from his forehead to his chin."

"We're not going to find this faggot that easy. Y'all might have to hit the strip clubs and jewelry stores, find out who's spending more than usual," Zay said staring out the passenger's window at the man posted in front of the L Room. There was a familiarity about him.

"I don't even think that's going to work. Whoever this silly nigga is, he's far from stupid. He had to do his homework to find the stash spots. Evan's sorry ass is going to tell me every dealer they ever hit." Zay opened the passenger's door and got out.

Moving toward the L Room's entrance, Zay kept his eye trained on the stranger. Although Donavan didn't identify him as the robber, in Zay's mind any new face was suspect. As he got closer, Zay thought, *It can't be.* "Reza?"

Reza looked from his phone. "Oh, shit, Zay, my man! What's really good, my nigga?" Grinning hard he dapped Zay and embraced him.

For sure Zay was in a horrible mood, but he and Reza had history. Fifteen years earlier, Reza was Zay's go-to cocaine supplier. The pair had more than a business relationship; they hung out and traveled together leisurely. They rightfully considered themselves friends.

Beaming Reza said, "I wondered if you still lived in Charlotte. I was hoping to bump into you."

"How long you been out?"

"Almost seven months. This is crazy running into you here. I thought that I would catch you in the strip club."

"I be in there every now and then, but not how I used to be. What you doing in the QC though?"

"I came down to visit this li'l broad I fuck with, waiting for her to get off right now. Yo, I might be staying out here for a while."

"Who is she?" Zay asked. "One of the waitresses or a manager?"

"No, one of the owners. Evan."

The mention of Evan's name ruined Zay's momentary excitement of seeing an old friend. "You fucking with that bitch?"

"Yeah, is she one of your pieces or something?"

"Fuck no!" Zay retorted. "My wife, Joey, is an owner too."

"You got married? Not you, playboy. All them hoes you had."

"Yeah, I had to put my guns on the shelf, but fuck all that right now. Keep ya eyes open around that bitch. She ain't straight."

"Sheesh." Reza whistled. "I know she has a past; hell, we all do."

Judging by Reza's tone and body language, Zay felt that Reza was speaking from experience. "What do you know about her past?"

"Our paths crossed a long time ago and not in a good way."

Zay knew that Reza had been robbed years ago by a male-female team around the same time that Evan and Gage would've been doing their thing. "Hold up, Reza. She wasn't the bitch who set you up?"

"Yes," he admitted reluctantly.

"And now getting down with her? With her? Where the fuck they do that at?"

"It's not so black and white with me and Evan. On the inside I converted to Islam. I learned to forgive. Back then she was young and that bullshit nigga she was with had her mind. He was going to kill me and she didn't let him."

"All that sounds good but you wouldn't be with her on some revenge type shit playing mind games with her?"

"Yo Zay, you know me. You know how I get down; if I wanted some get back I would've just got it. I don't play no games."

Being that Zay did know Reza to be no-nonsense and direct, he accepted his word. For now. Something just wasn't right about a man being able to forgive such a grave transgression. "Reza, just stay on point. Snakes don't change; they just shed their skin."

The L Room's double glass doors flew apart, capturing the men's attention. Cee steamrolled out with Joey at her heels, shouting, "Cee, wait a minute. Please hear me out."

Cee suddenly halted causing Joey to almost run into her back. Spinning around on one heel Cee faced Joey down. "What is it you have to say? What! What! What!" she yelled.

"I just wanted to tell you I'm sorry and—"

"Your sorry don't mean jack shit to me."

"But, Cee—"

"Shut up and listen for once! It's my turn to talk! What you done hurts the worst because you have a husband! Standing here with no doubt in my mind I can tell you if our roles were reversed and Zay had died that night, if I had an inkling," she said, and held her index and thumb up to Joey's face, pressing them as close together as she could without touching, "the smallest idea about the who, the what, the when, the where, or the why, I would've come to you, even if I was 99.8 percent sure about the who, the what, the when, the where, or the why. So there is nothing you can say to me to rationalize that bullshit you did. I never thought that I would live to see the day that I would say this to you." Cee paused to make sure she was truly conveying what she felt. "I hate you. I fucking hate you."

***

The footage of Joey and Evan fighting played out on a thin sixty-five-inch smart television that hung on a honeysuckle family room wall in the home of John Doe's girlfriend. Sitting on the edge of a brown suede ottoman, money from the robbery at his feet, John Doe stared at the smart TV with a wide smile plastered across his face. He loved seeing the destruction that he was causing in the women's lives.

"Damn, Joey fucking Evan up." He pulled on the blunt. "I didn't even know her pretty ass could fight."

"Oh, you think she pretty?" His girlfriend slapped him upside the back of the head.

"Just because I say shawty is pretty don't mean I want her. I hate both them bitches."

"I know, baby. I'm just playing with you." She stood up, a turquoise lace bra and matching thin V-string thong was all that she donned on her smooth mocha skin. "Told you that you would love it," she said crossing the room. Reaching up she powered the plasma off. "Enough of this."

"You did a good job. You always do. Come here." He patted his thighs.

Obligingly she sat on his lap and locked her arms around his neck. "What's up, boo?" she asked sexily anticipating and hoping that he was ready to have sex. She loved making love to him.

"Like I was saying you have been doing your thing. Without you none of this shit would be going as smooth as it has. I think it's time for you to have a little break from it all. We're going to take a long vacation and spend some of this money." He picked up a stack of money and fanned it.

"I don't know if I can get vacation time off this soon. We have a few big events coming up."

"Man, listen, it's not like you're going to be working there much longer. After I get the rest of my money and kill Evan, we're done here!"

"Yeah, but in order for the plan to work I need to keep my job."

"Tell them someone died in your family and you need some time off."

"Yeah, that will work. I think in my contract I get two to four weeks of bereavement leave."

"I'm going to take you to Vegas and Beverly Hills." He scooped up ten banded stacks of money and laid it on her lap. "I want you to spend all of this on yourself."

"Thank you, but I don't need to do that. I just want to be with you."

"That's why I'm going to spend it on you, because I know that you don't care if I do or don't. You'll be with me. That's why I love you so much, Isadora."

Chapter Eleven

"You expect us to believe you don't know anything about the disappearance of Dawhar Bradley?" a tall white detective with a buzz cut stated to Zay, who was seated across the table from him in the small interrogation room.

"I don't any have any expectations. I told you I don't know anything about that man or where he is."

"Detective McIntyre," Scott Fleishman, Zay's attorney, stepped in, "my client has been more than cooperative in speaking to you when you didn't even have sufficient evidence to bring him in for questioning."

"Your client threatened to kill Bradley in roomful of police officers."

"That may be true indeed, but we've already given you his alibi and a complete list of respectable people to confirm with for the time that you're saying he disappeared."

"And when my partner gets done running them down we'll be done here."

"Are you charging my client?"

"Not yet."

"Well, we're done here then. Let's go, Mr. Tappens."

The door opened and in walked Detective Wells, a man of medium height with bulging muscles. "I just spoke with three senators, a governor, two mayors, and a police commissioner who all vouch for this guy for that whole week!"

"Senators and a governor." Detective McIntyre scoffed. "It must be some type of prank."

"No, it was the real thing," Wells replied. "We are done here now and thanks for your time."

Fleishman and Zay left the room. Shortly after, the original investigators on the assault case, Detectives Robbins and Blankenship, filed in. "What is so special about a guy that he has politicians and a commissioner alibiing for him?" Robbins wanted to know.

"I don't know," Wells replied, "but they all said that he was at the same week-long golf tournament with them that closed out with some ritzy gala."

"I want to know more about this Zavian Tappens," Robbins said. "Something about him just doesn't pass the smell test."

"Would you give it a break already, Robbins?" Blankenship said. "You're still pissed that your football hero was exposed for the rapist he is."

"Excuse us, ladies." Wells laughed. "I would love to stick around for this little marital spat, but we followed the lead. It was a dead end and we have to go look for people who are really missing."

On the way out McIntyre stopped and told Robbins. "Dawhar Bradley may be just a fugitive on the run. I know his wife thinks he's missing."

"How is he on the run when he hasn't withdrawn any cash, used a credit card, and his car hasn't been seen?"

"The guy is a multimillionaire, so no one know how much cash he had on hand. At the end of the day this guy is a rapist and if those girls had been a year or two younger he'd be a pedophile. Let the fugitive taskforce locate him." He patted Robbins on the back. "Okay, buddy?"

"That's fine, but I'm still going to look into this Zayvian Tappens."

***

As soon as Joey saw Zay and his attorney step off the elevator into the lobby of the Trade Street police station lobby, she went over to him. "Are you okay? What did they want?"

Zay wrapped his arm around her shoulder. "Not here, baby. Let's get in the car first."

It had been a contentious two and a half weeks for the couple. Since she'd revealed Evan's secret to Zay he'd barely spoken to Joey. If and when they did speak it was with regard to their children or the welcome home party for Zay's older brothers that was less than twenty-four hours away. Joey's home was not the only place filled with tension as a result of the revelations of Evan's past. At the Luxe the three former best friends were not speaking. All business was handled by the managers underneath them.

"Let me drive," Zay said as the couple approached Joey's Panamera, which was parked on the street a few blocks from the police station. "I have places I need to go."

A nervous wreck, Joey happily turned the keys over to him. She would not be able to calm her nerves until she knew what the police had brought Zay in for. When Joey arrived home from dropping the kids off at school, Zay was being placed in the back of an unmarked Dodge Charger. Immediately calling his attorney she'd followed the car all the way down to the station and waited with no knowledge of what was going on.

Joey fastened her seat belt. "What is going on, Zay? What did the police want with you?"

"They questioned me about Dawhar."

"Oh my God, are you serious?"

"Yes, but they don't have anything."

"How do you know?"

"'Cause there is nothing to have and them detectives were from missing persons, not homicide."

"When I saw them putting you in the back of the car I didn't know if they were the narcs, the feds, or the DEA. I thought I was going to have an anxiety attack."

"I didn't know you cared."

"What in the hell is that supposed to mean?"

"You haven't had much to say to me since we got back from Miami, like you got a reason to be mad. Like I hid something from you and your spots got robbed."

Joey was tight. Inhaling deeply she folded her arms across her chest. "You shut me out. Every time that I've tried to make small talk you give me the cold shoulder. The only time you've said more than three words to me is to tell me something you want at your brothers' party. I only respond to the way you treat me. I'm not going to beg and grovel for you to talk me."

"You should try it sometime instead of being so stubborn."

"You're crazy as hell, Zay. I'm your wife and I'm scared as hell of this maniac who's stalking Evan. He's saying I owe him money. What if he tries to do something to me next? This is a time when we should be banding together; instead we're at odds. I'm confused and I'm lonely. I need you to tell me it's going to be all right. I need my husband."

Hearing that she needed him was always enough to melt him. Zay never wanted her to feel as if she needed him and he wasn't there. He reached over and held her hand.

"I apologize. I should've never let it go this far. This shit is stressful though; trying to find this nigga who robbed my spots is like chasing a ghost."

"I know. Evan has tracked down every dealer they robbed and even put a private investigator on them and it's not any of them."

"What do you think about Reza?"

"What do you think about him?" Joey shot back. "He's your dear old friend."

"I think he's on the up and up. If he wanted revenge he would've just beat the hell out of her or killed her."

"Whenever I see them together on the property, he seems like he's really into her."

"Every time I try to figure this shit out my damn head start hurting and it's banging extra hard now right 'cause I haven't eaten today."

Joey reached over and massaged his temples. "Why don't you stop and get something?"

"I don't have time. I gotta meet with this man and sign this paperwork so everything will be straight for my brothers when they get out this evening. After I'm done with him we can go to the crib and you can whip me up something good."

"I wouldn't mind doing that, but I gotta get to the Luxe. There is a lot of work to be done to prepare for your brothers' party tomorrow tonight. Isadora won't be back until tomorrow, so I've had to help Bev with every little thing."

"I'll only be a second in here." Zay pulled into an office development and parked the car. "When I'm done we can swing by the house so I can get my truck and you can go on to work."

While waiting for Zay, Joey went through her business e-mails and returned calls. A group text popped onto the screen of Joey's smart phone, and she opened it and was shocked to see pictures of her children at school. Pictures of Zay and Jason out and about came across the screen, followed by shots of Joey, Evan, and Cee inside different areas of the Luxe. The message beneath the photos read: **Pay me my money, or one of these people will be hurt.**

Joey got out of the car, and rushing toward the office building she stumbled and fell onto the concrete. Bursting out of the glass double doors in a hurry after receiving the same message, Zay came to her aid. "How did you fall?"

"I was running to show you this." She held out her phone.

"I saw the text already."

"What are we going to do?"

"I'm about to send him a message back." Zay typed and sent a text.

Joey read the message when it popped up on the screen: My wife don't owe you shit. I've never been extorted in my life and I'm not about to start getting extorted by a text message gangster.

"Zay, do you think that was the right thing to say? This lunatic could go after the kids."

"We could pay money that you don't owe and he could come after us or the kids."

"Oh God, he's sending another message." Joey read it: "'Send $2 million to this account #234878956010 at the Caribbean National Bank, Cayman Island's Country Swift Code FCIBKYKY by five p.m. tomorrow or else.'"

"This nigga is out his mind."

"Zay, take me to get the kids. I wanna make sure they're okay. I'll take them to work with me until we figure this thing out."

"Ain't nothing to figure out. We're going to have to go on extra guard 'til we find this nigga. We not paying that money. Evan can pay it. This is her problem and she can pay it again and again when he decides that he wants more money."

"I think there may be someone who can help us."

"Who?"

"Kane told me about this chick who's real good at finding people. I think it's time I reach out to her."

***

After retrieving the kids from school, Zay drove to the Luxe Enclave to drop his wife and their children off. Before pulling off, he asked Joey, "You feel okay here? I know the pictures of you inside your office shook you up."

"At first I thought that he'd gotten inside and taken those pics, but I can tell by the angles that they're from the security cameras." Joey waved at two security guards who were patrolling the property on a golf cart. "I called the tech guy who installed the security system; he said it sounds like we were hacked. He's already in there trying to see if we were, and if so, he can trace it."

"Cool. When I get with Jason I'll bring your car back, but I still want you to call me when you're ready to leave so I can follow you home. Give me a kiss."

Joey leaned into the driver's window and kissed her husband passionately, happy to be in accordance again. "I love you."

"I love you too, baby. Call you in a little while." Zay drove away.

"Ewww, Mommy, you kissed Daddy in the mouth!" Joey's daughter, McKinley, sang out teasingly. "Yucky!"

"They had to kiss for your big head to get here!" Joey's oldest son, Braden, said.

"What do you know about kissing?" Joey quizzed.

"He kisses his girlfriend after school," the youngest boy, Axle, said.

"Oh, so Mr. Braden has a girlfriend." Joey smiled at her blushing son.

A white BMW 750 pulled up to the curb and out jumped Dawhar's wife, Leska.

Joey looked to the sky. *What now?*

"You slut whore," Leska screamed coming at Joey. "What did your husband do to my Dawhar?"

"My husband didn't do shit to that rapist. He should have, but he didn't."

"My husband is no rapist. All you whores seduced him and then screamed rape!"

"I have no time for this nonsense. I don't argue with fools. Bye, Felicia, and get the fuck off my property."

"Who is Felicia?"

"You, bitch! Now, bye."

"I'm not going anywhere until you give me some answers."

"Leska, for real leave before I beat ya ass worse than Cee did the last time."

"Ain't going down like that this time," a tall, stout woman said emerging from the passenger's seat.

"That's right," another tall, clearly overweight woman said, getting out of the back seat.

"Braden," Joey said to her son, "take your brother and sister inside now." She looked around for the patrol guards she'd seen earlier, but they were nowhere in sight. "Hurry, get them inside."

Braden picked up McKinley. "Come on, Axle. Run and go to Auntie Cee's." The kids ran into the spa. Once inside, Braden put his baby sister down and ran room to room until he found Cee in her private suite, styling a client.

"Auntie Cee, they're going to hurt my mommy. You have to call for help!" he screamed.

"Calm down, Braden. Who's going to hurt your mommy?"

"Three ladies." He held up three fingers. "And two of them are really, really big."

Cee looked over and saw Joey's other kids standing in the doorway. She quickly grabbed her purse from under her station, telling her client, "I'll be back and you kids stay right here. Do not move."

Outside Joey was not cowering away. She was an experienced fighter. She knew whenever it went down to grab

Leska and do her dirty. "What you thought, Leska? That bringing these two big country biscuit-eating bitches with you was going to scare me?" Joey asked, "You still going to get your ass molly whopped, so I suggest you burn the road up."

"You got a real smart mouth," the big-boned passenger said.

"Do something about it."

The big woman charged Joey, but stopped about a foot away when she saw Cee aiming a .380 right at her.

"Back your big ass up. What the fuck is going on out here?" Cee asked.

"Not shit," Joey replied. "This bitch up here tripping again."

"Leska." Cee shook her head. "You again? The last ass whipping wasn't good enough?"

The big woman backed up toward the car. "Leska, you my li'l cousin and I love you. But I'm not down to die behind this shit." Both passengers got back into the car.

"I just want her to tell me where my husband is," Leska cried out. "Her husband did something to him; that's why the police picked him up today. Now tell me where he is."

"Look, bitch, that nigga ain't here," Cee said.

"I would think as a woman who's lost her husband you would have some sympathy for me."

"Don't you dare compare our situations. My husband died a real man with an impeccable reputation. Your husband is a rapist who left your dumb ass to go on the run instead of standing to face his charges."

"This is far from over," Leska seethed at Joey then got into her car and sped away.

"This day just cannot get any crazier," Joey said aloud.

"What was that about?" Cee asked.

"The police think something happened to Dawhar. I guess he's missing or something. They picked Zay up for questioning, but he don't know nothing about where Dawhar is," Joey lied, protecting her husband's secret. "I'm glad those two big bitches didn't get a chance to get some licks in on me. Thanks for saving my neck. That was big, considering."

"Considering what?"

"The last thing you said to me was you fucking hate me."

"Yeah, I did. Sorry about that." Cee blushed. "I'm past that though. I was so angry at y'all that day all I could see was red."

"I couldn't tell that you're past it. This is the first time that you've spoken to me in over two weeks."

Cee put her gun into her purse. "I was going to talk to you today. I've been dealing with a lot. I had to get myself in order first. I had to get my little cocaine issue under control. Even though I was beyond pissed with y'all that day, I could see the hurt in your eyes when the coke spilled out and I felt ashamed. I went to a meeting and I haven't gotten high since that day."

"That's so good." Joey hugged Cee. "Snorting powder is not a good look for anybody."

"I know. I'd been binging out for a couple of weeks just trying to absorb the pain."

"I wish you would've come to me, but that's neither here nor there now. If you ever need to talk or want me to go to a meeting let me know. I'm here."

"I know that you are."

"How are you feeling about Evan right now?" Joey asked Cee. "Have you talked to her?"

"No, her crazy ass wrote me a ten-page letter telling me why she was sticking up those dudes back then and apologizing. I'm going to talk to her though. I don't hate her either. Wait a minute." Cee paused. "Did you see that group message with the pictures?"

"Hell yeah; that's why I took the kids out of school and brought them up here with me."

"Maybe I should have one of the trips pick up Shelby and PJ."

"You should, and keep them in the house for a few days until this blows over."

"What makes you think it's going to blow over soon?" Cee asked.

"I'm about to make a call that I should have made two weeks ago."

"Hey, Joey," a Indonesian man of medium height called out as he exited the Luxe headquarters carrying a black computer processor.

"Hello, Iwan," Joey greeted him as he got closer. "I didn't know you were here already."

"I was nearby when you called."

"Excuse me," Cee interrupted, "but I have to get back to my client and I'll make sure Braden and the little ones are okay."

"I'll be in there in as soon as I'm done out here." Returning her attention to Iwan, Joey asked, "Did you find out who hacked into our security cameras?"

"No one."

"Are you sure?"

"I'm positive," Iwan answered. "Although there is something fudgy going on with the hard drive that's linked to the security cameras."

"Fudgy? What does that mean?"

"I believe that it's been tampered with. I installed a new hard drive and I'm going to take this one with me and see what's going on with it."

Later that evening Jason and Zay stood in baggage claim of the Charlotte/Douglas International Airport, awaiting the arrival of their older brothers. Tony and

Rico Tappens had been released that morning from Manchester Federal Prison in Kentucky. Jason and Zay had not told anyone that the older Tappens boys would be home on this day. Everyone else in the family was expecting them in another twenty-four hours. Jason and Zay beamed with pride when they saw their older brothers descending the escalator. Rico and Tony were tall, slim, and athletically built. Tony's skin was the color of a toasted almond and Rico's was the color of dark honey. Both older Tappens brothers were in their early forties, but neither looked a day over thirty-three.

At the bottom of the escalator the brothers hugged tightly, smiling so hard that all thirty-two teeth in each of their mouths could be counted. "It feels damn good to be free," Tony announced with tears in his eyes still having a hard time grasping that he was free after eighteen years.

"It does indeed." Rico nodded, checking out every female in view. His eyes locked in on white girl in denim hot shorts with an ample backside. "Damn, these bitches don't even wear clothes no more, and when did white girls grow these humungous asses?"

Everyone laughed at Rico who was known to be the most animated of the four brothers. On the way to the parking deck Tony and Rico looked around in amazement at the modern automobiles, fashion, and technology. They felt as if they were in a time warp. Jason unlocked the doors to his Denali XL via remote.

"This you?" Rico asked wide-eyed.

"Yeah."

"This thang here is beautiful," Rico said. He was even more impressed by the interior of the truck, prompting him to ask his little brothers, "What da hell is y'all doing out here? I can tell y'all getting plenty of money."

Laughing, Zay answered, "Don't worry about what we do; just sit back and kick your feet up. We got you." Zay went into the glove box and handed his two older brothers cell phones and $10,000 each. "A little something."

"Y'all definitely getting it," Tony stated. "Thanks for the paper, but what the hell is this?" he asked holding up the cell.

Laughing in unison Jason and Zay replied, "It's an iPhone."

"I don't even recognize Charlotte now," Rico said getting out of the truck in front of Dorenda's house. "I can't believe they tore down Boulevard Homes."

"Me either," Tony said.

"That ain't nothing," Zay said. "Fairview Homes, Piedmont Court, and Dalton Village are gone too."

"These crackers not playing no games," Rico said.

Jason tapped a few times on his mother's door. Moments later Dorenda opened the door in a floral black and purple silk house dress. "Zay, Jason, I wasn't expecting you boys. Come on in." She turned to walk away.

"Wait, Ma," Zay said.

"What is it?" Dorenda turned around.

Jason and Zay stepped apart so that Dorenda could see in between them. "Hey, Mama." Tony and Rico smiled.

"Ahhhhhhhhh!" Dorenda screamed looking to the sky. Tears fell from her eyes. "Oh Lord, my babies are free. Thank you, Lord."

Tony and Rico ran up the steps and wrapped their arms around their mother, holding on to one another as all three cried tears of joy. As happy as Tony and Rico were to be free, no one was happier in the room than Dorenda to have all four of her sons together. Dorenda went to each one of them and touched their faces.

"My prayers have been answered. Why didn't you boys tell me you were coming today? I would've cooked a big meal for you."

"We wanted to surprise you," Tony said.

"And we didn't want you to cook," Jason added. "We're taking you out for dinner."

"I don't want to eat out," Dorenda said. "I want to eat here so we can talk and laugh as loud as we want. I already started making food for the dinner tomorrow. I'll make some more stuff and we can eat here."

"Okay, Mama, we doing it however you want to do it. We can eat here and do dinner out tomorrow before the party," Zay said. "I'm going to get Joey and the kids."

"Yes, get all my grandchildren here. Tony, Rico do your daughters know you're home?"

"They're on the way over," Jason answered for his older brothers. "They don't know that Tony and Rico are here yet though."

"Good, good," Dorenda gushed. "All my sons and my grandchildren here in my house at one time. God is good. God is good! Yes, He is!"

Chapter Twelve

"What's wrong, baby?" Reza asked Evan. The way she was moping around her bedroom-sized closet getting dressed in silence, he couldn't help but notice that she was sad.

"I'm a little down."

"About what?"

"Everything. My two best friends hate me; this stupid-ass stalker is destroying and scaring the shit out of me at the same time. Tonight I have to put on a brave face to go and provide my best service at a party for the brothers of the person who can't stand the sight of me."

"Cee and Joey don't hate you. They're rightfully upset and hurt, but y'all will get past it. You're a different person now and you've kept it real when shit hit Front Street. I know Zay; eventually he'll get over it too."

"I hope so," she said slipping into a white Missoni knit mini tank dress. "Can you zip me up please?" Evan turned her back to Reza.

Slowly moving the zipper upward, Reza said, "Zay is the only person who knows you robbed me."

"You told him? Why?"

"He put it together. It wasn't hard to figure out. He was my stickman back then."

"Wow, stickman, there's a word I haven't heard in a long time."

"Yeah, that's that VA slang. Anyway Zay thinks I'm seven-thirty for dealing with you. At the same time when I told him you deserved a pass because you were young and dude had your head fucked up, I think he understood."

"Hmmm, I don't know. Zay has never really cared too much for me." Evan stepped into a pair of metallic gold Blahnik pumps. "Joey thinks that I don't know. I could always tell by the way he looked at me. I can only imagine what he thinks of me now."

"Enough of that depressing shit. I got some good news today."

"What kind of good news?"

"My parole officer approved my transfer."

"Yaaaay." Evan beamed. "Finally something that I can be happy about." She grabbed his face and planted a soft, sensual kiss on his lips.

Holding Evan by the waist he looked her in the eye. "You wanted me to stay; now you got me. So treat a nigga right."

Eyes twinkling Evan smiled cheerfully. "I wouldn't dream of treating you any other way!"

Reza took her hand and led her over to an upholstered cream and white paisley sleigh bench in the middle of her enormous closet and sat down. "When I say treat me right, I'm not just talking about some 'cater to me' type shit. Treat me right means be one hundred with me at all times. Despite our past circumstances I'm rocking with you and I know a lot of people wouldn't understand that, but it's not for nobody to understand but us."

"Since you're being clear with me I have to ask: you're not staying with me because of what I have to offer, are you?"

"Go ahead, yo." He pulled his hand away from hers. "You asked me to stay and I don't want shit from you. Like I told you before I wasn't stupid. I put up plenty of paper for that rainy day that I knew would come eventually."

"Didn't mean to offend you, but you have to understand even I wonder from time to time how you could be with me after what I did to you."

"I'm not as devout to Islam or on my din as I should be, but I learned a lot from my religion while I was on the inside. I don't think or rationalize on a basic level. And I don't have to explain to anyone how I can or why I love you."

Shocked, Evan's eyes widened, and her heart thumped wildly against her chest. "Did you . . . did you just say that you love me?"

"Yes."

She threw her arms around his neck. "Oh, baby, I love you too."

"Why didn't you tell me?"

"I didn't want to scare you off. You know how you men are when women start throwing the L word around."

"I guess I have to keep reminding you that I'm not most men. I know it's time to go, so let me get to the point."

"Okay," Evan agreed.

"I have some people I can reach out to from back in the day who can definitely find out who is stalking you. Not only will they find them, but they will eliminate them. Before I reach out to them I have to know that you have been one hundred with me about everything."

"Of course I've been honest. I've told you all my deepest secrets, things that until recently I hid from my two closest friends for years."

"Because of our past, you can't afford to keep anything from me, and I'm warning you only this one time, do not cross me. Yes, I love you and for reasons I can't seem to put in words, I'm deeply in love with you. But, I swear on the eyes of my children if you cross me the consequences won't be nothing nice."

***

"Everybody almost ready?" Zay asked entering the family room of his home, fastening a diamond cufflink on his white linen button-up.

"I'm ready," Tony replied. He was a beautiful sight, his brown skin cloaked in all white Bottega Veneta. Fresh out of the barber's chair the one blade on his Caesar and the trim on his beard were exquisite.

"Rico's and Jason's pretty asses still upstairs getting dressed." Back together only close to forty-eight hours the brothers were paired up how they were when they were younger. Tony and Zay, the two levelheaded brothers, would often be found in deep conversation; while the two cowboys, Rico and Jason, would be off to the side sharing tales of wild women and drunken nights.

"You need some help with that?" Tony pointed to Zay's wrist as he continued to struggle with the cufflink.

"Yeah. Joey usually hooks them for me."

"Damn, I can't believe we still haven't met her yet, as much as you wrote and talked about her the last ten years."

"She's been busy working on the party for you guys; that's why she didn't come to Mom's house with the kids and me. She didn't even leave the Luxe last night, because everything has to be to her perfect standards. You want a drink?" Zay asked as he went behind the wet bar.

"I don't even know why you asked; pour me a double. Shiiit, I'm trying to make up for eighteen years of forced sober living."

Chuckling, Zay pulled out four cognac snifters and a $3,800 bottle of Richard Hennessy. "I bought this," he said, and held up the Hennessy, "a year ago and I counted down the days and hours 'til you and Rico would be released and I would crack it open and share a toast with my big brothers." Zay poured a double shot in each snifter and handed one to Tony. "One toast while we wait on them two slow asses won't hurt the moment."

"It sure won't." Tony raised his glass.

Zay raised his glass. "To the last of a dying breed. You and Rico took that eighteen on the chest and did the time just like real niggas supposed to."

The brothers tapped snifters then drained the liquor from them.

"I'm proud of you and Jason," Tony said. "You held it down out here and from the looks of this mansion and everything else I've seen, my little brothers have done very well."

"Yes, we have, and the thanks go to you. Everything that I know about this treacherous game I learned from you." Zay refilled the snifters.

"Yeah, you may have followed my map, but what you boys built requires a strong hustle and extreme intelligence: two things that come from within."

Zay blushed from the recognition by his older brother, who'd also assumed the role of father figure when their father passed. "I appreciate that especially coming from you."

"I'm still a straight shooter and I give props where they are due." He took a sip from his glass. "I'm curious about a few things but if you don't want to discuss them I understand."

"Ain't nothing I can't or won't discuss with you."

"How much white do you have to move in a month to afford a place like this?"

"I don't fuck with cocaine. Stepped up to the major leagues and got into the dog food game."

"You moved on to heroin?"

"Yeah. A little over five years ago, my connect showed me that the real paper was in heroin. One brick of the boy is equal to three to four bricks of quality coke."

"Charlotte has changed," Tony said. "This wasn't much of a heroin city when I left."

"It still isn't. People around here still prefer that white girl," Zay responded. "Most of my business in the city comes from the east side, and the Greenville neighborhood. It ain't much to brag about though. We do real good in Greensboro, Winston, and Durham. Those three spots are money in the bank. Nothing compares to the money we make in the Maryland, DC, and Virginia area. I've stacked crazy cake from them places."

"A dude from B-more who was locked up with us was worth a billion off that dope, but the nigga ratted when they got him. He shitted on his workers and gave up the name of his supplier from across the water."

"That's a damn shame." Zay shook his head. "Made all that money and turned into a fuckin' rat."

"Ay, I know it's some room for Rico and me to make a few dollars with you and Jason."

"Nah, it's not."

Furrowing his brow, Tony frowned at his little brother's answer. No was the last thing he expected to hear. "Damn, it's like that? You can't put ya family on?"

"Of course I could put you on and risk you going back to prison for the rest of your lives. Catching twenty years in your early twenties is totally different from catching twenty in your early forties. Or, I could give you the money that we put up for you two. I'm not talking a couple of hundred stacks either. I'm talking a few million each."

Tony choked on the liquor that was gliding down his throat, and he coughed roughly a few times. "A few?" He coughed again. "A few million? Y'all getting that kinda paper?"

Zay nodded his head.

"I appreciate it, man. I ain't going to say no to it. A hundred stacks would have done me fine. I know that you had to hustle hard for that money. It's not going hurt your pockets?"

"Not at all. I've had a great run. Even if it did hurt my pockets I'd do it for you and Rico. Y'all took care of us. I'm also doing it for Mama; I want y'all to stay free for her. That's enough money to buy a crazy house, a nice whip, and start a business. I own a few businesses that I can give y'all the blueprint to and you two can stay out the game."

When Tony went away to do his time he knew that his family would be okay, because Zay was bright and a natural hustler. But the things that his younger brother had accomplished in the past two decades amazed him. He tapped the rim of his glass. "Hit me again, li'l bro."

Zay topped Tony's glass off with two more shots.

Tony raised his glass. "When I left you were a boy, and now you're a real man. Better than that you're a self-made man. I'm so proud of you and thankful for you."

Once again the brothers tapped glasses and tossed down the shots.

"Could you keep the money thing between us?" Zay asked. "I really wanted to surprise the both of you with it. I knew that it was going to be hard. I knew that one of you was going to be coming at me about getting on, I just expected it to be Rico first."

"Oh, don't worry; he'll be coming at you real soon," Tony replied. "Hell, he probably up there in Jason ear right now." Tony was amped about the money, but there were other things that he'd picked up on and he wanted to get answers to while Rico was not around. It wasn't that he was being sneaky; he just didn't want to discuss sensitive issues in front of Rico. After eighteen years on the inside Rico was still a hothead and easy to fly off the handle. There were many days that Tony had to talk him out of impulsive and poor decisions that could've prolonged his time in prison or landed him on death row.

"Zay, what's going on with this football nigga who tried your wife?"

"He done."

"Done like what?"

"He dead."

"You did 'im?" Tony quizzed.

Zay looked his brother dead in the eye. "Yeah."

"Didn't know you had the heart for the murder game. I thought it was a situation you might want me to handle."

"You got a lot to learn about me, big bruh. I don't like killing. But, there is not a man walking these streets who can violate any member of my family like that and think they gon' continue to breathe."

"Okay, okay, and what's with this dude y'all looking for who robbed ya spots?"

"That's a long story and nothing that I want you to worry about. I'll fill you in on that tomorrow. Right now it's time to party."

"Damn right," Rico announced, entering the room, dapper in a white Versace tux with navy lapels and navy Mauri gators. Without a bowtie, his shirt was unbuttoned down to the third button. "What's that new shit they saying now? Time to get up."

"No," Jason said following Rico into the room, "it's 'turn up' and I wouldn't miss hearing that dumbass term if no one ever said it again."

They were overjoyed just by being able to be together. The brothers burst into laughter as if Jason's response was the funniest thing ever said.

"Ayo," Zay said, "we gotta go. Joey's texting me they ready to start the dinner at the L Room."

"What's the L Room?" Rico asked. "I thought the party was at the Luxe."

"It's all in the same place," Zay answered. "Now get a glass. I want to make a toast before we leave." He raised his glass. He motioned his snifter toward Tony and Rico.

"You two stepped up as teenagers to fill the shoes of our deceased father. Because of your love, guidance, and discipline, Jason and I stand here as men. I love you. I mean we love you. And, because you took such good care of us, even putting your life on the line to do so, it is now time for us to take care of you. Tonight, I toast to my big brothers, Tony and Rico: the last of a dying breed."

The brothers arrived at the Luxe Enclave in two different chauffeured vehicles. Jason and Rico were in an impressively beautiful white Rolls-Royce Phantom Drophead Coupé with the top down. Zay and Tony traveled there in an equally extravagant white Rolls-Royce Ghost. Getting out the car, Rico was visibly awestruck by the size and the magnificence of the Luxe Enclave. He looked at Tony who was walking up. "Y'all own all of this?"

"This isn't mines; this is my wife's and her friends'."

"Yeah," Tony interjected. "But we all know that you made it happen."

"No, I didn't have anything to do with it. This is all them. The money that my wife put in was money that she made from promoting."

"Wow, that's crazy," Rico said looking around at the three eloquent beige brick, marble, and stone buildings and the gorgeous greenery in the late spring sunset. "I thought this was going to be like one building. This place is like an upscale office park."

The Enclave grounds were flanked by additional security who were hired in case John Doe decided to strike. They were not the run of the mill, either. The firm that was hired dealt in high-profile security and black ops.

The L Room's doors opened and out walked Joey in a white Philipp Plein tight-fitted, short split-sleeved, studded-shoulder mini dress. The white Zanotti Cruel

Summer six-inch heels on her feet elongated her slightly bowed but well-toned legs and gave her infinite curves. Joey's red mane was laid for the gods in long, wavy curls and M. Latrice had flown in from Miami and slew her makeup. She was so striking that Zay, her own husband, had to do a double take.

"Gat damn." Rico whistled. "Who is this bad-ass bitch?"

Jason elbowed Rico in the side. "That's Joey, Zay's wife!"

"Oh, shit. My bad, baby bro," Rico said to Zay. "I knew she was pretty from the wedding pictures that you sent, but they didn't do her any justice and her dress was white, but it wasn't fitting like that one."

"You straight," Zay said in a trance, staring at Joey as she came toward them. When she got near, he grabbed Joey by the waist, pulled her close, and spoke softly into her left ear. "Damn, baby, what you trying to do tonight?"

Blushing she replied, "I guess that means I look good in this dress."

"Yeah, you looking too good in this little ass dress. I think you might need to take it off."

"Not." She playfully pushed him away. Turning her attention to Tony and Rico, Joey said, "Welcome home!" She embraced them each. "I've heard so much about the two of you from your mother and brothers."

"We heard a lot about you too." Rico scanned her up and down. "But we didn't know it was like that."

"Ayo," Zay said giving Rico the side eye, "that's enough, bruh."

Everyone laughed.

After exchanging a few more pleasantries with her newly acquainted brothers-in-law, Joey said, "Well, welcome to Luxe Enclave. Before the party starts we have dinner waiting in the L Room. I wanted to fill your stomachs with food before you start filling them with liquor." Hand in hand with Zay, Joey led the way inside to a small event room. When she opened the door a crowd around forty to fifty family members and friends yelled, "Surprise!"

Tony and Rico were happily shocked and trilled to see so many aunts, uncles, cousins, and people from the past. For more than two hours the older Tappens brothers reminisced with the people they grew up with. Their young adult cousins, who were children when they caught their time, fascinated them. Noticeably absent to Tony was their mother's sister, Fran, and her son, Isaac. Growing up Isaac often stayed with them while his mother worked third shift. Four years younger than Jason, Isaac was like a little brother to all of them.

While walking Dorenda to her car after the dinner, Tony asked her, "Ma, where is Auntie Fran and Isaac?"

"You know Isaac in the hospital."

"For what?"

"He got shot."

"When?"

"Two weeks ago. He was in a coma for a week. Didn't Jason and Zay tell you?"

"No. Who shot him?"

"We don't know. Some fool broke in and tried to rob him," Dorenda replied, oblivious to the real reason behind her nephew's shooting. "I'm on the way to the hospital to pick up Frannie now; she's going to stay over at my house tonight to get a break from the hospital. You and Rico should come over for brunch and then we can go to the hospital to see Isaac."

"Okay, Ma." Tony kissed Dorenda on the cheek and hugged her. "Get home safe and text somebody to let them know you made it. Don't text my phone though; I'm still trying to figure out how to work that thing."

"I'll send Zay a message when I get home and don't you boys drink too much."

"We'll try not to, Ma."

"Good night, baby." Dorenda got into her navy Lexus LS 460 and backed out of the parking space.

Tony watched his mother drive off into the night, and when Dorenda's taillights were out of sight he returned to the L Room. All of the older relatives had left. Only a few guests who were staying for the party at Luxe remained, and they were sitting at the table with Tony's three brothers enjoying cold bottles of champagne. Tony leaned over to Zay, and said, "Let me holla at you for a minute."

"Sure, big bruh," he said and got up and stepped a few feet from the table with the eldest Tappens.

"Why didn't you tell me about Isaac?"

"We just wanted you and Rico to enjoy this night before we put all that in your head."

Tony knew that something was amiss with Zay. A light went off in his head and Tony asked, "Did he get shot during the robbery at ya spot?"

"Yeah," Zay replied reluctantly.

"Why are you being so hush-hush about this robbery with me? What is really going on?"

"Listen, that robbery wasn't just a simple lick by some local; it's more to it. I haven't told you because I know how you are. You're going to try to step in and help. Besides, it's something that I don't even want you worrying about right now. The only thing that I want you to do tonight is have a ball, bag a few bitches, and get pussy from all of 'em if you can."

"A'ight," Tony responded, "but tomorrow I want to know everything. You been holding this family down solidly, and now that I'm home any niggas who even think about fucking with you or this family, I'll put 'em in the ground personally."

Joey came over and interrupted before Zay could respond. "Excuse me, baby." She rubbed the small of Zay's back. "I need to borrow Tony over at the table for a second." Both men followed Joey over to the table were Rico and Jason were still sitting with a few guests.

"I have to head over to the Luxe now and judging by the line outside it's going to be insane tonight so I wanted to introduce you two," Joey said and pointed to Tony and Rico, "to a few people who will be taking care of anything you need." Joey waved the Luxe staff over. "Guys," she addressed the staff, "this is Tony and Rico. Tonight is their night and we're going to give them the five-star treatment. Familiarize yourselves with all the faces at this table, with the exception of the ones you already know of course." She smiled. "Everyone right here will be in Tony and Rico's VIP section," Joey said addressing the table. Joey began introducing the staff, starting with two pretty, sexy women dressed in metallic silver bra tops, matching hot pants, five-inch platform pumps and white bunny ears.

"This is Nicole and Sicily, your bottle waitresses. They are assigned to your booth only. Whatever you need they will be at your beck and call."

"Anything?" Rico asked eyeing Sicily's thick brown thighs then winking at her. Sicily didn't mind the overt flirting; he was a possible come up in her mind. The older females on staff had been talking about Tony's and Rico's history in the city, even mentioning that the elder Tappens probably still had money.

Shaking her head Joey continued, "This is Bev, my right hand. She is over all operations at the Luxe so if you have any problems and you can't find me, Bev will take care of you."

Strutting meanly in a white-on-white David Koma sleeveless body con print dress and purple Brian Atwood strappy six-inch heels, Isadora entered the room. A few steps behind Isadora, Cee and Evan walked in. Cee dazzled in a white curve-hugging Jean Paul Gaultier long-sleeve knit dress, and gray and white Lanvin platform pumps. Her short hair was sleek and sophisticated slicked back and her face had been wonderfully beaten by M. Latrice also. A large silver chunky chain-link necklace lying close to her neck made the outfit perfect.

"And this is my left hand." Joey beamed. "Isadora is second in command to Bev, as well as over all of the VIP hostesses and waitresses."

"Hello." Isadora waved flashing a brilliant smile.

"What's up, chocolate." Rico swooned forgetting about the waitress he was exchanging googly eyes with seconds earlier.

"You," Isadora flirted back.

He is definitely a Tappens man, Joey thought. "Okay, y'all can do all that later. These ladies have a lot to do." Bev, Isadora, and the waitresses exited to go back to the Luxe.

"Last but not least," Joey said, "I would like for you to meet my two best friends and business partners. Evan and Cee, this is Tony and Rico."

The four exchanged handshakes, "nice to meet you's", and "how are you's."

"I hate to rush, but I have to get over here and make sure everything is in order. See you guys soon and once the party gets going I'll come to your section and pop a few bottles with you!"

"Yo, what's up with blondie?" Tony asked eyeing Evan hard as she walked away.

"She ain't shit," Zay replied dryly. "Stay the fuck from around her at all times."

"Damn, I didn't say I want to marry the girl; you just told me a few minutes ago to get as much pussy as I can."

"Yeah, but, my nigga, not that pussy."

"She that awful?"

"The robbery you keep asking me about happened because of some bullshit she did."

"Well, I'll be damned."

Immersing himself in the conversation, Rico asked, "What about the pretty li'l one with the short hair?"

Zay looked at Jason and smiled, then replied, "That's Cee; she's the one whose husband got killed here. You better refer all questions about her to Jason though. He says they're just friends, but . . ."

"What's good with her, Jason?"

Side eyeing Rico, Jason replied, "Cee is completely off-limits."

Drake's "Started from the Bottom" blasted through the Luxe's high-tech sound system as the DJ yelled into the mic, "If you started at the bottom, let me see ya fucking hands in the air!" The 3,000-plus crowd of people dressed all in white was enthralled by a good time of drinks, dancing, and shining when the DJ made his next announcement. "Ah, shit. I just got the word the men of the hour are in the buildiiiiiiiiiinnnnnnggggggg! Welcome home, Tony and Rico. Ladies, show my dudes some love and twerk something for them." He dropped Busta Rhyme's "Twerk" song remix, and the crowd went crazy.

Rico and Tony were greeted with hugs and kisses from females they'd known before going away, females they didn't know, and skimpily dressed females who were young enough to be their daughters. Dudes gave them pounds and embraced them as they made their way through the club and up to their VIP section on the second level. The club was filled with people who actually knew the brothers, knew of them, and people who knew that it was going to be a banging party.

Both brothers were beyond amazed at how nice their sister-in-law's club was. When they'd gone away clubs were not tricked out in such a luxurious manner, especially not in Charlotte. Not only had the city come a long way, but so had the nightlife. Rico was completely blown away by what the chicks were wearing or lack thereof. Pointing at different women dressed in sheer or teeny, tiny ensembles with no bra or panties beneath them, Rico told his brothers, "I thought them bitches at the airport had little ho outfits on; these bitches in here is damn naked."

"Wait 'til we take you to the strip club after this." Jason cheesed. "That shit is totally different now. Them hoes don't be having on nothing but a string between they ass, if that."

Proud of the job that Joey had done thus far, Zay looked around with a big grin on his face. He couldn't wait for Tony and Rico to see the rap acts that were about to take the stage. Joey had brought in the brothers' two favorite rappers from the era before they went to prison. Following their performances the two hottest rappers presently at the top of the billboard charts were set to perform a medley of hits. As with every big event at the Luxe, Joey moved around the venue making sure that everything was as close to perfect as possible, especially for the celebrity performers. Because of Joey's hospitality, special attention to detail, and prompt payments, celebs loved to work her events even before she opened her own club.

A small room behind the second-level VIP area served as a food station for Tony and Rico's VIP guests and the performers. The L Room staff set the room up like a classic 1950 burger joint, complete with authentic decor. Those who were allowed to access the exclusive food room had the choice of gourmet chicken, beef, or turkey burger, jumbo-sized onion rings, and steakhouse fries. Although the staff had the pop-up burger shop running smoothly, Evan played the room close. She didn't want to interact too much with Zay and she surely wasn't in a partying mood. In addition to the stress that John Doe was causing her, Evan's stomach had been cramping badly for the last few days, and if she stood on her feet too long she became woozy. The night wasn't all bad for Evan though; she had Reza. He stayed by her side for the better part of the night, and the only time he strayed was when he went to chill in the VIP with Zay.

The club was a movie and Tony and Rico felt like the stars of a real live motion picture. They went ballistic with excitement when the rappers performed. Tony and Rico were even more geeked when all four of the rappers wanted to party in their VIP sections. The entertainers were familiar with the elder Tappens boys from articles that had been written about them in *Street Dons* magazine. When the brothers got busted eighteen years earlier, Tony and Rico were the youngest among twenty-eight people indicted in a multistate cocaine trafficking ring. The streets praised them for being the only two on the case who didn't rat.

With the performances over and all of the VIP guests and celebs enjoying themselves, Joey decided that it was time for her to kick back a little. On her way up to the second level she literally bumped into Kisa. Happy to see her, Joey smiled and gave Kisa a once-over. Kisa was stunting hard in really short white Balenciaga short shorts, a white long-sleeve backless blouse, gold Tom Ford six-inch knee-high Grecian gladiator heels, and a big brown and gold python clutch by Gucci.

"Yo, bitch, I can't stand your fly ass," Joey said. "You smashing every chick in here right now."

"I try, I try," Kisa jokingly replied. "You look like a bag money though in that Philipp Plein."

"Thanks. Did you just get here?"

"No, I've been here for a little while."

"Why you didn't find me when you got here?" Joey questioned.

"I knew you were busy, and we were straight anyway."

"We?"

Kisa stepped to the side revealing a gorgeous young woman with milk chocolate complexion, and a bounty of soft light brown curls reminiscent of seventies' disco hair crowning her heart-shaped face. She was casket sharp in a sexy white fitted Moschino suit with skinny pants and Jimmy Choo crystal-jeweled platform pump sandals. "This is Mish," Kisa introduced.

"This is Mish?" Joey asked, surprised with raised brows. *Damn, I didn't know killers came this beautiful. She doesn't look anything like she sounds.*

"Yes, I'm Mish." She extended her hand.

"Nice to meet you in person." Joey shook her hand. "I didn't expect to see you until tomorrow. I'm glad you're here now though. With the way this shit been going down you being here early don't hurt nothing."

"Nice to meet you too."

"Y'all come on up to the section. We'll pop a couple of bottles, and discuss a few things."

"Okay." Kisa followed Joey. "Mish is going to stay, but I have to leave in forty-five minutes."

"Why?"

"I have to pick Sin up from the Air Center; he's coming in from Amsterdam."

Heads turned when the three ladies entered the VIP area; all eyes were mainly on Kisa and Mish. Although their section was filled with pretty, scantily dressed women, Tony and Rico almost tripped over one another trying to get over to Jason to find out about the two jaw-dropping beauties. Sitting next to Jason on the couch, Cee laughed as the brothers stumbled toward them. Holding up her hands she halted them.

"We already know what you want," Cee announced. "That one," she said and pointed at Kisa, "she's very married and the other one, we don't know who she is. Y'all are going to have to ask Joey."

Both drunken brothers made a beeline for their sister-in-law. Inebriated and drained, Zay flopped down on the couch next to Cee and Jason.

"What are those two drunk niggas up to?" He nodded toward his older brothers.

"Trying to find out who shorty with Joey and Kisa is," Jason replied.

Studying the unfamiliar woman, Zay said admiringly, "I don't know her, but she is bad."

"Yo," Cee squealed, elbowing Zay in the ribs. "Your wife's best friend is sitting here."

"Ain't nothing wrong with looking, and I see you sitting here with Jason. Hope I didn't interrupt anything."

"No, you are not interrupting a thing! Jason and I are just friends. I don't know why y'all don't believe us."

"Y'all might just be friends right now. We can all see you both want more than friendship though."

Joey walked over and took a seat on Zay's lap. "Are you guys happy with the way the party turned out?" she asked Zay and Jason.

Nodding his head, Jason raised a pink bottle of Ace toward her. "You did a great job sis-in-law!"

"You sure did, baby," Zay told her. "Thanks for making this happen for my brothers. They're having the time of their lives."

"That's all that matters."

"Is that one of Kane's cousins?"

"No, that's the person that I called about Evan's problem."

"What is she going to do?" Zay asked skeptical of the brown beauty.

"Kane said she's one of the best hitters she knows. I'm going to chop it up with her in my office in a little bit so that she can track this clown-ass nigga down."

"I hope that she is that good. I'll pay her whatever. She don't even have to kill that nigga; just find him and bring him to me." Zay slipped his hand beneath her tiny dress and massaged her inner thigh. "What's up with you though?" He kissed the side of her neck.

"I'm good." She blushed biting down on her lower lip.

"I want to go home and do some things to you."

"What kind of things?"

"Things like this." He pushed her thong to the side and tickled her clit with the tip of his finger.

Creamy liquid rolled down Joey's walls as pleasure sparked through her body. Panting in his ear she said, "I thought y'all were going to the strip club."

"I was going with them until I saw you in this dress. Ever since the dinner I've been thinking about how good you look in this. I'm ready to get you out of it."

"Hmm, and I'm ready for you to take it off of me."

A VIP bouncer tapped Joey on the shoulder.

"Yes," she said over her shoulder.

"Joey, security down at the entrance needs you. There is somebody named Iwan asking for you."

"Tell them to let him in. I'll be right down. Baby," she said to Zay, "I need to run down to the door. I'll be right back."

"Nah yo, let somebody else handle whatever it is." With the tip of his finger he circled her opening.

Joey's body shuttered, she eased his hand from beneath her dress. "Baby, I have to go, but I promise I'll come right back." She rushed down to the lobby and found Iwan nervously pacing. "Hello, Iwan." Joey greeted him with a handshake. "What brings you here this late?"

"I'm sorry to interrupt your event. I tried calling your cell and I thought that you needed to see this right away."

"See what?"

"It took me all day, but I got to the bottom of your security camera issue. You were not hacked. Someone edited out hours of surveillance and fixed the time stamps so that the interruptions wouldn't be noticed."

"Is there a way to find out who did it?"

"That's what I wanted to show you." He held up an iPad. "She thought that she'd deleted the surveillance, but I was able to pull it off the hard drive. I compiled the missing clips into one video." He tapped the play symbol and handed the iPad to Joey.

Staring at the screen Joey's jaw dropped and her heart skipped a beat or two, when she saw Isadora sneaking into her office and other offices that she wasn't supposed to be in. The video ended with Isadora entering the security room where the surveillance equipment was housed.

"Is this all?"

"Yes."

Joey held up the iPad. "Can I hold on to this until tomorrow?"

"Sure."

"Thank you, Iwan, you probably just saved my life."

Angry that his demand for money had been refused, John Doe planned to snatch Joey, Cee, or Evan from the Luxe Enclave. His plan had been thwarted by all the extra security on the property. Since his kidnapping plans had gone awry, John Doe decided to make noise in a different way. In the dead of the night John Doe stood in the middle of the street outside of Dorenda's Dilworth home. All of the lights were off, everything in and around the house was quiet. John Doe dialed Dorenda's home phone and let it ring.

A few moments later, the darkened house lit up. John Doe ended the call then pressed the smart phone's camera icon and began recording. He aimed the Desert Eagle that he held in his right hand at the house, he pulled the lever, and sprayed the home with all nine bullets. Seconds after the shots stopped a bloody, gurgling scream came from the home. His job there was done.

Tucking away the burning hot pistol and walking briskly, he cut through the backyards of several homes until he reached East Boulevard where his car was parked. Hopping in the car, he quickly ducked down to avoid being spotted by one of the police officers in the caravan of eight cars that was flying up East Boulevard with their sirens blaring. Once the police vehicles were in the distance, John Doe sat up, started the engine, and calmly drove away.

"I know who took the pictures from security cameras," Joey told Zay out of breath. She'd damn near sprinted from the lobby through the packed club up to the second floor.

"Who is it?" Zay asked instantly sobering up a little.

"You'll see soon; just get Cee and Jason up to my office and wait for me."

Joey went over to the pop-up burger joint and told Evan, "Go to my office. I have something to show you, and bring him too." She pointed at Reza. Suspicious of Evan's guy she wanted to see his reaction when she revealed Isadora as the mole. Next, Joey went to Isadora, who just happened to be in the company of Tony and Rico. Poker face on, Joey smiled ever so politely.

"Hey, I don't mean to interrupt, but um, Isadora, I'm about to entertain some of the special guests in my office and I need you to bring up a bottle Ace, a bottle of Hennessy Privilege, and a bottle of Ace rosé."

"Damn, sis-in-law," Rico said. "We not invited to the private party?"

"Of course you are," Joey covered quickly.

"I'll go grab those bottles for you," Isadora interjected before turning to leave.

Rico grabbed Isadora's hand. "When you bring those bottles to her office, I want you to stay and finish our conversation."

"Sure." She smiled sexily then switched off.

Disgusted Joey rolled her eyes and with her brothers-in-law in tow she headed to her office, grabbing Mish along the way. Those who'd already gathered in the office were talking among themselves when Joey entered; wasting no time she got right to the point. "Iwan, the tech guy came by. He figured out how this person got the pictures from the security feed. It was an inside job."

"By who?" Evan wanted to know.

Joey held up the iPad and just as her finger hovered over the play icon, her office door opened. Carrying a tray with two bottles of champagne, Hennessy Privilege, and a bucket of ice, Isadora sashayed in.

"Wow," Joey said in surprise. "You got here fast."

"I pulled these from the stock on this floor; I figured it would be quicker than getting it from the club level and having to move through the crowd." Isadora set the tray atop Joey's desk.

Joey went and stood next to Isadora. Placing her hand on the middle of Isadora's back Joey patted her and said, "Thank you so much, Isadora. You always go over and beyond your duties."

"You know I don't mind, Joey."

"Well, I do." Joey snatched up the bottle of Privilege and with brute force bashed Isadora over the head. The bottle shattered, soaking Isadora's hair and face with cognac. Moaning in pain and eyes burning, Isadora crumpled to the floor.

"Ayo. What the fuck?" Rico gasped totally taken aback. He looked over at Tony, who was staring at Joey in disbelief.

Joey knelt down, grabbed a handful of Isadora's hair, and yanked her head from the floor. "Who sent you, bitch?"

Dazed, but aware, Isadora cackled wickedly. "Fuck you."

Joey slammed Isadora's face against the floor then lifted it up. "One more time, who the fuck sent you, bitch?"

Blood gliding from her nose over her mouth, Isadora smirked. "Ya dead grandmother."

Joey angrily slammed her head against the floor several times until she lost consciousness. Standing up, Joey examined the blood that had splattered on her. "Fucking idiot bitch! My damn dress and shoes are ruined."

Mish came and stood next to Joey. Looking down at Isadora, in a Spanish-coated Southern accent she said, "I believe getting answers is more my forte than yours; would you like for me to go to work on her?"

"Sure would."

"Are there any tools in this building?"

"Yeah, go out of here and make a left and at the end of the hall the maintenance closet is the last door on the right. The maintenance staff tool boxes are inside."

Mish left the office. Evan and Cee began bombarding Joey with questions. "Who is that woman?" Evan asked.

"Someone who is going to help us get down to the bottom of this bullshit that you've dragged us into."

"Joey," Cee said. "How do you know Isadora has something to do with it?"

"Get that iPad off my desk."

Cee got the tablet and held it up for all to view it. While everyone watched quietly Joey explained what Iwan had told her. She kept a keen eye on Reza; judging by his expression he seemed to be just as surprised as everyone else.

Mish returned with a red metal toolbox. She picked Isadora up and sat her upright in a chair. Using cable wires that she'd found in the maintenance closet, she tied Isadora's wrists to the arms of the chair, and she bound her ankles to the chair's legs.

The room was completely silent as everyone watched to see what was about to happen. Zay told his older brothers, "Maybe y'all should go to back to the party."

"I'm good," Rico replied taking a seat on the mint green leather couch. "I want to see what this chick about to do." He pointed at Mish. "And I want to see how long she's going to hold up," he said nodding toward Isadora. "What is this all about anyway?"

"It's a long story," Jason replied, joining Rico on the couch.

Soon all five men were seated. Evan and Cee stood off to the side and Joey stood a few inches behind Mish. Mish uncorked a champagne bottle, and placing her thumb over the opening she shook it vigorously, and then sprayed the bubbly in Isadora's face. "Wake up, wake up!" Mish said.

Isadora bolted awake, and stunned from the liquid that shot into her face she gasped for air.

Holding her hands behind her back Mish spoke calmly to Isadora. "My friend here," Mish said and cocked her head toward Joey, who was standing over her shoulder, "she has some questions for you."

"Fuck you and your friend!"

"Wrong answer." Mish shoved a towel into Isadora's mouth, brought a hammer from behind her back and whacked the right side of Isadora's collarbone so hard that it cracked audibly.

Everyone in the room cringed. Grimacing in pain, Isadora bit down on the towel as tears dripped from the outer corners of her eyes.

Mish snatched the towel from Isadora's mouth. "Let's try this one more time. Joey wants to know who sent you."

Deeply in pain Isadora winced, and, breathing heavy, she looked at Mish through squinted eyes. "Fuck you, fuck her, and the rest of these muhfuckas."

Again, Mish plugged her mouth with the towel and this time she struck Isadora's left collarbone.

Soaked in a mix of liquor and blood, Isadora nearly blacked out from the pain, but she still had no intention of giving up a name.

Zay's and Jason's phones buzzed with text notifications; they both opened a message that was identical: Don't want to pay me? Okay!

A video message popped up on the phone, and recognizing the still image of their mother's home they pressed play. Zay's heart dropped at the sight of a gun aimed at the house. When the gun on the screen began firing shots Zay's phone fell from his palm, and in less than a second he'd gotten off the couch, zoomed by Mish, grabbed Isadora by the throat, and squeezed it, cutting off her air.

"I'm not going to play this game with you!" he exclaimed through closed teeth. "Who shot up my mother's house? Tell me or I will kill your ho ass." He applied more pressure. Veins popped from the side of Isadora's head and her eyes bulged from the sockets as she gasped for the air that she was totally separated from.

Joey moved in and tried to remove Zay's hands from Isadora's neck. "Baby, listen to me. I know you're pissed, but if you kill her we will never know who's behind this."

It took some seconds for Joey's words to register with Zay, but once they did he slowly slid his hands from Isadora's neck.

Jason stared at the video for a second time in utter shock with his mouth wide open. He felt a slither of relief that his daughters were not at home, but he couldn't be overjoyed since he knew that his mother was. The video disappeared as his phone rang and Mom appeared on the screen. He hurriedly answered.

"Hello, Ma, hello?"

Hysterical Dorenda cried, "Jason, I've been trying to reach y'all. My house has been shot up. Frannie got shot."

"Is she alive?"

"They just took her back for surgery."

"What hospital are y'all at?"

"Carolina's Medical Center, but Jason why would someone do this to my home? Why?" she pleaded.

"I don't know, Mama. Just hang on. One of us will be over there."

Angrily glaring down at Isadora as she coughed uncontrollably in dire pain, Zay asked Jason. "What did Moms say?"

"Her house was shot up and Aunt Frannie got hit; she's in surgery."

An already real situation got extra real for everyone in the room, especially for Tony and Rico. The clouds of liquor that the brothers' minds were engulfed in suddenly started fading away. Rico stood up.

"Mom's house got shot up? The fuck is going on around here?"

"No more stalling, Zay," Tony said and walked over to his brother. "What the hell is this all about?" he demanded.

Zay cut his eyes over at Evan. Ashamed, she looked away. "Let her tell you," he said and pointed at Evan. "I don't feel like telling nobody that dumb shit right now. This is her bullshit anyway; we've all just been pulled into it."

Tony and Rico turned their attention to Evan.

Joey picked up Zay's cell and began the video. As it came on she had a thought. "Hold up, I know how to find out who sent her; but before you start talking to them," she spoke directly to Evan, "tell Rahmel to take a couple of guards and go over to the CMC for my mother-in-law." Joey flew out of the office, and in her heels she sprinted to the office that Isadora and Bev shared. She looked behind Isadora's desk and spotted the brand new $14,000 pink Ralph Lauren Ricky bag that she'd complimented Isadora on earlier in the evening. At the time it had run across Joey's mind she'd never seen Isadora carrying a bag that cost more than $3,500. Joey had wondered if Isadora had purchased it or if it was a gift. Now, she knew that it was more than likely bought with the proceeds from the robbery.

Joey opened the purse and took out what she was looking for: Isadora's iPhone. She knew that like everyone else in the modern world, a person's entire life could be found on their smart phone. Joey pressed the phone's home button only to find that the phone was locked and could only be unlocked with Isadora's fingerprint. With Isadora's personal items in hand, Joey rushed back to her office.

"I got her phone," she announced, entering through the door. Joey handed Cee the purse. "Go through her bag to see if it's anything in there that can tell us something."

Feeling the onset of defeat, Isadora frowned and dropped her head.

Joey held the phone next to Isadora's right hand that was still bound to the chair arm. "Press the button," she told Isadora.

Isadora closed her hands into a fist and squeezed them tightly.

"Yo, open ya fucking hand, 'cause I'm not about to struggle with you."

Refusing, Isadora squeezed her hand tighter; therefore, Mish stepped back in and slammed the hammer against the top of Isadora's hand twice. Howling in pain Isadora involuntarily uncurled her hand. Joey grabbed her index finger, and pressed the phone's home button instantly opening the phone. Telling the story of her shady past Evan stood in a semicircle surrounded by Tony, Rico, Jason, Rez, and Zay. Joey went over. "I know she's explaining this situation, but she need to go through this phone with me right now." Holding the phone up where they both could view it, Joey scrolled through the short list of contacts. "Ev, do you recognize any of these names?"

"Nope."

Joey closed the contact list and opened up the phone's photo album, and she scrolled through an array of tiny pictures of Isadora's recent vacation to Beverly Hills and Las Vegas. Most of the pictures were of Isadora posing next to sights and landmarks. *This sure doesn't look like a funeral to me,* Joey thought continuing to scroll down until she happened upon a picture of Isadora with a man standing behind her, holding her at the waist. Joey tapped the picture box enlarging the image on the screen. Her mouth fell ajar and her heart stopped. She recognized him and so did Evan.

All of the color slowly drained from Evan's face as she stared at the screen wide-eyed. Taking a half step back, Joey cocked her head to the side and sourly glared at Evan. "What kind of shit is this, Ev?"

"I dunno. I don't understand," Evan replied never taking her eyes off the screen. She couldn't pull her eyes away from the man's face. He was a little thinner than she remembered and he'd obtained a thick scar that ran diagonally from the left tip of his hairline, across the outer edge of his right brow, stopping at his temple. Yes, there were a few differences, but there was no doubt in Evan's mind as to who he was.

"What are y'all looking at?" Cee asked moving toward the pair. She took the phone from Joey and squealed. "That is fucking Gage!" She looked at Evan then to Joey and back at Evan. "You said that he got killed! What kind of games are you playing?"

"Let me see that." Zay extended his hand to Cee. She placed the phone in his palm. Jason and Reza flanked at his sides to get a view.

"That is that nigga," Reza spouted upon laying eyes on a face that he would never forget.

With her mind racing at warp speed Evan stood frozen as every eye in the room zoomed in on her. *How can he be alive?* she thought. *I shot him in the head for God's sake. I watched him die.*

"Evan!" Cee yelled. "Snap the fuck out of it and tell us what is going on."

Though badly battered and covered in blood Isadora displayed a smug smirk. "Give her a minute," she spoke up. "She's confused; she thought that she killed both of them."

"Killed the both of who?" Joey questioned bewildered. "Evan, what is she talking about?"

"Don't act like you don't know," Isadora spat.

"Yo, you shut the fuck up, okay?" Joey retorted. "I'm talking to Evan."

"And I'm talking to you and I've been waiting a long time to confront you three bitches."

"About what?"

"The night Evan murdered my brother, Marshawn, and tried to kill his friend Gage so that you whores could take his stash."

Zay glared at his wife. "So you were a part of this grimy shit?"

"Hell no, I wasn't; she is lying!"

"I'm not lying. My brother was killed and more than six million dollars was stolen from his home. And I saw you three bitches there. It was twelve years ago, but I remember it like yesterday," Isadora closed her eyes and envisioned one of the most horrible nights of her life while continuing to talk.

May, 2001

Isadora pushed her brand new candy apple red Mitsubishi Eclipse through the quiet streets of Sugar Loaf with the music blasting. It was graduation weekend for most of the colleges in and around Atlanta. The clubs were going to be jumping extra hard, and Isadora was ready to hit the scene and show off her new wheels. First, she had to stop by her big brother's home for some cash. She was the apple of Marshawn's eye. There was nothing that he wouldn't give his baby sister. The 2001 Eclipse had been a gift from him just for completing her first year as a computer science major at Emory University.

Turning on the dead-end street that led to Marshawn's palatial home, Isadora saw three cars exiting the cul-de-sac. She knew that they had to be leaving her brother's home because it was the only house in the circle. Isadora looked at the female driver of each car as they passed by. Three pretty faces in luxury cars. "Strippers," she hissed. Isadora could only imagine what they had been doing at her brother's house; *Probably a foursome,* she told herself. Entering her brother's home, Isadora called out to her brother.

"Marshawn!"

He didn't answer.

"Marshawn," she hollered out again.

Still no answer.

Isadora followed a ticking sound to the theater room in the rear of the home. "Oh God, noooooooooo!" she shrilled at the sight of her brother's bullet-riddled body. She backed out of the room, scared that someone could still be in the house. Isadora ran to her car, locked herself inside, and called 911. When the paramedics and police arrived Marshawn was pronounced dead, but they found Gage on the second floor. He'd been shot twice in the side of the neck and once in the head. One bullet was lodged in his neck; the second bullet went straight through his neck. The bullet that he'd taken to the head circled around his brain and exited through the front of his skull. Barely alive from the loss of blood and the trauma from the bullet slamming against his head he was rushed to the hospital. Gage survived surgery but slipped into a coma afterward.

Although Isadora didn't know Gage, she assumed that he was a friend of Marshawn since he'd been shot as well. She stayed by his hospital bed for three days and when he awoke from his coma Isadora's face was the first thing that he saw. The doctors sent her out the room immediately so that they could check him out. Standing in the hallway, Isadora overheard a nurse on the phone notifying the homicide detectives that Gage was awake. When the doctors left the room she rushed back in; she had questions that she needed to ask before the police showed up at any minute.

Isadora leaned close to the bed. "I'm Isadora, Marshawn's sister. Were you two friends?"

"Yes," Gage responded in gruff whisper, his throat extremely dry from his long slumber.

"Who did this to you?"

"Evan."

"Is that a man?"

Gage shook his head side to side.

"A woman?"

He nodded his head up and down.

Isadora remembered the three women who drove past her on the way to the house that night. With everything that had happened she'd forgotten about seeing them. "Was she with two other women?"

Gage thought about it and the last thing he remembered before completely losing consciousness was hearing Evan on the phone with Joey directing her to the house. He'd been double crossed by Evan and her friends. The detectives swept into the room before Isadora could ask him anything else and put her out. When Isadora returned to the hospital next day, Gage had concocted a brilliant story about what happened that day. He told Isadora that Evan was there as Marshawn's date and that they were waiting for Evan's friends to arrive. Gage said that he left to go to the store for blunts and when he returned Marshawn was dead. He said when he went to search the house for the shooter, Evan shot him. Isadora ate his story hook, line, and sinker.

Isadora visited him every day until he was released from the hospital and during those visits they established a foundation to a friendship that led to a full-blown love affair.

Returning to the present from her trip down memory lane, Isadora opened her eyes and stared her directly at Joey.

"Don't ever tell me that you were not there."

The daggers that Zay was shooting at Joey were piercing every inch of her body. Cee noticed the anger that Zay was aiming at Joey and since Evan seemed to be choking on air, she spoke up.

"Zay, you know I've never been down with that street shit, and would not have been there. We did go to that house that night, because Evan called us and said she was in trouble. When we got there she said it was a drug deal gone wrong and Gage was dead."

"It was a robbery and cold-blooded murder!" Isadora shouted.

"That it was," Evan said coming out of her trance. "But, your facts are all wrong."

"So you say, bitch. I know you killed my brother."

"I put your brother out of his misery, because the nigga you're so in love with put a few bullets in him first. He was dying anyway. I just made it come faster."

Isadora sat stunned and it was written all over her face.

"Awww, you look so shocked." Evan smirked. "Gage didn't keep it real with you? Allow me to tell you the real. Gage was my man and we robbed drug dealers the same way we robbed your brother. I was tired of robbing, but as long as I was with Gage he wouldn't let me stop. Therefore, when I saw the perfect opportunity to drop him, I took it."

"So what, he lied? Getting back at you is something we both have in common and that we live for."

"You're a fool."

"I'm a fool who let you live. I've had so many chances to murder you. That morning in front of the building, I could've murked you instead of just making you pass out. I should've burned your precious L Room down while you were still inside. If I wouldn't have waited for you to come out, no one would have interrupted me. You and that building would be ashes right now."

It only took a millisecond for what Isadora said to register with Cee. Cee went to the cabinet where Joey kept her gun and retrieved it. Everyone was so caught up in both Evan and Isadora's audacious admissions, they didn't notice what Cee was doing. Cee went over to Isadora and placed the muzzle of the gun against Isadora's temple.

"Say it again."

"Say what again?"

Trembling, she said, "The part about burning the L Room down."

"What about it?" Isadora asked annoyed.

"You said you tried to burn it down."

"Yeah, I tried."

"Then it was you who killed the security guard and my husband?"

"Yeah, it wasn't personal though. It was either me or them."

"It wasn't personal?" Cee hit her across the side of the head with the pistol. "Well, this is." She put the gun back to Isadora's head.

Joey wrapped her hands around Cee's gun hand. "Don't do it, sis," Joey begged. "I know you want to, but you can't. This isn't for you; it won't feel the way you think it will."

"I think it will feel pretty damn good to put a bullet in the head of my husband's killer." Cee tightened her grip around the gun and as bad as she wanted to she couldn't bring herself to mash the trigger.

Joey eased Cee's hand down until the gun was away from Isadora's head. She gently took the gun from Cee. Upset that she was unable to carry out killing the person who'd taken the life of her husband, Cee ran out in tears and Jason chased after her.

Isadora laughed. "Y'all some ol' pussy-ass bitches. I just told the bitch I killed her husband and she couldn't pull the trigger on me."

Joey backhanded Isadora. "Shut your mouth, before I give her the damn gun back!"

Isadora's phone rang out; Evan picked it up from the desk. It was a text from a person listed as G. Assuming that is was Gage, Evan opened it and read it: "'Baby girl, you on the way home yet? I got some shit to show you! Bet these muhfuckas pay up now.' I think Gage just sent her this." Evan showed the text to Joey.

"Oh, so he feeling himself now? Let's see how he feel about this." Joey snapped a picture of Isadora in her horrid state and sent it back to Gage with the message: Hey, Gage, is this your bitch?

Awestruck, John Doe, better known as Gage, stared at the phone in disbelief. "They got my baby," he muttered and with the back of his hand wiped away the tears that were streaking down each side of his face. Not only was he hurt by seeing Isadora badly beaten; he was beyond blood-boiling angry. It was sadistic and twisted that Gage was carrying out a relationship with the sister of the man he too murdered just as much as Evan had. Though he'd come to know her under a well-calculated lie, she was his everything and he loved her more than any other woman, including Evan.

Gage was going to rescue her and he planned to kill anyone who got in his way. He knew that there was a 99 percent chance that Evan had told Isadora the truth about him. He didn't care if Isadora no longer wanted to be with him or never spoke to him again in life, but he was going save her. Gage mapped out a plan in his mind as he veered his car down Interstate 485. *They wanna play this game?* He told himself, *I'm the master at this.* Being ever studious, Gage knew just where to go to grab one of their loved ones.

Pulling into the parking lot of the Piper Glen townhomes he shut the car lights and parked in front of a three-story end unit. Quietly he crept up to the door and, bam, he kicked the door so hard it fell off the hinges.

"What the hell!" A tall, slender twenty-something guy yelled jumping up from the couch where he'd been sleeping with his girlfriend.

Gage struck the young man with the butt end of his shotgun knocking him out cold. The girlfriend screamed loudly.

"Shut up." Gage put the barrel of the sawed-off shotgun in her face. "Get up."

She did as she was told.

"Let's go." Using the gun, he pointed toward the door. Keeping the gun on the girl, he guided her to the trunk of the car. Gage popped the trunk, shoved her in, and closed it. There was no way that he could go to the apartment that he shared with Isadora. He was sure that someone was probably there waiting for him. Gage found a dope haven motel on the east side. A broken-down cruddy place like this was perfect: somewhere he didn't need identification to check in, and all the guests were too locked into their own criminal behavior to notice him.

After securing the girl in the skin-crawling motel room that had bed bugs for sure, Gage placed a Facetime call to Isadora's phone.

Zay, Joey, Evan, Reza, Cee, Tony, Rico, Mish, and Jason were huddled in the sitting area of Joey's office plotting their next move when the Facetime alert chimed on Isadora's phone. Seeing that it was G sending the alert, Evan picked up the cell and pressed answer. Collectively, everyone held their breath as they waited for the call to connect.

Gage popped up on the screen, and he smiled wide when he saw Evan. "Hello, beautiful, I'm guessing you never expected to see me again."

"If I never did it wouldn't be a day too soon."

"Whoa, shawty, that's no way to talk to the man you tried to kill, and you should be a little humble."

"Humility for bastards was never my strong suit."

"Ha ha ha, you're still the same sad-ass sidity bitch."

"Gage, what do you want? It's time for this dumbass game to stop. Joey and Cee had nothing to with what went down. What is it going to take for you to go away? Money? What? Just name it."

Gage was done playing too; it was time to get what he'd come for. "I want Isadora, the six million that you stole from up under me at that last lick, and I want you."

Zay snatched the phone. "Look, patna, that money that's between you two, but if you want your bitch come see me, nigga. It's a whole lotta shit you gotta answer for!"

"What up, Zay? It's been a long time, my man."

"Fuck you, ol' fuck-ass nigga."

"Damn it's like that? After all the bricks you bought off me back in the day. I actually felt bad about hitting ya spots and shooting up ya mom's house. It wasn't personal." Shaking his head, Gage sighed. "But I had a feeling that you were not going to agree to my terms. That's why I took out a little insurance policy out." He turned the camera on Taleah, one third of Cee's triplets.

"Uncle Zaaaay," Taleah, bound to a chair, cried out. "Please help me."

Hearing her child's voice, Cee jumped up. "What the fuck? He has my baby," she said and snatched the phone and peered at her helpless daughter. "Don't be scared, Taleah; we're going to get you, baby," Cee said unsure of how they would even begin to go about saving her.

Gage popped back up on the screen.

"You dirty muhfucka, let my baby go!" Cee demanded.

"I plan to do just that, once I get what I asked for. Now let me talk to Isadora."

Hastily, Cee handed Joey the phone, only obliging him in hopes that he wouldn't harm Taleah. "You take the phone to her, because if I do I'ma kill that grimy bitch while he watching."

Joey held the phone up so that Isadora and Gage could see one another.

"Damn, Dory," Gage winced upon seeing her face. Isadora's eyes were two thin slits, and she was lumped up like an amateur who'd gone toe to toe with a heavyweight champion.

"Gage," she mumbled through swollen lips. "They got me."

"Shhh, baby, it's okay. I'm coming to get you. Hold tight."

"Gage?"

"Yes?"

"They told me that you were not Marshawn's friend, that you were at his house with Evan to rob him. Is that true?"

Shamefully, Gage dropped his head. "It is true, but—"

"No," Isadora cut him off, "no buts. It doesn't matter; I know that our love isn't a lie."

"I swear it's not a lie."

Joey turned the phone around. "Enough of that bullshit; what do we have to do to get Taleah back?"

"I told you what I want and you already got my banking information. Discuss it with your folks and when y'all ready to make it happen hit me back."

Joey turned to the group. "So, what do we do?"

"Pay the money," Cee replied. "So I can get my daughter back."

"Yeah, but he wants Evan, too."

"Give her to him," Cee screamed pointing at Evan. "This is her infested horse shit and my family will not keep paying the cost! I've lost my husband and I'll be damned if I lose one of my children."

Joey glanced at Zay. By his expression she knew that he shared Cee's feelings.

"There has to be another option. Cee, I feel you. I love Taleah as if she is mine, but Evan is one of us. She has done some terrible things, but we can't hand deliver her to her death."

"Hey, I am sitting right here." Evan raised her hand and then she looked at Cee. "I can admit that I'm one selfish bitch, but I was there when you gave birth to that girl and her sisters. And, I have loved all three since that day. So nobody has to make the decision for me to go. I'd already decided that I was going when we heard her voice." Standing, Evan paced the floor while talking. "I have four million in liquid cash that I can transfer to Gage's account; the rest of my money is tied up in CDs and bonds. If y'all could put the other two million up, I'll go to him. I can handle Gage."

"Look, Ev," Cee said and faced her friend. "I didn't mean to come off so harsh as if your life means nothing to me. Joey's right: we should try to see if there is something else we can do other than turning you over."

"Gage was always greedy," Joey offered. "Why don't we play into his greed and offer him an additional million and tell him to settle up with Ev on his own time."

Mish stepped forward. "If you don't mind, I have an idea."

"Of course we don't mind," Joey replied.

"Not in front of her though." Mish nodded toward Isadora. "Is there somewhere we can move her to?"

Joey checked her watch; it was a little past four a.m. "It's too risky to move her right this minute. Bev might still be counting up and the cleaning crew doesn't finish until five. How about we just move to the conference room?"

Everyone filed out of the office, with the exception of Tony and Rico; they stayed behind to keep an eye on Isadora. In the conference room everybody took a seat at the oblong table. From the head of the table Joey asked, "Mish, what do you have in mind?"

"If dude will agree to your offer and you have the banking information I can get the money back, once I take care of him. I think that this is the best plan, because if you," she said and looked at Evan, "go with him, I may not be able to get to him before he kills you. I will get him."

"You sound very confident," Zay said to Mish, curious as to whether she was really as good as Kisa claimed her to be. He'd really wanted to call Asaad's people in on this situation, but Zay didn't want to indebt himself any further to his connect than he already had.

"I am confident; this is what I do and I have one of the best hackers in the world on my team. She'll have the money back into your accounts like it never left, minus a ten percent recovery fee. I can also take my hit fee out of that money."

"That's not a problem as long as you deliver; the paper isn't an issue," Joey remarked. "In the Luxe payroll account we have right at two mill that we can transfer, so that puts us at six. We need to be able to offer an additional million."

"I got that covered," Cee said. "Petey's life insurance checks have all cleared."

Joey initiated a Facetime call to Gage. "Let's see if he'll bite."

Grinning evilly Gage came on the screen. "Y'all ready to make this happen?"

"Not quite yet. I have a counter offer."

"I'm not into negotiating on this here, but I'll listen."

"Look we can't just give you Evan; if you catch her on your own great. So instead of handing you Evan, we're offering you another million on top of what you're asking."

"Joey, Joey," Gage chuckled. "You were always the business-minded one out of three musketeers. The only way I'll walk away without Evan is you good people give me ten million."

"Ten! We barely scraped the seven together!"

"That's not my problem. You have two options if you want your friend's daughter back. Pay the six million and hand over Evan or pay the ten mill."

"We'll do the ten million," Cee shouted out.

Joey looked at her and mouthed, "How?"

"I can cover it. It's available in my account."

"We'll pay the ten," Joey told Gage.

"I know Evan is in the room. Hey, Ev, if you can hear me your friends must love your shady ass."

"More than you ever did," Evan retorted.

"One day, we'll have a chance to rehash history before I put three bullets into your skull. For now, send my money to my account. Then meet me on the tarmac at the Wilson Air Center by the jet waiting for takeoff, at five thirty-five sharp. Bring Isadora and I'll bring this sweet little thing. Don't try no silly shit," Gage warned with the wave of a finger. "If you do, Cee will have twins instead of triplets."

Chapter Thirteen

The entire crew went in three different vehicles to Wilson Air Center. The five men traveled in Cee's Escalade. Carrying a small arsenal of guns, Mish rode shotgun with Evan in her Jaguar. With Isadora tied up in the back seat, and Cee in the passenger, Joey drove her Range straight to the tarmac. They pulled alongside the only idling jet and waited for Gage to arrive. All agreed that it wasn't a good idea for Evan to go onto the tarmac, because Gage could possibly get aggravated and kill her on the spot. From a distance Mish and each of the men positioned themselves in different spots hoping to get a clear shot at Gage.

At exactly five thirty-five Gage arrived in silver 750Li and parked opposite Joey. He stepped out of the car in and yelled out, "Where's Isadora?"

Joey got out. "No good, playboy, we sent the money, so you let us see Taleah first and then you can have your foolish-ass bitch."

"No manners." Gage went to the rear of his car and opened the trunk. Slowly he pulled Taleah out the trunk, to her feet, and with the muzzle of his gun shoved into the side of the extra-large beige overcoat that she was draped in he escorted her to the front of the car.

Excited Cee jumped out the truck and ran toward them screaming. "Taleah!"

"Mom!" Taleah shouted gleefully.

Gage turned the gun on Cee,. "Un-uh."

Cee stopped on the dime.

"You see your daughter. I didn't harm a hair on her head, even though y'all worked my girl over damn good." He kissed Taleah on the cheek. "Now bring Isadora to me and if anyone thinks about shooting me," he shouted out for those whom he knew were nearby to hear. "If I get shot, she'll be blown to pieces." He opened Taleah's overcoat, revealing four short metal capped pipes connected to a plastic box strapped to her chest by duct tape.

Every person who had a gun pointed at Gage lowered their weapons. No one dared to take a shot that would endanger Taleah's life, or anyone close by.

"Nooooo." Cee doubled over with both hands covering her mouth and tears flooding her face.

"Ain't no need for all that whooping and hollering, li'l mama. You see this?" He held up a little black remote with three buttons. "This only has a range of four hundred yards. So, once I'm high up in the sky you won't have a thing to worry about."

Pulling Isadora by the arm, Joey led her to within five to six feet of Gage.

"Come here, sweetheart," he told Isadora.

"Not yet." Joey yanked Isadora back. "Same time, Gage; fair exchange, no robberies."

"You right," he replied then suddenly with brute force he shoved Taleah in Cee's direction.

Taleah fell to her knees at her mother's feet. Cee threw her arms around her child; holding Taleah tight Cee rocked side to side caring absolutely nothing about the bomb wedged between their chests.

Joey released Isadora's arm and nudged her forward. "Go."

Hands tied behind her back Isadora slowly limped her sore body over to Gage. Exhausted, dehydrated, and dirty she collapsed against his chest and sobbed. He embraced her.

"I know they hurt you bad. It's almost over now; we just need to make it on to this jet and we'll be home free."

Gage tucked the pistol into his waistband, not even bothering to untie Isadora, assisting her up the steps and onto the jet. Gage spun around on the top step and clearly holding the bomb remote he announced, "Good doing business with you girls, and please let Evan know that I will see her soon." Stepping backward he boarded the jet, and moments later a crew member retracted the steps and shut the door. The plane taxied to the nearby runway. After receiving clearance for takeoff, the jet sped down the strip and rose steadily into the early morning sky.

Joey watched as the jet got smaller and smaller as it ascended in higher and higher. Sitting on the asphalt, Cee cuddled Taleah in her arms as they both sobbed deeply from the gut. Evan, Mish, and all the guys converged on the tarmac. Glad to see Jason and Zay, Taleah cried out to them, "Please get this off of me."

Neither men knew shit about bombs, but here was a girl who was like a daughter to them; therefore, they had to do something. Both men felt that if one of their children was in Taleah's current predicament they would want someone to at least try. With the circumstances surrounding the situation, calling the law in had to be an absolute last resort.

"I can't diffuse a bomb," Zay said. "I'm not even going to front. We maybe can get it off of her real quick and throw it in those trees." He pointed to a wooded area that outlined one side of the tarmac.

"Yeah, that might work," said Jason. "I just hope this muhfucka really can't blow it up from the plane. Cee." Jason spoke softly to the distraught mother. "You're going to have to let her go so that we can see what we can do."

Reluctantly, Cee slowly released her child.

Bending down Zay told Taleah, "Carefully open up the coat."

Following his directions, Taleah grabbed the coat's lapels and pulled them apart. Immediately, Zay and everyone else became suspicious of the bomb's authenticity. A view of the device up close revealed that the multicolored wires were not running intricately from the beige box to the pipes. It looked like a pile of random wires were just glued to the box and to the pipes. Mish leaned in and tapped the pipes and the box with the tip of her nails.

"Let me guess," Zay said. "You know about bombs, too?"

"I don't know how to make them or diffuse them," Mish responded. "I've handled enough of them to know that this one not only looks fake, it feels fake. Listen," she said and tapped the device again. "It's hollow; there is nothing inside of it." Unexpectedly Mish ripped the device from Taleah's chest. Holding it in the air she shook her head. "He got us with a fake."

"Damn." Tony chuckled. "You gotta give it up to this dude; he is quick on his feet."

"Man, fuck him," Jason spat then asked Mish, "How you supposed to catch up with him now?" He looked her up and down. "Him and that bitch could be flying anywhere in the world in a matter of hours."

Mish was used to men doubting her ability as a hired killer because of her gender and appearance. Jason was giving her the doubtful look that the other men had. Smiling her words came out wrapped in sarcasm: "They could be. Since I do know what I'm doing, before they land I will know where they landing."

"Jason," Joey interrupted. "She's the best; she will get them. As for right now we need to go before security or the police come."

A black Benz G-Wagon drove up and the dark, tinted window rolled down. Behind the wheel, dressed in a gray tank and gray sweatpants, Kisa nodded at the small group.

"That's my ride," Mish said. "Joey, can we discuss a few things real quick?"

"Sure."

The two women stepped off to the side. "The ticket for the hit on the guy is one hundred thousand, and like I said before I can take it out the money when my hacker gets it back."

"That's cool."

"What do you want me to do about the girl?"

"Is the price the same for her?"

"Same price."

"One second." Joey called Evan and Cee over to the private conversation.

"Cee, what do you want her to do with Isadora?"

"Put a bullet in the middle of her head for my husband."

"Okay, then there you have it," Joey told Mish, then directed her attention to Evan. "The fee for her service is two hundred thousand and plus the ten percent recovery fee will come out your money."

"I have no problems with that. I just want it to be over. Whatever I need to pay to get this psychotic nigga out of my life once and for all."

"That's what it is then," Mish said. "When it's done I'll bring confirmation." She got in the car with Kisa.

"Ay, Joe," Kisa called out. "Everything worked out for you?"

"Only time will tell, thanks for the referral though."

Lightly smirking, Kisa nodded her head, chucked the deuces, and peeled off.

Evan stopped Cee and Joey as they were walking away. "I wanna say something before you leave."

Both women paused and silently gave her their undivided attention.

With a noticeable awkwardness in the air Evan began. "Um, I know what a lot of people think of me especially now that my past has been aired out. I want y'all to know that I'm truly sorry for the pain and trouble that was brought to your families because of what I did and I deeply regret hiding things from my two best friends."

Stoic-faced, Cee and Joey stared at her with no response.

"Also, I really appreciate that after everything you suffered because of me, you still cared enough about to protect me from Gage."

Dead silence.

"So, I guess whenever y'all are ready we can discuss where we go from here personally and business wise."

Still nothing.

"Well, talk to you girls later."

As Evan passed, Cee grabbed her hand. "There is nothing for us talk about with regard to our friendship or The Luxe Group."

Saddened, tears welled up in Evan's eyes. "I deserve that." She wiped a plump tear off of her cheek with her finger. "I'll have my attorney contact yours to figure out how to split the conglomerate up."

"That's not what I meant. There is nothing for us to talk about, because nothing has changed. Our businesses will remain a conglomerate." Cee placed her hand on Evan's shoulder. "Our friendship isn't just a friendship. We are sisters, three girls from the west side, from the dirt, and at the end of the day we are all we got. Yeah, you fucked up royally and it may take awhile for everyone to get over the things that happened. I'm highly upset, but you will always be one of us and I love you." Cee pulled Evan close and embraced her tightly.

Evan planted her face against Cee's shoulder and let out a good shoulder-heaving cry. Joey wrapped her arms around her best friends, and she kissed Evan's cheek. "I'm pissed with you, but I love you, Ev, and I always will."

"Ayo," Zay shouted. "Hate to interrupt y'all li'l moment, but we gotta blow." He dapped Reza. "We need to get up soon."

"On the real, my nigga."

"I can tell you really down for Evan. Just remember keep one eye up at all times."

"No doubt."

"What a welcome home this has been," Tony said sitting on a stool eating breakfast on the center island in Joey and Zay's kitchen.

"I can't even put last night into words," Rico added animatedly. "I mean, we went from the best party ever to being in the middle of some wild gangsta movie type shit."

From the opposite side of the island Joey and Zay laughed at Rico. It felt good to laugh after all the recent occurrences. Finding out that Gage was behind it all had brought a small sense of closure. They wouldn't be able ascertain full closure until they knew that Gage was eliminated. "It isn't always like this," Zay said to his brothers. "We live a calm family life."

"That's right," Joey added.

"You ain't just plain Suzy Homemaker," Rico joked at Joey. "Not the way you were handling business last night."

"Every now and then Joe-Joe from the west side creeps out." Joey smiled. "I have to keep that bitch tucked deep inside 'cause she ratchet!"

Rubbing the back of Joey's neck, Zay shook his head and laughed. One of the things that he loved about his wife was her quirky and sometimes dark sense of humor. He missed moments like this with her. Now that all the Gage and Evan drama was hopefully behind them, he prayed that many stolen moments like this were in store for the days ahead. Zay took his hand from behind her neck to answer his vibrating phone.

"Hello?"

"Hey, Zay," his attorney Scott Fleischman greeted him. "If you got a minute to spare I need to speak with you."

"Go ahead, I can talk."

"No, not over the phone. I'm having breakfast at the Pancake House on Charlottetowne Avenue. If you can get over here kinda quick before I have to be in court we can talk."

"I'm on the way." Zay ended the call and stood up.

"Who was that?" Joey asked.

"My attorney; he needs to see me."

"Do you need me to go?"

"You might as well come; he close to the hospital right now." He looked at his brothers. "Since I gotta make a stop, if you want y'all can take one of the cars and go ahead to hospital to be with Mom."

"I don't feel like driving," Tony replied.

"Me neither," added Rico. "I don't have a problem waiting while you stop. Besides, Moms called before we started eating. She said Aunt Fran is stable and resting, so she's going home to shower and get some clothes."

"Jason." Cee shook him lightly as he lay asleep on the couch in her bonus room.

"Yeah." He stirred awake looking around trying to remember where he was.

"I didn't want to wake you. I know that you're dead tired."

"I'm straight." He slowly sat up. "Just dozed off for a minute."

"A minute! More like two hours."

"Damn, I been asleep two whole hours?"

"Yes, sir, and you can go back. I woke you only to see if you wanted something to eat. I'm going to get the kids something." Cee sat on the couch to put her shoes on. Just out of the shower, makeup free, in a black YSL logo shirt and black leggings she was glowing youthfully. "I'm going to Salsarita's and Showmars. Which one do you want?"

"Neither really, but I'll take a flounder and shrimp from Showmars. How is Taleah doing?"

"She's doing better. She stopped crying for now and I think that's because PJ and Shelby are up. Those two are smart. They know that something is going on."

"How did Talia and Tanine take the news?"

"They were relieved that she was okay. The trips can always sense when each other is in trouble or hurt. Tanine and Talia had been trying to reach Taleah all night and morning 'til we got here."

"Wow; what about her boyfriend?"

"He is really shook up. He had some pounds of weed in the house, so whenever he woke up from being knocked out he was scared to call the police."

"Gage and that crazy bitch caused a lot of problems."

"Yes, they did," Cee agreed. "I can't believe Pete's killer was around me every day, attended his funeral, the repast, and gave my family a sympathy gift."

"Gage got that bitch head fucked all the way up, worse than he probably had Evan's. She didn't care that she been sleeping with one of her brother's killers for the last ten years."

"This entire thing has been ludicrous. I can't believe that all this shit has happened to my family over something that we had zero to do with." Staring off into space, Cee said in a low voice, "I should have killed her; I don't know why I couldn't."

"It was good thing that you didn't. You may have not gotten Taleah back. Not only that, witnessing a killing can haunt you for life. Doing the work yourself can destroy you."

"It doesn't seem to bother that chick, Mish."

"We don't know that, and even if it doesn't bother her y'all are cut from a different cloth. Mish is beautiful, with rough edges and hard interior. You," he said and stared at Cee while thinking of the right words, "you're gorgeous too, but you're delicate, honest, and soft. The things dudes like me want in a woman." He smiled continuing to peer at her adoringly.

"Why are you looking at me like that?" She blushed.

"No reason." He shrugged, really wondering if they could ever be more.

Cee reached out, cupped Jason's face, leaned over, and gently caressed his lips with hers. With the tip of her tongue she traced then parted his lips and kissed him fervidly. Feeling it, Jason sank deep into the kiss, only to pull back seconds later.

"What are you doing, yo?"

"What you wanted to do, but wouldn't because you've been trying to be such a perfect gentleman," Cee replied giving into the feelings that she'd developed for Jason. Her infatuation with him had been brewing for weeks. Not wanting to dishonor Petey she fought and did her best to suppress her wildly growing emotions. Now that things were at a fever pitch between them she could no longer hold back. "You didn't like my kiss?"

"I didn't say that. I don't want to go there with you while you're still grieving and all this other chaos is going on."

"I may be grieving for years to come, so if you don't go on we will never get to see what we could be."

"True," he agreed, "but—"

"But what? Look, I'm not trying to make you my man or jump in the bed with you. I'm not ready for either of those things. I kissed you because you're special to me, I appreciate you, and I wanna explore slowly, to see if we could be more than friends."

"I wasn't going to say that I didn't want to go there with you, because I do. You special to me too, but this is still Petey's house and I respect his memory. Kissing you, hell even having this conversation here feels creepish and weird."

"So ride with me to get food so that we can converse some more. Then after I feed the kids why don't we go somewhere that you feel comfortable and do a little more conversing and some more kissing."

"I'm with that." Jason winked. "I want to be clear before we cross this line that no matter what happens we should not ruin the friendship that we have right now."

"No doubt, and if I'm moving too slow for you and another woman comes along you want to pursue a relationship with, by all means go for it. I don't want what I'm going through to hold you up."

"You don't have to worry about that."

"Yeah, yeah, that's what you say now until some cute li'l young thing strolls by."

"Like I said Cee, that ain't nothing to worry about."

"How can you be so sure?"

"I only want you."

Deep in a Xanax-induced sleep Evan rolled over and reached out for Reza. He wasn't there. Eyes still closed she patted the mattress; when she didn't feel him she opened her eyes, and saw that the right side of the bed was empty. Rising up a little she looked to her left. Reza was sitting in a sky blue upholstered wingback chair with a Glock .380 resting on his lap leering at Evan. Spooked she sat straight up.

"Reza, what's wrong? Did you hear a noise or something?"

"Only the sound of a snake slithering."

"Huh?" She frowned, groggy and perplexed, and said, "What are you talking about?"

"You."

Evan glimpsed down and saw an empty bottle of Patrón on the floor next to the chair leg. "Oh, so that's why you're tripping?" She yawned, pointing at the bottle.

"Nah, that ain't why!" he shot back.

"What's the problem then?"

"You."

"What could I have done? I've been asleep since we got here."

"You did the very thing I told you not to do." Reza sneered.

"What!"

"You lied."

"About what?"

"Last night before the party, I asked you if you had been completely honest with me about everything and you said yes."

"And that wasn't a lie."

"I'll give you that. It wasn't exactly a lie, but it was a lie by omission."

"So what did I omit?"

"That you killed or thought you killed your boyfriend and the dude y'all were sticking up."

Leaning back against the plush white crystal-tufted suede headboard, Evan inhaled deeply and with the roll of the eyes she exhaled audibly. Since Isadora had broadcast the truth to everyone about Gage's attempted murder, Reza had been a little standoffish. Evan attributed his quietness to the seriousness of the circumstances.

"I kinda had it in my mind that I'd take that secret to the grave with me."

"Bet you did. You shot that nigga three times in the head and neck like he was nothing to you. I can't help but wonder if you betrayed the man you loved like that, what could you do to me one day?"

"I killed him 'cause he was hitting me and he didn't want to stop doing robberies."

"I'm sure not wanting to share that six million with him didn't have anything to do with it."

"Getting Gage that night was about chance and opportunity."

"If dude would've gotten his hands on that six million he would've retired from robbing."

"You don't know Gage. He wouldn't have flipped the money. He wasn't a hustla; that's why we had to keep doing those licks. Gage loved to spend big, and then add in his love of cocaine and gambling. That six million would have been gone in less than two years."

"That's probably true, but the money was a big factor. Admit it."

Evan shook her head. "No."

"Admit it!" Reza screamed aiming the gun at her.

Terrified, Evan yelled, "Okay, okay, it was a big part of my decision. I saw the money and I knew that was my chance to get away from him. I was miserable with him. He'd become nothing more than a violently mean coke addict. He was never going to let me go." Tears streaming down her face Evan cried, "I would never do that to you."

Reza lowered the gun. "That's a shame I have to put the pistol on you to get the truth. After what I heard in that office I just don't think I can ever have any kind of trust for you. I was stupid to think that this could work when I knew that I could never fully trust you." He raised the gun and aimed it her again.

"What are you doing?"

"Killing you before you kill me."

"If you kill me you will murder your child," she warned.

"Huh?"

"I'm pregnant."

Reza squeezed the gun's lever. Three loud blasts rang throughout Evan's mansion, shattering the serene silence.

Zay pulled opened the glass door to the Pancake House and bumped into his attorney as he was leaving.

"What's up, Scott? How is everything?" Zay extended his hand.

"Pretty good." Scott shook Zay's hand. "Glad you made it before I took off."

"It was a wreck on seventy-seven. I got stuck in one of those spots where I couldn't get to an exit. What's going on though?"

"You remember Detective Blankenship, the white detective from your wife's assault case?"

"Yeah."

"He's my frat brother and college roommate. Blankenship isn't a dirty cop. He does give me the heads-up whenever it involves my clients."

"So what, they still think I got something do with Dawhar's disappearance?"

"No, the police have issued a fugitive warrant on him. However, Blankenship says his partner, Detective Sanders, is borderline obsessed with Dawhar."

"The black detective?" Zay asked.

"Yes."

"Ya man ain't lying. That detective was acting like groupie around Dawhar."

"And it seems that he's still a fan and for some reason he blames you and your wife for Dawhar's downfall."

Zay twisted his face. "You have to be kidding."

"Unfortunately, I'm not. Sanders wanted to know who you were that such respectable and affluent people alibied you. He's been digging."

"What did he find?"

"Nothing of evidentiary value. He knows your net worth and he doesn't believe all your money is clean; therefore, he's given your name to the narcotics unit to be looked at."

"Are you fucking serious?" Zay looked up at the sky shaking his head. Just when one issue was close to being fully resolved, here was something else that he deemed as bullshit being tossed at him. "Un-fucking-believable."

"That joint taskforce between the narcotics unit and DEA that was put together a year ago just went to the grand jury with some major charges on a lot of people locally and nationally." Scott looked Zay directly in the eye and sternly warned, "You need to be careful, because when the indictments come down people are going to be looking for deals. The investigators are going to be tossing your name at them asking what they know and have they done business with you."

"And all it takes is a few of them to lie and they'll hit me with conspiracy charges."

"It isn't that simple anymore; DAs now have to have actual evidence," Scott stated reassuringly. "If you've never been caught with any drugs, caught discussing drugs on wire taps, and you have a legitimate income that matches your lifestyle, the testimony of a would-be coconspirator isn't enough." He looked at his watch. "I have to get going; we can finish this my in office later. In the meantime, watch your back and keep your hands clean."

"Thanks, Scott." Zay shook his hand once more and headed toward his car.

The previous night's events had finally taken a toll on Rico and Tony; the recently freed brothers were both sound asleep in the back seat of Zay's car. From the passenger seat Joey had been on pins and needles while watching her husband talk with his attorney. She could tell by Zay's demeanor during the conversation that the news wasn't good. Silently, Joey prayed that the police were not coming after Zay for Dawhar's murder.

Zay was only halfway in the car when Joey started questioning him. "What was Scott talking about?"

Still processing the information himself, Zay didn't say anything. Looking at Joey he came very close to lashing out at her. Feeling that if she'd listened to him about Dawhar, the chain of events that had been set off by the assault on her would have never happened. He had to remind himself that it could have happened even if she had taken heed to what he said.

Joey rubbed his thigh. "Baby, are you okay? What did he tell you?"

Wisely, he continued to sit quietly, thinking before he spoke. Just as much as he'd been ready to blame her seconds earlier, as her husband he still needed to protect her. In order not to scare or extremely stress her, Zay chose not to divulge all that he'd been told. Keeping it light, he replied, "Scott was just telling me that I need to lay low for a while and not to get caught up in anything."

"Why?"

"It's indictment time."

Chapter Fourteen

Gage and Isadora had flown straight to Belize, the country where Isadora's mother resided. Shortly after Marshawn's murder, their mother left the States and vowed to never return. Five years had passed since Isadora had visited with her mother. Visits for Isadora were hard, because after her brother's death her mother went through an arrested development. After Marshawn died the world went on for everyone else, but it completely stopped for his mother.

Isadora's mother's home and life was a shrine to Marshawn. Being in her mother's home was like reliving her brother's death each time she went there. It was too much for Isadora to deal with, and after every visit she'd return to the States and slip into a deep depression that would last for weeks. Upon returning from the last visit five years earlier Isadora decided that it would be her last. Though she stopped visiting, Isadora spoke with her mother by phone weekly and sent money monthly.

The couple had been in Belize for a week but had yet to see Isadora's mother. After being away for so long Isadora didn't want to show up at her already fragile mother's door swollen and covered in bruises. Instead of going to her mother's home in Belize City, they went to Cayo Espanto, Belize; a private luxurious five-star resort island. The resort comprised of seven waterfront villas and only accommodated eighteen guests at a time, which was great for them. They were able to get the only bungalow over the water, which totally isolated them from the other guests, giving the couple the seclusion that they desired.

Under the influence of Percocet and hydrocodone Isadora slept the first few days, only awaking to eat, bathe, and get spa treatments. Her face and body benefited greatly from the rest and by the fourth morning Isadora had recovered almost 90 percent from the bad beating she'd received in Joey's office. Isadora spent the other days lying up with Gage, enjoying the resort's white glove butler service. Although they had been alone for six days in a bungalow, only a little over 1,000 square feet, they had not talked in depth about the gigantic neon green elephant in the room: Gage's true role in Marshawn's death. However, they did touch on the subject lightly on the jet ride to Belize, and that was just to agree to talk about the ultrasensitive topic at a later date when their emotions had calmed.

On the couple's eighth and last evening at the resort, Gage had the staff set up their meal on the dock of the bungalow while Isadora was asleep. When she awoke, Isadora's mood was a little salty, but she thought that his gesture was nice and romantic. During the beautiful dinner beneath the Caribbean sunset, Gage talked nonstop about all the different ways he wanted to spend their newly acquired millions. He mentioned extravagant homes, $100,000 cars, and jewelry including a twenty-carat flawless diamond engagement ring for Isadora.

Gage might as well have been talking to himself, because Isadora had checked out of the conversation and the meal as soon as he started talking about the money. Isadora sipped flute after flute of champagne while watching Gage's mouth move, but she didn't hear a word he said. During a brief break in his soliloquy, Gage finally noticed that Isadora's mind was not there.

"What's up with you, Dory? You haven't said a word or touched your food."

"I know that we agreed to talk about my brother's murder when we get back to the States, but I need to know something before I can go on another minute with you."

Gage huffed; he didn't want to ruin the evening with the topic, but he knew that he owed her as many answers as she had questions. Not to mention he was interested to see where she was mentally on the issue. "Ask me whatever you want."

"Evan admitted to me that she fired the shots that killed Marshawn, after he had been shot by you. I've grown up since my brother died. I know that robbery goes hand in hand with what he was and that things can go left during one."

"Are you asking did I shoot your brother?"

"Yes. No. I mean, yes, did you shoot my brother?"

"Isadora, I did shoot your brother in the leg to keep him off of me, not to kill him."

"Did you go there planning to kill him?"

"Hell no. I did plenty of jobs and no one ever died until Evan did that bullshit. It may be hard to believe, but murder is bad for robbers too. A simple stickup is just that, but killings always attract police. Robbing your brother was never personal; it was strictly business."

No matter how much Isadora tried to justify, rationalize, or make excuses she had to admit that Gage was just as guilty as Evan of murdering her brother. And there she sat madly in love with him. Deeply conflicted she stood up.

"I thought I was ready to talk about this and clearly I'm not. I'm going to lie back down for a li'l bit."

Gage rose up. "You want me to come?" he asked nervously.

"Not really and I'm not angry or mad. I just want to be alone."

Isadora disappeared into the bungalow leaving Gage confounded. He couldn't fathom which direction their relationship was going to take. Gage didn't want to think about or imagine losing Isadora. He hoped with every fiber of his being that she'd stay, because he truly loved her, and if she could not be happy with him he would not hold on to her. Gage had already decided that he would give her half the money and let her go. Feeling that it was best to give Isadora breathing room, Gage grabbed the bottle of champagne and stretched out on one of the plush beige outdoor loungers at the edge of the dock.

Lying back and staring up at the stars, Gage drank from the bottle as he tried to think of the right words to say to Isadora to keep her in his life. His thoughts were interrupted by creaking wood beneath feet. Over his shoulder he said, "You changed your mind about lying down, babe?"

There was no answer.

"Dory, I know that this shit between us is crazy, but please don't shut me out. You're all I got." Gage got up so that he could see Isadora, but he was stunned to come face to face with a lean, curvy figure in a head-to-toe black scuba suit. For a moment he was transfixed by the beautiful eyes and soft lips peeking from the facial cutout. Snapping out of his trance, he asked the mystery woman, "Who the fuck are you?"

Silently she glared at him and made a swift movement with her hands toward his torso. Gage saw her coming at him, but she was so quick that he couldn't get out of the way or block her. He attempted to swing at her with the champagne bottle, but he couldn't move.

"What the fuck?" he questioned aloud as the Dom Perignon bottle slipped from his hand and hit the wooden dock making a loud thud. Gage's entire body locked up and he fell face first onto the wood making an even louder thud. He could not move a joint, limb, or muscle from the smallest to the largest due the succinylcholine-filled needle that had been jabbed into the side of his abdomen. The poisonous paralytic was a nasty little monster; it would take five to seven minutes for him to die. Still fully conscious, Gage would experience every excruciating second of his lungs slowly collapsing and his heart grinding to a halt.

Concerned by the loud noises, Isadora stepped into the bungalow's doorway. "Gage, are you . . ." She saw him stretched out on the dock and the scuba-suit-clad woman over him. "Oh God!" she screamed in a panic, and the murderous female glanced up, turned toward Isadora, and locked eyes with her. Immediately recognizing Mish, Isadora froze in fear.

Mish stepped around Gage's body and moved expeditiously down the dock's walkway to the bungalow's entry.

A burst of survival adrenaline surged through Isadora's veins; she spun around, and made a desperate dash for the bedroom to get a gun that was stashed beneath the pillows on the bed. Crossing the threshold Mish raised a silencer-capped pistol and fired off two hollow-tip bullets. The back of Isadora's head exploded from the impact, splattering a mixture of brain matter, skull chips, and blood on the bed and walls. Death was instantaneous.

Mish went back out onto the dock to check on Gage. It appeared that he'd already slipped into the afterlife. With Gage's history of surviving the impossible Mish wanted to be sure that he'd cross to the other side. She placed the silencer's muzzle to the back of his head and pulled the pistol's lever four times for good measure. Satisfied that her job was done, Mish slid the gun into a holster on her inner left thigh. She dipped down into the water and swam a quarter of a mile to a waiting jet ski.

Sitting atop the jet ski was Mish's longtime business associate, Nacinda, a wildly attractive Belizean-Creole woman in a bikini top and cutoff shorts. Mish climbed onto the rear of the jet ski and Nacinda sped the three miles across the rough dark ocean to her lavish San Pedro beachfront home. Before going into the house, Mish peeled off the scuba suit and gave it to Nacinda to be burned in the home's backyard fire pit.

While Nacinda discarded the evidence, Mish went into the house and took out her untraceable satellite phone. She dialed the number to another satellite phone. It rang a few times and then Joey answered, "What up?"

"It's done," Mish stated.

Joey smiled. "Good."

"That paper will be back where is supposed to be by morning."

"Nice. Wonderful doing business with you."

"If you ever need me, you know what to do."

"We may need you real soon." Joey sighed.

"Damn, y'all got more issues already?"

"I think that some are about to rise."

"Why you feel like that?"

"It's indictment time."